THE JURY ROOM—
BEHIND CLOSED DOORS

Naomi pointed to Frank. "Look at him, he never says anything. He just sits there and votes guilty every time. That's not deliberating. That's just being stubborn and prejudiced from the beginning."

Naomi got up and went over to Frank. "Isn't it true, Frank, that you just don't like me or anyone? All these months we've ridden together in the car you've never talked to me once. You probably hate me so much you vote guilty just to be spiteful to me."

Frank looked at Naomi but he said nothing.

Naomi waited.

Frank took a deep breath and looked away.

Naomi screamed, "Talk to me! Don't turn away from me! Don't you have the guts to face the truth?"

Also by Victor Villaseñor

WILD STEPS OF HEAVEN
RAIN OF GOLD
MACHO!

JURY

The People vs. Juan Corona

Victor Villaseñor

A DELL BOOK

Published by
Dell Publishing
a division of
Bantam Doubleday Dell Publishing Group, Inc.
1540 Broadway
New York, New York 10036

ISBN: 0-440-22333-4

Printed in the United States of America

Published simultaneously in Canada

March 1997

10 9 8 7 6 5 4 3 2 1
RAD

With gratitude,
to Ronal Kayser and Charles Bloch

Principals in the Corona Trial

THE DATES

The Trial: September 11, 1972—January 10, 1973

The Jury Deliberation:

January 11, 1973, through January 18, 1973

THE LOCATION

Superior Court of California in and for the County of Solano, Fairfield, California

THE INDICTMENT

Twenty-five counts of murder committed in Sutter County, State of California

THE DEFENDANT

Juan Vallejo Corona, 38, labor contractor, Yuba City, California

THE VICTIMS

1. Kenneth Edward Whitacre

2. Charles Cleveland Fleming
3. Melford Everett Sample
4. Unknown
5. Donald Dale Smith
6. John Joseph Haluka
7. Unknown
8. Warren Jerome Kelley
9. Sigurd Emil Beiermann
10. Unknown
11. William Emery Kamp
12. Unknown
13. Clarence Hocking
14. James Wylie Howard
15. Jonah Raggio Smallwood
16. Elbert J. T. Riley
17. Paul Buel Allen
18. Edward Martin Cupp
19. Albert Leon Hayes
20. Raymond Reand Muchache
21. John Henry Jackson
22. Lloyd Wallace Wenzel
23. Mark Beverly Shields
24. Joe Carriveau
25. Joseph J. Maczak

THE DEFENSE

Richard E. Hawk, 39, Attorney at Law,
Concord, California

THE PROSECUTION

Dave Teja, 38, District Attorney,
Sutter County, California
Bart Williams, 38, Special Prosecutor,
Sutter County, California

Ronald Fahey, 40, Chief Deputy District Attorney, Sonoma County, California

THE JUDGE

The Honorable Richard E. Patton, 52, Superior Court Judge, Colusa, California

THE JURY

Ernest (Ernie) Phillips, 53, Vacaville—retired U.S. Air Force sergeant; jury foreman

Faye M. Blazek, 66, Vallejo—retired teacher

Richard (Rick) Bremen, 26, Vallejo—welder at Mare Island Naval Ship Yard

Frank J. Broksell, 58, Vallejo—retired toolmaker at Mare Island Naval Ship Yard

Laurent (Larry) Gallipeo, 41, Vallejo—civilian employee at Hunter's Point Naval Ship Yard

Matthew (Matt) Johnson, 54, Vallejo—retired Marine Corps master sergeant

Victor Lorenzo, 45, Vacaville—grocer

George W. Muller, 43, Fairfield—ex-Air Force sergeant presently a civilian employee at Travis Air Force Base

James (Jim) R. Owen, 39, Vallejo—metals inspector at Mare Island Naval Ship Yard

Donald Rogers, 60, Vallejo—retired machinist at Mare Island Naval Ship Yard

Naomi Underwood, 61, Vallejo—retired civilian employee at Mare Island Naval Ship Yard

Calvin Williams, 51, Vallejo—school janitor

WITNESSES MENTIONED DURING DELIBERATIONS

Physical education teacher (not named)

Mr. Kagehiro—discovered the first body

Mrs. Vallejo—Corona's tenant who testified he fixed her screen door

Deputy Sizelove—with the Sutter County Sheriff's Department

Mr. Khera—Mr. Kagehiro's neighbor

Mr. Cummings—carpenter who kept daily work log at the Sullivan Ranch

Expert on tire tracks from the U.S. Treasury (not named)

Ray Duran—foreman at the Sullivan Ranch

Mr. Sullivan—owner of the Sullivan Ranch, where Corona was contractor

Clerk at Del Pero's Meat Market (not named)

Undersheriff Cartoscelli—with the Sutter County Sheriff's Department

Dr. Rooney—pathologist with the Department of Criminology, State of California

Dr. Ruth Guy—expert on blood types

Mr. Pervis—offered a job by Corona

Jose Raya—offered a job by Corona

Terry Pasco—handwriting expert with the Department of Criminology, State of California

Sidney Goldblatt—handwriting expert from the U.S. Treasury

John J. Harris—handwriting expert from Los Angeles

Byron Shannon—saw Corona offering work to some of the victims

CORONA FAMILY

Gloria Corona—Juan's wife

Doña Candida Corona—Juan's mother

Pedro Corona, Felix Corona, Natividad Corona —Juan's brothers

Juan and Gloria's four daughters

Foreword

On May 20, 1971, the body of a man was dug up by sheriff's deputies in an orchard near Yuba City, California. He had been brutally murdered. Over the next two weeks, twenty-four more bodies would be discovered within three square miles. All had been savagely killed. On May 26, 1971, before the authorities knew the extent of the crimes, Juan Corona, a labor contractor, was arrested. He was subsequently charged with the largest mass murder ever attributed to one man in the history of the United States.

Reading the newspaper accounts, I thought, "No one man could have done all that. I wonder why they arrested him?"

I drove up from my home in San Diego to Sutter County in northern California to investigate. After interviewing the sheriff and driving around and seeing the wealth of the local farmers and the poverty in the

Mexican work camps, I decided maybe Corona was innocent and had been arrested because of racial prejudice.

I parked my van, which was my home, in a trailer camp for ten dollars a week and began hunting out the facts. One interview led to ten more, two conflicting stories required twenty more questions. I began to get a feeling for the rural community referred to as the "Fruit Bowl of the United States." I began to understand the history of the area: the Gold Rush; the Indians; the importation of the Chinese; then, more recently, the arrival of Mexican workers hired by the agriculturists.

I started visiting the Corona family, the defense, and the prosecution. Many times I drove out to the location where the bodies had been found along the Feather River and, as I learned more and more, the more unreal the mass murder became to me. Not only could I not believe that one man could have done all of this, but I couldn't understand why none of the victims had been missed by family or friends.

By the time the trial began—fourteen months later—the defense and the prosecution knew me well but . . . they didn't trust me. Each side thought I worked for the other. And the Corona family and their supporters were very angry with me because I was a Chicano and yet I wouldn't join their cause.

The defense obtained a change of venue to Fairfield—sixty miles nearer San Francisco—and just as jury selection was completed and the trial was starting, I went to Guadalajara, Mexico, to see exactly where the Corona family came from and to visit Juan Corona's older brother Natividad. After what I had found out in Mexico, and with the many confusing things that were brought out in the course of the trial, I was no longer so sure that

Corona was innocent. But it was still beyond my comprehension how one man could have committed all those murders by himself. "Hell," I thought, "the digging of the graves alone would have been a full-time job. And all that killing—how could a married man with four small daughters and a full-time job have done it and still appear to live a normal life?"

I began to look at the jurors—ten men and two women—and think, "Are these people going to be in for a tough job when they start deliberating!"

The trial dragged on from one incredible, confusing fact to another equally incredible and confusing fact for five months, covering a sea of circumstantial evidence. I watched the defense and the prosecution, each with its professional ax to grind, and each day I grew to distrust attorneys more and more and have less and less faith in our legal system.

On January 11, 1973, the case went to the jury, and I suddenly realized that the most important aspect of this mass murder trial would be the jury's deliberations. For how could twelve people, picked at random, begin to consider such a weird case as this? And each day they stayed out—a total of eight—increased my desire to learn what they were going through.

Then, on the eighth day, the verdict came in, shocking the news media, and myself as well. I decided to go along with some twenty newsmen to the home of Ernie Phillips, the foreman of the jury, because it was inconceivable to me how any jury could have arrived at any verdict, guilty or innocent, in this case. But as I listened to Ernie Phillips explain himself so calmly and with such sincerity as the newsmen bombarded him with questions, it hit me . . . here was a man who had tried to do his best.

Here was a man who had no ax to grind, no professional gain in mind, a man who honestly tried to rise to the situation and who was taking the full responsibility for his actions.

Then I decided to interview as many jurors as I could. That same day I saw two more and each was as sincere and open as Ernie Phillips had been. Yet each was troubled and confused and angry. It seemed that they too hadn't much trust in attorneys, or perhaps much faith in our courts of law. Their story became all the more engrossing. I decided to write a book from their point of view.

Over the next seven months, I interviewed all twelve jurors. At first many of them didn't want to speak to me, some because I'm Chicano and they figured I must be with the Coronas and my interviewing was a trick. Others were exhausted; some simply never wanted to speak about the case again. But I continued trying until I had spoken with every juror, with some as many as nine times.

Rick Bremen, the youngest person on the jury, had taken notes during deliberations and was very open and truthful . . . even when the truth didn't flatter him. Faye Blazek and Ernie had almost complete recall and were very generous with their time. Naomi, whose recollections many times contradicted the other jurors', was one of the most helpful persons on the jury. For rightly or wrongly she caused me to check and recheck my information more than did any other juror.

I accumulated over sixty hours of taped conversations with the jurors, two thousand pages of handwritten notes, and dozens of charts of the various seating arrangements in the jury room during those eight days.

I learned a lot about the human mind and this thing called memory. I found out that four people could each recall a specific incident on a specific day as having happened quite differently. When one juror said, "That never happened," or "I didn't say that," I had to go to three or four or five other jurors to find out how many could recall that particular detail. I learned that if one juror could not recall ever having made a certain statement, if I walked around the room as I read my notes and re-enacted what I had pieced together, very often that juror would say, "Oh, yes, now I remember! Sure, I did say that."

After seven months of research, I began writing this book. After nine months of writing, I returned to re-interviewing jurors, checking, rewriting, rechecking. Finally, I felt confident that what I had reported—even a minute detail like a woman looking in her purse at a certain time on a certain day—was as close to the truth as is humanly possible.

In becoming close to all the jurors and their families, I regained a respect and admiration for my fellow man. And I also came to the realization that this is not just a story about one jury but is, unintentionally, the record of an extraordinary test of our jury system

—Victor Villaseñor

JURY

First Day—
Thursday, January 11, 1973

"You do solemnly swear that you will take this jury to some secret and private place and that you will not converse with them about the case, nor allow anyone else to do so, and when they have reached a verdict you will return them into court by order of the Court, so help you God?"

The bailiffs responded to Judge Patton's charge by saying "Yes," and the jury of two women and ten men stood up. Carefully, one of the bailiffs ushered them out of the courtroom and into the jury room in back of the courthouse. He told them that the physical evidence of the case was of such magnitude that the Judge deemed it necessary for them not only to use the jury room for their deliberations but also the courtroom, which would be theirs as soon as it was cleared of newspaper reporters, television men, Corona family, and the general public.

The bailiff left and the twelve jurors were alone.

The year and a half of police investigations was done, the five months of trial were over, the closing arguments of the prosecution and defense were finished, the Judge's instructions were completed, and the entire trial of eighty days, a hundred and seventeen witnesses, nine hundred and eighty exhibits, and nine thousand and some odd pages of transcript was finally theirs.

The jurors paced the room. Not one of them was looking forward to what they were about to do: deliberate on the largest mass murder—twenty-five dead men had been found—ever attributed to one man.

Adding to the tension were the crowds of spectators and newsmen from across the nation and abroad, all awaiting the verdict outside the courthouse.

On the long table in the jury room were a large electric coffee pot, an odd assortment of mugs and cups, and a half-empty carton of doughnuts. None of the jurors had known each other before this trial, and over the last five months coffee and doughnuts had become one of the few common grounds between them. Each of the twelve chipped in a dollar a week, and Rick Bremen—the youngest juror—bought the doughnuts and made the coffee.

It was good coffee. Four jurors were very particular about their coffee and so the first thing these four did was have a cup.

The ages of these ten men and two women ranged from twenty-six to sixty-six, and they had just about that wide a range in life's experiences; yet over the past five months they'd come to know each other in a way that people rarely do.

A few now gathered at the window of their second-story room, looking past the lawn to the sidewalk where the supporters of the accused, Juan Corona, marched around carrying signs. Some of the placards read "Juan Corona Is Innocent," others "Sheriff Whiteaker Is the Murderer."

Speaking loudly in a nasal voice, Donald Rogers said, "Those demonstrators and their signs are stupid. No way on earth could the sheriff be the murderer."

A couple of other jurors agreed and said it was ridiculous how the number of demonstrators had increased—that now it wasn't just the Corona family and a few friends, it was an assembly of hundreds of people rallying for a cause.

An older juror added that the pickets seemed to be getting increasingly long-haired. A younger juror asked what was wrong with that.

Ernie Phillips, fifty-three, wearing a sweater over an open shirt, stopped sipping his coffee and said, "Long hair or not, our freedom of public assembly is one of our most important constitutional rights." Two of Ernie's four children were in their teens.

Matt Johnson laughed. "Yeah, that's right, Ernie. But what gets me is why do they always have to march around counterclockwise?"

Many of the jurors joined Matt's laughter. Ernie did not. Because he was over fifty, Matt's long hair and full beard put off several of the jurors.

Rogers spoke again. "Well," he said in his loud Texan voice, "I guess we can all start talking about the case now. Ah, we don't want to be standing here milling around like sheep!"

George Muller, a small man with a quick sense of

humor, said, "I got to go to the john. So don't bring in a verdict while I'm gone, Rogers."

Victor Lorenzo and Larry Gallipeo, two of the less talkative jurors, burst out laughing. Rogers grimaced and brought out a big cigar. He was the only juror who smoked cigars and many of the nonsmokers resented him because of this.

Someone knocked on the door.

Naomi Underwood answered it, and there was Ed Hehr, the head bailiff, who had been with them since the beginning of the trial.

"Well, folks," said Hehr, "the courtroom has been cleared. You people now got the run of the place. Courtroom, hallway, bathrooms, jury room, everything except that little room down there where I got the three alternate jurors tucked away."

"Poor men," said Naomi.

"Oh, I don't know," said Faye Blazek as they walked down the hallway. "I'm so tired that I wouldn't mind trading my place with any one of them."

"I wouldn't trade mine," said Naomi. "After listening to all that evidence for nearly five months they're going to miss out on all the deliberations."

Faye didn't respond. Aside from being the only women on the jury, Faye and Naomi had very little in common.

Empty, the courtroom seemed larger and felt very different to the jurors. The defense table and the prosecution table had been butted together in front of the judge's bench and twelve chairs placed around them. But the jurors just walked about, feeling out the lonely strangeness of this room that had been so alive with television and newspaper men, attorneys, witnesses, and spectators.

In a corner, apart from the other jurors, Faye was

talking to Jim Owen and Calvin Williams. Faye, who was not only the most formally educated juror but also the oldest, was asking Jim if he would accept the position of foreman if she nominated him.

"Well," said Jim, "I don't know. It all depends on what the others want. I mean, I don't really want to serve but . . . sure, if it comes to me, I'll serve." And he smiled, looking tall and handsome. At thirty-nine he was the second-youngest juror.

"Good," said Faye, "because I don't think I want Ernie or Matt to be foreman."

"Why not?" asked Calvin. Calvin was the only black on the jury, and he and Jim had become very close over the last five months; they both liked to read the Bible after lunch when most of the jurors took a walk.

"Well, because they're too obvious," said Faye, glancing across the room at Ernie and Matt, who were drinking coffee. Beyond them Rick, also with a cup in his hand, was swiveling in the judge's chair.

Seeing Rick in the judge's chair, Faye looked at him disapprovingly and then continued. "Matt was in the Marines for thirty years and Ernie was not only in the Air Force—God knows for how long—but the man just talks so much that we'll never get anything done."

Rick stopped swiveling in the big chair and, leaning forward over the judge's bench, said, "Hey, you can't see anything directly below the bench from up here. That means Judge Patton couldn't see the defense and the accused."

Matt laughed, nudging Ernie. "I guess the Judge missed half the show."

"Not really," said Ernie, "for the things we saw going on between the defense and the accused aren't evidence and we should not consider them in our deliberations." Saying this, he walked toward the two butted tables.

Matt shrugged.

Rick got up from the judge's chair, coming around the tall bench.

Frank Broksell, a white-haired man with thick-rimmed glasses who had been staring with annoyance at Rick, quit his vigil and walked toward the tables.

Victor and Rogers, both big men, stopped thumbing through the pile of evidence on the clerk's desk and also moved to the tables.

Returning from the toilet, Larry and George came across the spacious courtroom. Even though Larry was past forty, he wore mod clothes. George didn't; he, like Ernie and Matt, was an ex-military man.

Good-heartedly, Jim was telling Faye not to worry, that things would surely work out.

"Yeah," said Calvin, with his head down, "I agree that Ernie does like to talk a lot but"—he raised his head, looking at the white-haired woman—"I recall that he talks good sense most of the time."

"Yes, I guess you're right," said Faye, "but . . . oh, I just wonder if anyone else will ever get to voice an opinion."

Laughing, Jim put his arm around the retired teacher. "Ah, come on, Faye, I know none of us are very happy with what we have here, but please, let's not get downhearted before we even begin." And Jim turned her around, walking her toward the tables where the jurors were assembling.

The large empty courtroom hummed with a nervous tension. It wasn't only that these twelve people didn't like what they were about to do, but over the past few weeks they'd begun to get on each other's nerves. Twice, for example, the janitor had been called in to oil a chair after one juror had accused another of making the chair squeak just to be annoying.

"Well," said Ernie, "I guess the first thing we do is elect a foreman."

"And you're it!" bellowed Matt in a thundering voice.

"I second it!" yelled Rick.

"Here's Hawk's chair," continued bellowing Matt. "It's the biggest one. So sit right down, Ernie, and this spot will now officially become known as the foreman's place."

"Hey, hold on one minute," said Ernie "We've got to hear from all twelve people." He glanced around the tables. "Are there any other nominations?'

Fay looked at Jim, who winked at her and shook his head. Faye pressed her lips, not saying anything.

"Well, okay," said Ernie, "I don't really want to, but if elected I'll serve to my utmost—"

"Ah, sit down!" said Matt.

"Wait," said Ernie, "let's go slow here." And he didn't sit down. "We've got to have a vote. We can't just rush into this thing."

"Yes sir," said Matt, and he smiled to himself and moved away from Ernie. Matt had done what he wanted to do. He'd gotten the focus away from himself and over to Ernie. He'd been half afraid that someone would nominate him and he didn't want to be foreman on this case in any way, shape, or form. In his opinion it had been a long, screwed-up case. In fact, he had told his wife and some friends at home that this case would go down in history not as the largest mass murder ever committed by one single man but as the most fucked-up mess ever presented in a courtroom.

* * *

When all the jurors were seated Ernie asked if anyone had any ideas on how to begin their deliberations. Several jurors began to speak but then stopped. Ernie stood up.

"Well, then, let me open this thing up with a few possibilities. Or maybe before I go into these preliminary suggestions, I should first indicate that I believe we should set up a few simple rules so no one person will end up doing all the talking." He smiled and rolled his eyes. "Wait. I know what a lot of you are thinking. You've got the look my wife always gets—'Is he going to talk forever?' Well, to set the records straight—like those attorneys kept saying all five months long—no, I'm not going to do all the talking, but you can sure bet I'll do my full share."

"Yes," said Faye.

"What?"

"I said, yes, I was afraid you would."

"Oh, hell," said Matt. "We all knew he would. That's no big deal. So get on with it. How do you suggest we start?"

Ernie cleared his throat. "Well, I don't know. The prosecution presented its case in ten phases. Their first phase was called body discovery—"

"That won't work!" cut in Rick. "They didn't keep all their phases in their original order. They kept jumping from body phase, to blood phase, to handwriting phase, and back again to body and blood. All the phases are completely mixed up. It would take us two months just to put them in order and relate them to their respective witnesses."

"Well, then how about doing it by the victims?" said Rogers. He was hard of hearing and shouted without realizing it. "There were twenty-five first-degree murders! We could start with them!"

"You can't call them first-degree murders," said Faye in a soft but firm voice. "That's part of our—"

"Why not?" yelled Rogers. Naomi, who was sitting next to him, jumped and edged her chair away. "The attorneys all stipulated and the Judge said that when all the attorneys stipulate—"

Matt rolled back in his chair and, with a twinkle in his eyes, gently began to stroke his beard.

The three or four talkers kept talking.

A few of the nontalkers—Frank, Larry, and Victor—noticing that Matt had leaned back, did the same.

Naomi looked from one talker to the other as though she were watching a tennis match. Her eyes gleamed with excitement.

The jurors were having the same problem the prosecution had had for over a year and a half before this trial began. How to present twenty-five murders, more than a hundred witnesses, and nearly a thousand pieces of evidence?

Attorney Bart Williams, who had been hired by District Attorney Dave Teja months after Juan Corona was arrested, stated publicly that the material relating to these murders had not been used to establish a case for the prosecution until he came into the case. Before that everything had been filed, or more likely not filed, and had been seen through the eyes of a police department collecting unrelated data. It had been a mammoth job for Williams just to get things in sufficient order so that a prosecutor could see what to present to a jury.

And Williams further said that half the evidence they'd

found could not be used in court, and half of what could be used had been so poorly recorded during the sheriff's initial investigation that it was hell to try to present it to the jury.

The talkers were still talking when Ernie, sitting directly in front of the judge's bench, tapped the table and said, "To begin with, from now on only one person speaks at a time and, for that privilege, you raise your hand. That's rule one. Rule two will be that each speaker will try to limit his comments to no more than five minutes. Rule three, the speaker, if he or she wishes, can stand up but they need not if they don't wish to. Rule four, let me see, oh, yes, no deliberations will take place unless all people are present and seated." He hesitated, then added, "Any suggestions? Anything that I said that doesn't seem fair? Or anything that anyone would like to add?" He glanced around. "Speak up. That's what we're here for."

Naomi raised her hand.

"Yes," said Ernie.

"Well, I just want to say that I think we're doing good. I've been on two juries before and I—I maybe don't look like it—but I read a lot of books, you know, mysteries, and I think we're doing fine."

"Why, thank you," said the foreman, "thank you. Any more comments concerning the rules of procedure before we get started with the actual case?"

Naomi shook her head; she was youthful with enthusiasm.

It was after lunch and Ernie was saying, "All right, it looks like we all survived our lunches. So let's begin where we left off. I believe we were discussing procedure of evidence versus procedure of victims. And by this I think we meant that we can either start by talking about the evidence, meaning the knives, the gun, the blood, the vehicles, and so on, or we can start with the first body that was found and then proceed to the second body, the third body, and so on through all twenty-five. Are there any suggestions?"

Not all the jurors were sitting down. Some seemed to be having difficulty finding a chair. Naomi, for one, was trying not to end up next to Rogers, with his loud, booming voice, and Frank was trying to sit with the less talkative jurors.

Standing there, Ernie watched as the jurors played musical chairs but neither he nor anyone else was really conscious of what was already beginning to happen. Personalities were becoming a distraction, and within a few days egos would sometimes be more important than actual evidence. Now, however, everyone finally found a chair and Ernie too sat down.

Faye raised her hand.

"Yes," said Ernie.

"Well, I've been thinking during lunch, and the biggest trouble I see is the evidence. Like Rick said, they didn't keep their original ten phases in order so we can't possibly deliberate from an evidentiary point of view. I believe we'll have to go by the victims."

"That's right!" said Rogers. "By the victims!"

"All right," said Ernie, "so we'll do it by the victims . . ."

Jim raised his hand.

"Yes," said Ernie.

"Well," said Jim, standing up, "how can we possibly do it by the victims? There are twenty-five and not all the evidence pertains to all twenty-five dead men. Some evidence only relates to one or two of the victims. Going by the phases makes more sense." Good-naturedly, Jim continued. "What I'm trying to say is . . . do we consider all the victims as a whole, or do we consider each victim separately? Secondly, do we consider all the evidence relating to all the victims or to each separate victim?" He smiled. "Oh, it's confusing, I tell you. This trial was so long and the Judge's instructions cleared it all up for me but only for a little while. Do you see what I mean, Ernie? How do we consider both the victims and the evidence? Collectively or separately?"

"We consider them dead!" said Rogers. Everyone turned to Rogers. "All those lawyers stipulated that these are first-degree murders and the Judge said if both sides stipulate, then we can consider it a fact!"

Victor and Matt burst out laughing. They were both big men. Rogers eyed them. Rogers, who was also a big man, wore glasses and always dressed in immaculate dark suits, white shirts, and conservative ties. He was a handsome man with elegant white hair and, with his cigar in his mouth, he looked forceful—and yet people were laughing at him.

Finally, with the laughter subsiding, Ernie turned again to Jim.

"Well," said Ernie, "I see your point, Jim, and, to tell the truth, I don't know how to consider the victims or the evidence. Maybe we should check someone's notes and see what evidence, exactly, was connected with which particular victim. Faye, you always took notes, do you happen to have that information?"

Faye moved uneasily in her chair. "I left them at home," she said. "After five months of taking notes daily I left them at home. I thought they told us we would get the transcript. I thought they told us—"

"It's okay," said Jim, who was sitting next to Faye. "Don't feel badly. I thought the same thing."

Faye was very upset. Tactfully, Ernie went on. "Anyone else have any notes?"

"I took some notes," offered Larry. "But they're not very complete. I figured like Faye and Jim. I thought they said we'd get the court transcript."

"Do your notes have any of the evidence listed in relationship to the victims?"

"No."

"Well," said Ernie, "we're back where we started from . . . how do we begin?" Rogers began to talk again. "No!" snapped Ernie. "No more about they're all first-degree murders. Man, we've got to go through the evidence, the facts, the witnesses, the whole ball of wax, and see if the accused committed them or not. It's beside the point, at this time, if everyone and his uncle agrees that they were premeditated horrendous murders or not." He stopped. He smiled. "Anyone else?"

Naomi raised her hand.

"Yes," said Ernie.

"Like you just said, how about the witnesses?" asked Naomi in a gravelly voice. She coughed, clearing her throat. She didn't like her voice when it got so low and gravelly. "Some of the witnesses were really interesting." Her voice was better now, and she smiled. Faye glanced at her, then looked away. "And these witnesses sure covered the facts," Naomi continued. "Especially all those experts with their scientific testimonies. They were my favorites. They were better than the victims or the evidence. One got educated when they talked."

"Yes," said Ernie in a soft voice. "That's true. The experts were educational. Learned in their respective fields of blood, handwriting, and pathology. Yes, I agree they were very interesting indeed, but I don't believe we can discuss this case to its best merital advantages by going through all—how many did the Judge say there were?—two hundred and forty testimonies by a hundred and seventeen different witnesses. Hell's bells, that's even more confusing than the twenty-five victims or the evidence itself."

Rogers raised his hand. Suddenly, Rick sat up and waved his hand also. Ernie turned to the younger man.

"Rick?"

"Well, going back to what Jim was saying, I think the answer to our problem can best be worked out by approaching it like Jim said. Only I'd like to add that it's one thing to just get started, to just discuss the evidence, and it will be a whole different matter when we start relating evidence and victims as a whole or separately to reach a verdict." Rick wasn't standing up, but he was sitting tall in his chair. He was a Vietnam veteran and, with his rolled-up shirt sleeves and his large well-developed arms, he was impressive. "In other words, I believe the Judge's instructions were that we are to consider each victim, each count, separately. That's why he gave Ernie these twenty-five different sheets of paper to sign when we reach a verdict. But . . . that's only for us when we bring in the verdict on each of the twenty-five counts of murder. I don't think he meant that when we discuss the case that we talk about the evidence separately. That would never work. So I suggest, following the case and the Judge's instructions, that we start with victim one, Whitacre, our only really fresh killing, then proceed to the evidence found at Corona's house and at the ranch camp. Because the evidence found at these two locations is general evidence dealing with all the murdered victims." He stopped and glanced around and then sat back. "To start with, I'm sure it will work. Procedurally speaking."

Ernie shrugged. "Well, I'm glad someone is sure about something. Any other suggestions or should I do some more talking and open up a few more—" Faye raised her hand. "Yes, Faye."

"I think Rick has the right idea. Jim did bring up the main problems to focus on, but I don't believe our dilemma ends there. Because, collectively or separately, what happens if we find Corona innocent of some counts and guilty of others? Did the Judge's instructions cover that?"

Matt raised his hand, and Ernie recognized him.

"Well," said Matt, "I think we've got an instructional problem, so why don't we call back the court and ask the Judge to reread his instructions?"

"Yes," said Ernie, "I guess that's what we'll have to do but . . . before we do that I'd like to find out exactly what we want to ask the Judge."

"You're the foreman, Ernie, so that's your problem," said Matt, sitting back and laughing.

"Thanks," said Ernie, "all I don't need is a friend like you. Man, we got problems and we haven't even started discussing the evidence."

Ernie called bailiff Ed Hehr to tell him they had an instructional question to ask the Judge. Hehr instructed Ernie to take the jurors to the jury room, and he would inform Judge Patton so that the Judge could summon the court.

Going down the hallway to the rear of the courthouse, Calvin asked Ernie why the whole court had to be called in for one small question.

Ernie said he didn't know why.

Matt laughed and said because judges and lawyers like to make a big deal out of everything so they can feel important.

Armed sheriff's deputies stood inside and outside of the court trying to keep order.

Over two hundred people still wanted to get into the courtroom but it was already packed.

The jury and the three alternate jurors were brought in and seated.

Superior Court Judge Richard E. Patton looked at them and as he spoke his voice sounded and resounded: "Ladies and gentlemen of the jury!" He enunciated each syllable distinctly. "Do I understand that you have a request to make of the court?" The jurors were attentive. All eyes were on them. "Who is the foreman of the jury?"

Ernie stood up and his blue eyes were small and he was very nervous. "I am, Your Honor," he said in a soft but firm voice.

The Judge looked at him, then spoke abruptly. "And what communication did you have for the court, sir?"

"We found, sir"—he hesitated, clearing his throat—"that at the outset of our deliberations we were at a loss to interpret certain instructions the Judge gave us at the end of our trial and we would like further clarification on a couple of these points."

"Will you state the matter of concern to you, Mr. Foreman?" said the Judge.

"Yes, sir," said Ernie, licking his lips and placing his hands down low against his sweater. One hand in the other. Squeezing each other. "It became apparent that the jurors were having trouble deciding in what manner do you try each case. For example, whether you consider evidence collectively or proceed from victim to victim and try each count separately." As he spoke, he kept moving his hands. "Or if you try all counts collectively and if anyone decides or has the opinion that the man was or was not guilty of one count, would he be innocent of all counts?" Ernie stopped, catching his breath as if to go on, but then he didn't say anything more. The room was silent. Sheriff's deputies, newsmen, Corona family, Corona supporters, general public, and of course the defense and the prosecution and the accused himself—everyone was looking at Ernie. Then it became apparent that he was not going to say anything more. He was simply standing there waiting.

"Please be seated, Mr. Phillips," said Judge Patton, and as Ernie turned his eyes met Juan Corona's. Ernie wanted to look away but didn't. He held, eye to eye, as he sat down, and the defendant, Juan Vallejo Corona, didn't look away either. "Well," the Judge was saying, "in response to this inquiry may I consult with counsel in chamber on the question presented?"

"Yes," said District Attorney Teja very quietly.

"Yes sir!" snapped Richard Hawk.

"Very well," the Judge said. "The jury will remain seated and the defendant and counsel will step into chambers with the court reporter and clerk."

Then, and only then, after the Judge had finished

speaking, did Juan Vallejo Corona lower his eyes as he got up to go into the Judge's chambers.

And Ernie, staring at Corona's back, felt an odd numbness start at the back of his head and travel down his neck and throughout his body. He was apart from everything, everyone, back to that day in World War II when his plane had been shot down over the English Channel. He wasn't remembering it so much as reliving it. In flashes. In feelings. As he came down in his parachute and all around were Allied aircraft and all below were enemy ships and here he came, falling, along with his whole crew. Falling. Gliding. And then he hit the water and his huge sheep-lined jacket absorbed a ton of water and he was sinking fast, deeper and deeper, when suddenly the lines of his chute tightened and jerked him upward. Breaking the surface he gasped and saw that his chute was caught in the wind like a sail and it was taking him, gliding him over the water, and now the wind was coming through his huge jacket and he was freezing and beginning to lose the feeling in his legs, his arms, his whole body, and then the numbness began at the back of his head and he was losing consciousness as the chute continued taking him out to sea. There was nothing he could do. He was helpless. He weighed a ton and this numbness, this state of not feeling, had consumed his whole body and it was now spreading to his skull and his head was going numb too. He was face up and only his eyes seemed to remain functioning and he could see the sky and the sky was a beautiful blue and it was filled with planes.

Someone was tapping him on the shoulder.

If it hadn't been for those little boys in that small skiff, he now thought, he would have just sailed out to sea.

Someone was speaking to him.

His chute had blown over the little boys' skiff and that had been his salvation.

Someone was still talking to him.

Slowly, Ernie wrenched himself away from his memories, from his thoughts of how those boys had fished him out of the freezing water, and returned to the present. He was here in the courtroom and someone behind him was speaking to him. Ernie turned around.

Jim Owen was saying: "I want to tell you that you worded our question correctly, but I was wondering if maybe it wouldn't be best to re-emphasize certain key points because, here in the courtroom, our question didn't seem to have the importance that—"

"Not now," said Ernie. "Wait until later. The press is watching us. It wouldn't be proper for them to overhear us."

Reluctantly Jim nodded and sat back.

Now the atmosphere was not the same as it had been during the long days of trial when the Judge took the attorneys into chambers. Then things had been so dull that often the jurors had made jokes among themselves which newsmen had overheard and expanded on, amusing everyone, even some members of the Corona family. But now the room was tense, silent, and the noise of someone moving in his chair carried across the entire court.

The meeting in the judge's chambers was over.

Juan Corona, a big, handsome man just under six feet tall, was the first to emerge. He wore a dark suit and tie and his jet-black hair was combed straight back. He spoke very little English. He was from Mexico, and he was not an American citizen but a green card holder. He'd made his living by hiring out crews of other Mexicans with green cards, which granted temporary citizenship to Mexicans so that they could legally be hired to work on American farms—for much less pay than an American would get.

In the audience was Juan's brother, Pedro Corona, and a few other Chicano friends who all stood up and yelled, *"De colores, hermano!"*

Juan tried to smile and wave to his friends but he couldn't. Instead he cringed, and placed his right hand on his stomach.

Hawk was following Juan and he smiled, motioning for Pedro and the others to sit down.

Then the three attorneys for the prosecution trailed in and each stood behind his chair.

The bailiff entered and ordered everyone to rise.

Briskly the Judge walked in and sat down.

The bailiff said, "The Superior Court of California in and for the County of Solano is now in session. Honorable Richard E. Patton, judge presiding. Be seated." The Judge smiled, glancing around as he always did while everyone took their seats.

"All right," Judge Patton said, "in response to the request of Mr. Phillips, I believe that this one instruction provides the answer which you seek, and I will read this instruction." He coughed, clearing his throat, and looked down, reading from a paper on his desk. "Each count charges a separate and distinct offense. You must decide each count separately on the evidence and the law applicable to it uninfluenced by your decision on any other count. The defendant may be convicted or acquitted on any or all of the offenses charge. Your findings as to each count must be stated in a separate verdict."

He paused and glanced up. "Very well. The jury will return to their deliberations. But first I will ask that an officer take the three alternate jurors to their places of custody and I will then ask that the regular jury be taken into the jury room and then I will have the main courtroom cleared so that it will be available for further use in deliberations." He sat up tall and final. "We stand recessed . . . subject to the call of the jury."

The Judge pounded the gavel.

Silently, the jury filed out of the court and into the jury room, but as soon as the bailiff closed the door they exploded into quick conversation—one group here, another there. And Ernie, going over to the window, watched. The jurors were angry, shaking their heads in disgust and indignation.

"It's not right!" snapped Larry, who was usually one of the least outspoken jurors. "Every time something important happens they go into chambers to work it out."

"Yeah," said Frank, also usually quiet. "That really gets me. Then after they talk it out behind that closed door they come back and just read a few legal-sounding words out of a book. They treat us like . . . uh, animals. No, like machines."

"Yeah," said Larry, "and I bet they don't act like machines in chambers. Back there I bet they talk and ask questions of each other like humans."

"I'd sure like to ask a few questions," said Victor, pushing his glasses up higher on the bridge of his nose. He was a powerfully built man, and he was shaking his head with such vigor that his glasses were slipping. "Ernie asked what we wanted but, dammit, in court it didn't sound as good and the answer didn't help us and now I can't even remember exactly what the Judge said."

"Yeah," said Frank. "They're the educated ones, the ones who know the law, and they didn't help us one bit. It's not right."

"You bet it isn't," said Larry. "Like now I can remember that the Judge said each charge is a separate count but he still didn't tell us if the evidence is separate or all together for each count, did he? I don't remember him answering that part of our question."

"He didn't," said Victor, "and I don't know how we're ever going to be able to discuss this case. Dammit!"

Across the room Faye was talking to Jim and Calvin. Jim was nodding and listening and then saying in a soft voice that yes, the Judge's instructions had not really solved their dilemma. "But what can we do, Faye? It seems the legal world only writes for other legally trained people. And it doesn't seem like we will ever have the opportunity to just sit there and talk to the Judge and have him answer our questions. The system doesn't seem to work that way. We have to call the whole court back in order to clarify one small point. It doesn't seem right."

"No," said Calvin. "It makes one feel dumb, or stupid, or something like that, to call the whole court back for one small question. I sure wish we could just talk to him, the Judge, you know, like people talk. Back and forth. Until each person understands the other."

"I agree," said Faye. "That's our whole problem. We're dealing with a one-way conversation and everyone knows that a two-way conversation is certainly superior."

"Right," said Jim, "that's it exactly. We should be able to talk until our whole question is understood."

At the door Naomi was talking to George, who was shaking his head and saying yeah, yeah, that he agreed with her. She kept talking and talking, and he said yes, she was right, ultimately they would have to arrive at their own interpretation of what the instructions were exactly, and yeah, it seemed like they'd almost wasted their time going in here.

"I believe we should've been given a copy of the instructions," said Naomi. Naomi liked that idea; she smiled and lit another cigarette. The excitement made her nervous and she was beginning to smoke more.

In the middle of the room was Rogers, smoking a fresh cigar and talking loudly, and Rick was in competition with him. They were by far the loudest. Then, in the middle of a sentence, Rick quit competing and went over to Faye, Jim, and Calvin.

At the window Ernie was swaying back and forth on the balls of his feet. He was not looking at the jurors any more. He was looking out of their second-story window. The Corona supporters were still marching, but Ernie wasn't thinking about them. He was thinking about Corona, the man, and yet he really wasn't—he was again out at sea, and these two young boys had him in their little boat and they were taking off his frozen clothes and wrapping his numb body in dry canvas. Then a German boat came up and took him prisoner. On the mainland the Germans loaded him and other American prisoners in the back of an open flatbed truck, while civilians from the village cursed and threw snowballs at them. But it made no difference to Ernie whether the snowballs struck his naked body or missed because he was so numb. Only his eyes and brain were still functioning, but when they got to the prison camp, it got so bad that even his eyes and brain quit functioning. The human species could do that when things got too terrible. The eyes and brain could turn off like a safety valve, preserving one's sanity . . . and Ernie now wondered if Corona, if in fact he did commit all these cold-blooded murders, did his mind now know about it? Or had Corona's mind canceled out, trying to keep its sanity, so that now Corona had no recollection of these murders.

Then Ernie wondered about Corona's wife, about Corona's daughters, and, having three daughters and one son himself, he shook his head. No way on earth could he himself have committed murder after murder . . . twenty-five mutilated bodies in a six- or eight-month period . . . without his family getting wind of something weird.

He stopped speculating. Hell, how could a non-murderer put himself in a murderer's frame of mind?

"Here," said Matt, offering Ernie a cup of black coffee. "You look like you need it. You're taking this whole thing too seriously." Ernie took the coffee. "You know, pal, what this whole thing really boils down to? It boils down to what we call in the military passing the buck." Then, lowering his voice to a whisper, Matt added, "Passing the buck quickly, before you fuck it up some more." He laughed and laughed. Ernie didn't laugh. "That's what they've done, Ernie. The whole legal bunch of them. Hell, that's what they've been doing to us since the beginning of this case. Playing their legally professional roles and passing it to the jury. Both sides. Acting like third-rate attorneys and hoping that we, the jury, will straighten up their fucked-up mess."

Ernie, rocking on his feet, began patting his middle-aged belly and then, finally, said, "You know, guys like you that turn hippie after fifty years of age have one thing in common."

"What's that?"

"You don't say the word 'fuck' with convincing indignation, even when that's your precise intent."

"Oh, you think so?"

"Yep, I think so. I mean, man, we're here with the largest mass murder this country has ever had and, I grant you, this case is not just fucked up, it's fucked, period, but we still have a responsibility. We're the jury, the jury system, and man, this system is no come-lately gone-by-tomorrow idea. It's as old as our western civilization and I tell you, I'll bet money, men like us, common people, have been straightening up this fucked-up world of professionalism since the first time things became screwed up enough to need these professionals to begin with."

Matt laughed, roaring with gusto. "Yes sir. But now, tell me, how are we going to go about this great and noble act of straightening up this 'hopelessly heterosexual' world of fucked-up professionals?"

And with the words "hopelessly heterosexual" Ernie burst out laughing and said, "That Hawk, that Hawk, ain't he something else?"

They were both loose now and Ernie was talking like the West Virginian he was and Matt was talking like the Bostonian he was, and now in this tension-filled room the memory of Hawk saying over and over again that these were homosexual crimes and his client was happily married and hopelessly heterosexual and therefore couldn't possibly have committed these horrendous murders seemed funny.

Both men laughed and throughout the room the

tension began to lessen. In laughter, men and women found a common ground.

There were three military men on the jury, and Fairfield, the location of this trial, was a military town which lay halfway between San Francisco and Sacramento just off Interstate 80.

Richard Hawk, the defense attorney, had won a change of venue from Sutter County, where the bodies had been discovered and the accused had been arrested. Hawk had publicly stated that Juan Corona could not get a fair trial in Sutter County because of the adverse publicity and the general small-town feeling toward Mexicans and other minorities, but that in Fairfield, with a wide range of people and a good proportion of ex-military men, who had seen the world and plenty of injustice, his client would get a fair trial and be found innocent.

The prosecution had not agreed; people were people, they said, no matter where you went, and Juan Corona would have got as fair a trial in Yuba City in Sutter County as he would get in Fairfield in Solano County—and he was going to be found guilty of twenty-five counts of first-degree murder.

But except for the defense and prosecution no one made such statements.

It had all been too long, too complicated, and the whole case was totally circumstantial. Not one single eyewitness had ever been found. And also, incredibly enough, no one had really missed any of the murdered men.

The jurors were all sitting around the two tables. A lot of talking had been done and Ernie Phillips was making a summation. "Well, then," he was saying, "do I understand that we all agree that the Judge's instruction answered the main part of our question but did not satisfy our particulars for the actual discussion?" A few nodded. "Good. Then do I further understand that we've agreed not to concern ourselves with the idea of a verdict at this time? That we've decided to simply start our discussion with phase one, discovery of the bodies, like the prosecution did but, unlike the prosecution, as we take each particular victim we'll also bring in any evidence from any given phase which happens to pertain to that victim which we are discussing." He paused. "Is that right? Is this what we've agreed to do? To start it off through phase one, victims, and then go around the table adding to that victim from any or all phases . . . whatever anyone happens to remember and thinks is factually pertinent?" Everyone nodded. "Okay then, to begin . . . victim one, Mr. Whitacre. Kenneth, I believe, was his first name. Now what do we know about Mr. Kenneth Whitacre?"

And having said this, Ernie took his chair, the large brown one, and glanced around. Several jurors had their hands up. "Let's go around the table to my right. Starting with George here and moving right around to Rick here on my left. Okay, George, what do you remember about Mr. Whitacre, victim number one?"

George sat up straight in his chair. "The first thing that comes to my mind is that woman." Victor burst out laughing. A few other jurors joined his laughter. George, small and lively, could start discussing even a murder case with a humorous twist. "Remember that woman who was a phys-ed teacher and she testified that she passed Whitacre walking along the road as she drove to school? She'd seen him wearing a big overcoat and the weather was hot and it looked like he was so sick and tired that he'd never get much further. That was in the morning, I believe, and he was walking along the road in an easterly direction by Mrs. Somebody's gladiola bushes." George laughed. "I remember that really well. The woman kept talking so fast that even the court recorder had to ask her to slow down and then she said, 'Oh, I'm sorry. My husband always tells me I talk fast too.' "

Most of the jurors were smiling but only Victor and Matt and Rogers were really laughing. Everyone seemed to remember the young physical education teacher very well.

"Okay," said Ernie. "Calvin, you're next. What do you remember about victim one, also meaning gravesite one?"

"Oh, I remember that teacher all right. She did talk. But also I remember her being so exact about the time she always drove by those gladiolas on her way to school. She said fifteen to nine, if I recall. And further up the street, about noon, that little girl that was sick and stayed home from school was looking out her window and she, too, saw that same man . . . walking along the road in a big gray overcoat, and she thought he looked sick too. She called her mother, the man looked so bad. He'd just stopped there on the side of the road. Like he couldn't go any further. Like he didn't even rightly know in which direction to go anymore." Calvin shook his head. "Poor man." And he said no more. So Ernie took over again.

"Yes, I remember that. The little girl's name was Gina Chapman." A few of the jurors looked at Ernie in amazement. How could he recall that little girl's name after five months and hundreds of witnesses? "She was a pretty little blonde girl and, man, was she nervous on the stand." He smiled compassionately. "Okay, next."

"Well," said Jim, who was sitting at the right end of the tables, "I remember what George and Calvin said. It was hot and Whitacre was lost and weary and he was wearing a gray or green overcoat. The woman and the little girl didn't agree on the color. And also I can't recall on which road he was seen. Was it on Sanders Road or on Eager Road? I believe that makes a difference. Because where his body was found the following day was—excuse me, Ernie, but do you mind if I get up and go to the mockup?"

"Help yourself," said Ernie. "That mockup board is part of our exhibits. Turn on the little button that lights up gravesite number one and get on with it, Jim. That's what we're here for."

The big twelve-by-eight-foot board was on a scale of one inch to one hundred feet. The map represented approximately three square miles of land five miles north of Yuba City, in Sutter County, a hundred and twenty-six miles northeast of San Francisco. All twenty-five bodies had been found within these three square miles, on both sides of Highway 99, which divided the map from north to south. The first two bodies were discovered west of Highway 99 and the other twenty-two, except for victim thirteen, were found east of 99 along the banks of the Feather River.

"Well, let's see. Kagehiro, the owner of the peach orchard where the first body was discovered, said his twenty-some acres lie right about here, just north of Eager Road. Eager runs east to west. And, yeah, Sanders Road, also running east to west, is the next road north of Eager. Larkin Road runs north and south, parallel with Highway 99, and connects Sanders and Eager on the west side of 99. Now, if Mr. Whitacre was seen here on Sanders Road at fifteen to nine and then again at noon and he was killed and buried over here that same afternoon . . . oh, I don't like thinking about this." Jim stopped, glanced around, then looked straight at Ernie and said, "Please, Ernie, maybe someone else best finish my turn." He came away from the board. "It's so easy to forget that *this is a murder trial.* I swear, there I was searching that map for roads and details just like one of those attorneys and I forgot what it was all about. That's terrible. People were killed . . . brutally. Time after time." Shaking his head, he sat down. "Ernie, do you see what I was driving at? One, we've got testimony about the man walking along until noon. Two, we've got testimony about Mr. Corona having a crew of workmen, all Mexicans, not any—white men, Anglos, whatever you wish to call us—working on the same ranch where the grave was later found. And three, we know through Mr. Kagehiro's testimony that Mr. Corona and his crew quit early that day. About noon. And four, we've got that big question of where did Mr. Corona go after he left with his crew? Did he drive by Mr. Whitacre as he took his crew back to the main ranch camp to the east side of Highway 99? Did he then—as Mr. Hawk suggested—go fix Mrs. Vallejo's screen door? Or did he then come back . . . alone . . . after dropping off his crew and . . ." Jim swallowed. "I mean, this first grave is important. I think we have to see if he's guilty on this first grave before we go on to the other twenty-four graves. A man's life and liberty are at stake." Jim shook his head, and the room filled with a heavy silence.

Even Ernie didn't say anything for a while. But then he said: "Well, Jim, we'll keep your words in mind. This is indeed a trying state we're in and, yes, I believe we all know and fully realize that a man's life and liberty are at stake." He hesitated. "Now, going on, you're next, Naomi. What do you have to add to victim one, Mr. Kenneth Whitacre?"

Naomi's eyes sparkled. She began to speak but then stopped and shook her head. "No, I pass this time." Her voice was low and gravelly. She coughed vigorously, clearing her throat. "I mean, I don't want to say anything yet." Her voice was better now, and she smiled. "Go on, go on, please. I want to hear. This is really interesting."

Ernie smiled. "Good. I'm glad to know we're interesting. Okay, your turn, Faye."

"Well," said Faye, "I've been thinking about victim number one and I'd like to say that all throughout these months of trial the prosecution and defense have always referred to these deceased men as numbers. As number one, number two, and so forth, and I always thought that was wrong. That these were not numbers, that these were people, but now as I heard you, Ernie, call victim number one by his name, over and over again, and I heard Calvin and George talk about him walking down the road I wonder . . . if maybe the prosecution wasn't wise in not reminding us all trial long that these twenty-five numbers were indeed real persons." She stopped and looked around. "In other words, I'm saying that for us to deliberate, to discuss this case objectively without getting emotionally biased, maybe we should do as the prosecution did and refer to these poor unfortunate men as numbers and not use their names very often. Or if we do use their names, then, please let us do it more discreetly." She looked about the table once more. A few nodded in agreement with her. "Nevertheless, to go on, what I recall of importance in connection to victim number one is first of all that Mr. Kagehiro testified that he found a hole in his orchard in the morning of May 19, 1971. That Corona on that same day was working in the capacity of a labor contractor. That the work was completed by noon. That he, Mr. Kagehiro, the owner of the orchard, brought beer and potato chips out to Corona and his crew. That the crew drank the beer and ate the chips and then Corona drove them off in his van, supposedly to the Sullivan camp across Highway 99 some two or three miles in an easterly direction. We don't have any testimony about which road Corona took. We also do not have any testimony if indeed Corona had the opportunity to see victim number one or not." She moistened her lips. "But we do have testimony by Mr. Kagehiro that in the evening of that same day he saw the hole, which he'd seen open in the morning, filled in. He became suspicious. He tried contacting the local police. The police didn't respond. The next morning, May 20th, he drove to the Live Oak police station and reported it. Later that same morning Deputy Sizelove from the Sutter County Sheriff's Department arrived. I think we all remember the testimony of how surprised they were to unearth a body. That was very clearly documented by Deputy Sizelove. But what was not made clear and is very important—like Jim said before we go on to the other victims—is not only the testimony of that gym teacher and that small girl but the testimony of Mr. Khera, that neighboring farmer, who said he saw Corona in a van. Alone. Late in the afternoon.

"Now, did Mr. Khera see Corona alone that same day that Corona worked for Mr. Kagehiro? Did the prosecution prove to us beyond a reasonable doubt that Corona did in fact, after he took his crew back to the Sullivan camp, come back to that area where he'd been working, west of Highway 99, where the body of victim number one was later found? I believe they didn't, and I further believe that we have to straighten out this first victim before we go on to the second or third or whatever." She stopped and sat back, looking very much the schoolteacher as she glanced around the tables to see how her pupils would react.

"Well," said Ernie, "Faye brought up some good questions, some provocative points for discussion, so now let's not stop, let's proceed. Man, it appears as if we've finally begun."

"Right!" said Rogers, who was the next juror to speak. "Let's keep going! But I want to say that I don't see why we have to straighten out this first body before going on. Hell, didn't we just all agree that we wouldn't vote or even think about a verdict at this time? That we'd just go on victim by victim and bring in everything we could remember? So I'm for going on." Eagerly, he leaned forward.

"There are twenty-five of them and the ones we've got really solid evidence on are number three, or E-3-5, or whatever you want to call the third body, and that last one, that number twenty-five himself. Those two are the ones that have the meat receipts with Corona's own name, and bank receipts with Corona's own name, and Hawk himself said that there are probably more bodies still out there with more of Corona's personal things." Sticking out his chin and smiling proudly, he glanced around the table. "Let's keep going, that's what I think. Hell, that fat prosecutor, Tejie, he said it all in a nutshell." Rogers always mispronounced Teja's name, which was East Indian. There were a lot of East Indians and Mexicans and Japanese in the farm area of Sutter County where the murders had taken place. "If they'd only had victim one for their evidence Corona would've never been arrested and we wouldn't even be here in court. So let's go on. The real evidence is up ahead." He stopped talking and sat back, tall, well-built, well-dressed, truly distinguished-looking in a good Anglo-American way.

"Thank you," said Ernie, shaking his head. "Well, it appears we are of two different opinions but . . . I believe that what we should do is—" Rick was waving his hand. "Okay, Rick, what do you suggest?"

"I suggest we do as much as we can in straightening out this first body and I, or someone, keep track of the evidence discussed, and then go on to the next, and the next, and not think of anything final at this time. Teja did in fact say that there would be no case against Corona if we were solely dependent on victim number one or any other single victim. And Ron Fahey, the other prosecutor, said in his rebuttal argument to Hawk that this case must be looked at as a whole. Not as this piece of evidence or that piece of testimony, but all the evidence and all the testimony as one larger picture of the whole."

"Right!" yelled Rogers, cutting in. "That's what I said that Tejie said and, right, Fahey said the same thing. We've got to look at the evidence as a whole. One big picture. I know. I paint since I retired and it makes all the difference in the world."

"Yes," said Faye, "but we must also deal more thoroughly with this first victim before we—"

"Hell," said Rogers, "we all agreed not to vote or think about a verdict at this time. So let's go on!"

"I don't believe Jim and I were referring to a decisive conclusion," continued Faye, "we only meant to emphasize that—"

"All of you are right!" cut in Rick, louder than Rogers and Faye. "But we need to take notes! And keep track of our points of discussion or we'll never remember where we agreed or where we disagreed!"

"All right, all right," Ernie said, drumming his fingers on the table.

George and Frank were looking at each other, shaking their heads. Calvin was also shaking his head. Victor pushed away from the table in disapproval. Matt drummed the table along with Ernie.

"You people have had your turns," Ernie was saying. "Now please, let's move on. You're next, Larry. What can you add to victim one? What suggestions do you have after listening to this spicy little bunch of fine, orderly people?"

"Oh, I don't know," said Larry. He was slender and the only juror other than Matt who wore colorful clothes. "I wasn't really listening to them. I was glancing through my notes while they were all talking at the same time and, interestingly enough, the witness I thought was so important to grave one I don't think has even been mentioned." All the jurors became quiet. "Cummings, the carpenter, remember him and how he kept a daily work log? I have in my notes that in May on the 18th, the 19th, and the 20th, Cummings didn't work at the main Sullivan camp on the east side of Highway 99. He worked those three days at the second camp off of Sanders Road on the west side of 99. And he testified that on one of those days, the 18th, 19th, or 20th, he saw Corona alone in his van . . . no, I think it was his pickup . . . anyway, he saw Corona turn off Sanders Road and drive through camp two and continue south into the orchards. And further testimony told us that you can drive through this second camp and through the orchards over to Kagehiro's property where that first body was found.

"So what I figure is this, that these days were in a man's work log and that's a lot better than people trying to remember dates and things that happened over a year and a half ago. And also this same route could've been taken not only to gravesite number one, but also to gravesites number two and thirteen. Still, I don't know if this is all that conclusive." He stopped talking and began glancing through his five-by-eight notebook. "That's all I have, Ernie. Thank you."

"Thank you," said Ernie. "Next, Frank, what can you add to body number one or to body number two, the first two gravesites which were found on the west side of Highway 99?"

"Oh," said Frank, smiling a small smile that grew and grew until it lit up his entire face. "I don't believe I'm going to be much help. I've never been one for talking. Even as early as high school I always found it extremely difficult to express myself. Especially when we were in groups, like the baseball team and other things like that." He sat up, and he adjusted his glasses and quit smiling. "I don't know how to express this but . . ." Now he wasn't smiling. "The single most important item in connection with gravesite one, I believe, is the tire tracks." He was a small man but he seemed to be growing bigger and bigger the more serious he became. "Of course, I fully realize that the prosecution had the wrong set of tire tracks for a while, then I know they mixed everything up . . . almost like a comedy and at the end barely got it straight, but still . . . didn't those last tire casts along with the testimony of that expert from the U.S. Treasury, who specializes in tire tracks and things of that sort, put Juan Corona's vehicle directly at gravesite one? I think so and I think this is very important evidence." Now Frank smiled and he was once again small and very kind-looking but . . . with his steel-gray crew-cut hair and his thick-rimmed glasses and his erect posture he seemed so strong and confident in his views that it would take a great deal to ever change his mind.

Victor, a grocer, was next and said he had nothing to say. He and Faye were the only jurors who had gone to college. He'd gone to Pepperdine in Los Angeles on a baseball scholarship.

It was Matt's turn and he got up, went to the pile of evidence on the clerk's desk, and said, "Look at all this stuff. Gobs of it. And I'll tell you, if we're really going to deliberate, as some of you I guess really think we really are, well then, I can foresee that in not too very long we're going to be getting into the actual pieces of evidence, and if so we're never going to be able to find any of the individual pieces, much less keep them in order, unless we have an index or something of that nature. Hell, just look at this mess. Those buck-passing professionals!"

Rick got up and began going through the papers in evidence to see if there was an index sheet. Matt assured Rick that there was none; he'd already gone through those papers immediately after lunch. Faye told Rick to be careful not to misplace the individual pieces. At this point, Ernie suggested they take a ten-minute coffee break and, during the break, Rick and Faye could go through the piles of evidence together, as a team, to avoid all problems, and he, Ernie, would call the bailiff and tell him that they needed an index.

The rest of the jurors began getting up and stretching. Deliberations had finally commenced.

After the index was brought in the jurors examined it.

It was a record of exhibits both for the People and for the defense. In the first column was the date a particular exhibit had been admitted; in the next was the exhibit number; in the third were the exhibits that had not been admitted but had only been marked for identification; and in the last column was a brief description of those exhibits admitted for evidence.

The jurors were beginning to get a feel for the case. Each piece of evidence seemed to be coming alive to them as perspectives changed again and again. All through the long trial they'd been silent and the attorneys had done all the talking but now, as they talked, the jurors were finding out a lot about themselves and about the case which they had never been aware of before.

Their deliberations had gone pretty well even though they'd reached no conclusions yet. They were just talking, going over the evidence, and trying to remember what they'd heard and seen during the five months of the trial, and surprisingly they were discovering that, as a group, as a collective memory, they were recalling much more than any one of them individually ever did.

At five thirty bailiff Ed Hehr knocked on the main doors of the courtroom to inform the jurors that unless they had something to bring to the court's immediate attention, their first day's work was over and they should start getting ready to go. Ernie said they had nothing immediate, and George jumped up and asked Hehr where they would eat and sleep, because he was hungry and tired and ready to go.

"Not so fast," laughed Hehr. "Your bus won't be here until ten minutes to six. What I'd like to do right now is fix you men up by roommates. Two people per room."

He took out a pencil and a notebook. "All right, who wants to be with who?"

Everyone was walking around and stretching.

The men began telling Hehr whom they'd like to room with. Rick turned to Jim: "Why don't we room together, okay?"

"Well," said Jim. There was a little hesitation in his voice but Rick didn't notice it, so Jim said, "Okay. Sure. Why not?" And he smiled. After all, they were both from Vallejo and they were the youngest jurors and they both worked with metal: Rick as a welder and Jim as an inspector.

"Oh, Matt!" yelled George, with open arms.

"George!" answered Matt, extending his hand.

And both men laughed, gripping each other's hands and Ed Hehr wrote down their names. They were both ex-military men and both liked to drink and eat and joke, so they were a natural combination. Everyone laughed along with them except Calvin, the only black on the jury. He was looking at Jim, his Bible-reading partner, but then he looked away and went to the bathroom, instinctively figuring that maybe it would be best to leave the room and let things kind of take care of themselves in his absence.

He left the room quietly, not allowing anyone to catch the feeling of what he himself was not yet completely aware of. Slipping out like a wise old buck deer that leaves the meadows and disappears into the protective canyons of darkness just before the hunting season begins. Each fall. An instinct in deer that developed in less than fifty years but as true, as solidly based in their survival psyche, as instincts which had taken ten thousand years to develop.

"Frank," Larry was saying, "how about us?"

"Fine," said Frank, "I'd like that very much. We drove to court together every day so we might as well room together. We don't seem to get on each other's nerves, do we?"

"No, not at all."

"Good," said Frank. He and Larry were in a car pool with Naomi. One week Frank used his small Dodge, another week Larry used his old Ford wagon. Naomi, a widow living alone, had no car.

Victor and Ernie decided to room together, since they were both from Vacaville and their kids went to the same high school.

"And besides," said Ernie, "I'm a good talker and you're a good listener."

"I have to be when you're around," laughed Victor.

Calvin was coming back into the room, slowly, cautiously. Ed Hehr was now asking who was left. Rogers looked around the room.

"Oh, Donald Rogers and Calvin Williams," said Hehr. "Well, I guess that takes care of all the men. And the women, that's easy enough. There are only two." Hehr closed his notebook. "Okay, I'll get out and let you folks do whatever you were doing"—he laughed—"then I'll see you all in the jury room in fifteen minutes. Any questions? Anything you'd like, just ask. A matron and another officer and myself will be with you people at all times, day and night. Oh, by the way, it's raining hard so I suggest you put your coats on."

After he left, the jurors began to mill about, doing nothing. Calvin watched and he saw Rogers, looking disgusted, take out a cigar and walk about the room, grumbling to himself. Calvin nodded in self-understanding.

Ernie, talking loudly, suggested that all the pieces of evidence be put away, all cups and mugs be taken to the jury room, and that everyone remember where they had left off so they could resume deliberations in the morning without confusion or disagreement. Then he officially adjourned the first day's session and reminded the jury not to talk about the case until tomorrow. He and Matt began picking up the pieces of evidence. There were almost a thousand of them, and so far they'd only referred to about half a dozen.

After the jurors had put on their coats and were going down the hall to the elevators, Faye dropped behind to speak to the matron, Georgia Wallis.

"I'd like to ask you something," said Faye.

"About the case . . . ?" Mrs. Wallis shook her head. "No, I'm sorry. We can't talk to you about the case."

"No, not about the case. About our room accommodations."

"Oh," said the matron, smiling, "then by all means ask me." Georgia Wallis was a young, attractive woman in her late twenties, quick to smile.

"I like Naomi," said Faye, "but she smokes too much. If at all possible I'd prefer not to room with her."

"Oh, of course," said Mrs. Wallis. "That's no problem. We were told that you are to be made as comfortable as possible. I'll take care of it. Don't worry about a thing."

"Thank you."

"Not at all. Thank yourself. It's you, the taxpayers, that make this all possible."

Faye pursed her lips, thinking that this was an odd statement. She realized the matron was only trying to be congenial, but she didn't like to be reminded about taxes. Faye and her husband, a special teacher for children with speech deficiencies, were building a beautiful home on the Mendocino coast, a wooded area three hours north of San Francisco, and the taxes were going up faster than they could finish building the house. Their dream house—and after all these years they might have to sell it before ever getting to live in it.

Outside the courthouse it was dark, cold, and raining. Pedro Corona was reminding the Corona supporters that it was important for the jury to realize that Juan Corona was not alone, that there were people who believed in him and knew he was innocent. That they had to demonstrate by their number that this trial was an injustice, that it was a politically racist trial! That Sheriff Whiteaker himself knew he'd arrested the wrong man but what could he do? He couldn't back out or Mr. Hawk would automatically win Juan's suit for three hundred million dollars against Sutter County!

Waiting near the bus were Juan Corona's wife Gloria and their four daughters, Juan's mother Candida, his brothers Felix and Alberto, and other relatives. Also waiting were Richard Hawk, his wife Geneva, and his legal aide Eddie Cray.

Sheriff's deputies in bright yellow slickers were asking the crowd of press and supporters to make room for the bus to drive out, but they left the Corona family alone. It was easy for them to tell who were family and who were Chicano supporters. All the Coronas dressed very conservatively, the men in suits and ties, the women in dresses and high heels. The Brown Berets and other Chicanos, on the other hand, had long hair and wore old faded Levi's patched with red and yellow flowers. Hawk had argued with many of the young Chicanos that Juan Corona did not consider himself a Chicano, but—in the oldest American sense—a real American, a man from a foreign country who had chosen to come to this country and make a better life for his family and himself. That Juan had but lately embraced the word "Chicano" in an attempt to gain some sort of personal identity. That Juan was a religious man, a conservative man, a family man, a man who had never let a mouth go by without sending money home to his mother.

The young Chicanos had replied that all that was fine but they would not be caught dead carrying around candles and kneeling down and praying. That if they were to support the Corona cause, they'd carry signs emphasizing injustice, politics, and racism. That, man, the world had changed, and crucifixes and candles were corny, degrading, and ultimately did not help to expose the real problems of economic servitude.

Hawk had finally agreed; a compromise had been reached, and there they were, the Coronas and the Chicanos, two very different types of Americans but both of Mexican descent.

Now the TV crews were in position, with cameras and microphones ready. Everyone was waiting for the jurors to come out of that rear door and walk past that armored car in the enclosed area on their way to the bus.

Just before they were to leave, the jurors were informed of the situation outside and told that for security reasons it was best—once the steel gate was opened—for them to keep in line and walk briskly to their bus.

"Any questions?" asked Ed Hehr.

"Yes," said Ernie, "but this isn't a question. Please, I'd like to say to all us jurors that I believe it would be advisable for us not to look at the spectators. It would be best for us to look down or straight ahead. We don't want a lot of people trying to guess or interpret what our facial expressions might mean."

Suddenly the jurors were outside. Cameras were popping, microphones being shoved at them. The crowd was moving, swaying, shouting, alive with the expectation of potential danger.

The deputies held.

There were yells of "Justice for Juan! *Justicia para Juan!*" And posters and flags and long banners were raised, waved, and pushed forward as far as possible.

The deputies held.

The jurors were in line, handing their bags to the driver. Then, as Victor and Larry boarded the bus, the four Corona girls were pushed up a little closer, two or three feet. And lights flashed, catching the photo for tomorrow's front page with the jury getting on the bus and Juan's four daughters standing there in the rain, eyes large and frightened.

Faye saw who pushed the little girls.

Frank, right behind Larry, saw who pushed them.

Ernie saw who pushed the girls and, being farther back, also saw who was behind those who did the actual pushing.

It was like a phantasmagoria of still-life slides, all being recorded by cameras, tape recorders, TV crews.

Then it was over. The jurors were in the bus and the bus was moving and the last face that was visible as the bus windows snapped by like little picture frames was Jim Owen's, his eyes sad as he looked through the rain-splattered glass at the Corona children and all the others standing in the rain and darkness.

Second Day—
Friday, January 12, 1973

It was January, mid-winter, and it was becoming one of the coldest, wettest winters in California history. Already nearly thirty inches of rain had fallen, and the normal rainfall was closer to twenty.

It rained all of that first night—a bad night for most of the jurors. They were staying at a Travel Lodge motel behind an all-night Sambo's pancake house on North Texas, one of the main streets of Fairfield, and the traffic was heavy all night long, especially the trucks in the early hours of morning.

At seven Ed Hehr started knocking on the jurors' doors. "It's time. You have forty-five minutes. At fifteen to eight we'll be going to breakfast."

"What the hell is this!" yelled Rick. "The army? I already did my fucking time."

Jim, Rick's roommate, didn't approve of swearing, so he didn't laugh or offer any words of encouragement as he normally did. He just got up quietly and went to the bathroom. Neither Jim nor Rick had slept well and then, about daybreak, when they had just been getting to sleep, the ceiling had begun to shake and pound as if it were about to cave in.

Someone was running in place in the room above them.

Someone was bouncing and moving and working out with incredible vigor.

Rick had cursed and threatened to smash the guy in the mouth, but finally he just covered his head with his pillow. Jim had gotten up and gone to the toilet and then returned to his bed to read his Bible and try to get his mind off the case.

The *someone* had been Calvin, who was fifty-one years old and had promised himself to keep in perfect physical shape and, as he'd done his morning exercises, his roommate Rogers had lain in bed and watched, first with surprise, then with annoyance and disapproval. But finally, as the exercises went on and on, he'd asked Calvin how old he was and when Calvin answered Rogers had whistled with real admiration, shaking his head as he looked at Calvin's almost-naked, dark-brown, sweat-shiny, good body, and he said no more.

At fifteen to eight Hehr came by again and told them it was time for breakfast and that they would have to go as a group. Arrangements had been made for the jurors to use Sambo's private dining room and go in by a back door.

Ernie and Victor were the first to come out. Victor was in the grocery business, so he always got up early. He'd slept well and had been up since five thirty. Ernie had not slept well. All night he had dreamed about his experiences as a war prisoner, about those first few weeks, about that time which his mind did not want to recall now, and he wondered what they'd done to him, and he further wondered about the human mind, the human species, and he wondered about Corona and all those dead men and then . . . he realized he was a juror, he was a man who was going to have to pass judgment on another man, and he didn't really like any of it at all. Not one bit. And so Ernie decided that after this trial was over he'd like to learn more about this man who was accused of twenty-five brutal murders. My God, some of them had been stabbed and chopped so many times their own families would not have been able to recognize them.

Why?

Why would a man do this to another man?

Good God.

Maybe after the trial he would go up to Yuba City and look at those orchards where the graves had been found.

He'd like to see the ranch foreman, Ray Duran, who had testified in court. He'd like to ask Duran a few questions, because he was sure that Duran knew a lot more than he had testified to in court.

In fact, Ernie and a few of the other jurors had agreed that all the Mexicans who worked on the Sullivan Ranch knew a lot more than they'd said in court. They had to. It was only common sense. Hell, how could a man, single-handedly, kill and bury twenty-five men with nobody seeing anything? Impossible.

The last of the jurors were coming out of their rooms into dark, drizzly morning.

"Good morning!" yelled George, moving about energetically. "Where are we going to eat? Man, I slept like a dog and I need some black coffee!" He turned to Ernie. "How'd you sleep? Ah, old buddy?"

"Not so good," said Ernie, shaking his head. "But what sleep I didn't get, Vic here made up for. Man, can he sleep. He tells me goodnight and before I can answer him he's sound asleep."

Victor laughed, raising his glasses on the bridge of his nose. "That's because I was afraid you'd start a speech, Ernie."

"Ah, come on, I don't talk that much."

"The hell you don't."

"Man," said Matt, "aren't we a congenial little bunch!" And Matt slapped Victor on the back and Victor, the only Latin on the jury, slapped Matt in return. Victor was as large a man as Matt.

Rick came up to them, talking loudly. "I had a miserable night! I wouldn't have slept a wink if it hadn't been for that night cap of George's."

"Ssssssh!" said George, putting his finger to his lips. "That's our survival kit."

The group of men who knew about the smuggled whiskey bottle laughed, but became quiet when the deputies came up. They all exchanged good mornings and then the officers and Mrs. Wallis walked the jurors across the shiny-wet asphalt to Sambo's.

There were a few newsmen in the front of the restaurant but they didn't see the jury go in the back door.

Some of the jurors didn't eat at all; others just had coffee and a roll. Their coffee-and-doughnut routine was hard to break. Rick suggested they take a dozen doughnuts to have with their coffee, but no one responded. Almost everyone was . . . not so much on edge, but not feeling normal. Not only had their daily routine of waking up at home and driving to the trial been disrupted, but their more or less comfortable role in the trial itself—sitting and listening impassively—had been radically changed. Now *they* were the ones doing the talking, the thinking, the remembering, and it was a taxing responsibility.

Breakfast went quietly. Matt, for one, kept pulling at his beard. He was not at ease. He missed his morning paper. All his life he'd read the dailies wherever he'd been stationed in the service, except when he was in a combat zone. Sure, he knew the Judge told them every day they were not to read papers or listen to the radio or watch TV but hell, the Judge only meant that in connection with the Corona case. Man was an animal of habit, and he wasn't about to change his habits overnight just because somebody told him to. So all trial long Matt had read his papers every day. The *San Francisco Chronicle*, the *Vallejo Times-Herald*, and sometimes the *Sacramento Bee* or the *Sacramento Union*. Only he'd always kind of skipped over those headlines that mentioned Corona, or mass murder, or more confusion in the confusion of the prosecution's case in Fairfield.

He smiled as he finished his coffee.

Those headlines were catchy, and often so misleading that in spite of himself a few times he'd read a whole article concerning the Corona case. Man, thought Matt, he wasn't the only one who thought this was the most fucked-up case ever presented in a courtroom. The press thought it was too. And his eyes twinkled as he recalled the day the prosecution had brought in all those little plastic bags of fingers, which they'd cut off the victims so they could fingerprint them for identification down at the state capital. Then they'd got all the bags and fingers mixed up, and Hawk had made a joke out of them in court. That Hawk, he was a feisty little fat fighter. Teja, he was big—probably six feet and two hundred and fifty pounds—and he'd got so mad he'd wanted to hit Hawk with Corona's big Mexican machete.

Matt laughed.

George asked him why he was laughing.

Matt asked George if he recalled those little bags of cut-off fingers.

Immediately George stopped eating.

Matt laughed again.

After breakfast, the deputies told them to go to their rooms and pack up. The bus would arrive in twenty minutes, at fifteen to nine.

George approached Ed Hehr and, with a smile, asked, "Were you a sergeant in the Air Force, by any chance?"

Hehr smiled and said, "Twenty years."

George stamped his foot and snapped his fingers. "Trapped again! Dammit!"

Hehr laughed and, opening the door, motioned for them to move along. George began to count cadence. Hehr smiled. He had a good face, and his eyes were alive and he was warm and friendly; the jurors could tell that he was a man first and an officer of the law second. He had that certain quality of self-confidence that gives a lawman the wisdom and perspective to know when to be tough and when to be warm and charming and, most essential of all, to know, deep in one's self, when to act one way and when the other. Some of the young deputies lacked this quality and never understood why they antagonized people with their orders while Ed Hehr seemed to accomplish his objectives with such ease and naturalness. He was a good cop, a professional.

Across town some ten blocks due west, closer to Interstate 80, which runs from San Francisco to Sacramento, was the rented house of Juan's wife, Gloria Corona. The house was only fifteen years old but it was one of those low-cost flat-roofed tract houses that after a few years would look flat and small and defeated. No amount of yard work or painting could save it.

A large "For Sale" sign was staked in the front yard.

All through the trial Gloria, her four daughters, and her mother-in-law had stayed in this small one-bath, two-bedroom house. Now they had been joined by some of Gloria's sisters-in-law and brothers-in-law for these decisive days of jury deliberations. Fortunately it was not as bad as it might have been because Gloria was accustomed to hard work and cooking for many people. During the busy months when Juan had been doing labor contracting, she'd risen at three o'clock morning after morning and ridden with him—she didn't know how to drive—the six miles from their home in Yuba City to the Sullivan Ranch north of town. There she'd put on coffee and cooked beans, eggs, and potatoes enough to feed sixty to ninety men. Then she'd begun making fresh flour tortillas from scratch, not only for breakfast but for lunch—three tacos per man.

She'd lifted sacks of flour and potatoes—Juan had helped her—that weighed a hundred pounds each, and used pots and pans of enormous size and weight. Vigorously, she'd worked for hours before the first signs of dawn. Vigorously, she'd worked through the spring and into the summer, when the pre-dawn hours were no longer cool and the temperature had risen to over a hundred degrees. Vigorously, in those months, she'd finished cleaning up after breakfast so that Juan could drive her home and she could attend to her daughters for a few hours before coming back to do the noon lunch and prepare for the main evening meal.

At home they'd had a young Mexican girl (an illegal alien from Mexico) caring for their daughters, but they'd never been able to get a girl, legal or illegal, to help her in the camp kitchen. That work was too hard and Juan, the man of the house, had explained that they'd have to pay too high a wage to get anyone. So instead Gloria—five feet one and a hundred and ten pounds—had done all the work for the past eleven years, only taking a few weeks off each time a child was born.

So, now, in Fairfield in their rented house, here she was again, up at five thirty putting on a pot of coffee, a pot of beans, and getting eggs and potatoes ready as she started preparing an enormous ball of dough for the tortillas for breakfast and lunch and dinner. At six thirty she woke her daughters, trying to get them through with the bathroom before their grandmother awoke. The elderly Doña Corona had a difficult time sleeping. Sometimes she'd pace the house until the early morning hours and not fall asleep until daybreak. Pedro Corona, who lived outside of the Twin cities of Marysville and Yuba City and commuted an hour and a half each way to Fairfield every day, tried to get his mother to come home with him but she usually declined. Pedro had seven small children, and his wife, a tall, handsome woman, was pregnant and their home was not much larger than this rented house. It was a difficult situation, but nothing compared to the way it had been at the beginning of the case.

Right after Juan was arrested, Pedro had taken Gloria and her daughters to his house, and that same day Rosario and her children had come to give moral support, and Alberto and his family had come, and Felix and his family had come, and that small house of Pedro's had sheltered and fed more than eighteen relatives for days on end.

Those had been the truly trying times. Juan had been arrested and newsmen and curiosity seekers were harassing them and they had a public defender who didn't speak Spanish. Old friends, people they'd known since 1952 when they'd first come to this area from Mexico, looked at them strangely or avoided them altogether.

But now, here in Fairfield, it was much better. Richard E. Hawk, a well-known criminal attorney, whose wife, Geneva, spoke Spanish, had agreed to defend Juan, and Hawk, true to his name, had clawed into their cause with beak and nail. Or, as Pedro and Gloria said, Hawk had saved the day. With Hawk on the case, the Sutter County Sheriff's Department suddenly quit giving the Coronas excuses and pushing them around. And then, within a few months, people stopped looking at them strangely. After all, they had a big-time attorney who flew in from the San Francisco Bay Area in his private plane. They had a man on their side who was not afraid to shout and demand or even—as he later proved—go to jail for their cause. In their estimation, Hawk was *un macho a todo dar*, and he was smart, too. He'd set up press conferences to tell the world that on the evidence Sutter County had they would never have arrested Corona had he not been a Mexican. That of course he wasn't saying that they'd arrested Corona *because* he was Mexican. "I'm not saying that at all," Hawk would tell the newsmen. "Hell, a police department can't do that anymore. But I am saying that if Corona had been an educated white

American or, more particularly, a rich local rancher, the sheriff would not have gone storm-trooping at three in the morning to the suspect's home. The sheriff's deputies would have gotten there at eight in the morning and said, 'Hello, Mr. Sullivan, we found a slip of paper in a grave on your property. Could you please explain this?' And Mr. Sullivan would have been given the chance to talk, to tell them where he'd been on May 20th, the day Kenneth Whitacre was killed.

"Believe me, I'm not saying Corona isn't a suspect; I'm saying that every man out there on the Sullivan Ranch is an equally good suspect. But Corona was arrested first. So no one else was ever investigated and anything which was found which pointed toward someone else—like Ray Duran or Sullivan himself—was ignored!"

In the Corona family's estimation, Hawk had brought the whole world around, first to a neutral position, then to their side. Now many people believed that Juan was indeed innocent and would soon be freed. Now the papers, the radio, and the TV were giving the Corona family words of compassion, understanding, and hope. These days, during the jury deliberations, were by far the best days they'd had since that nightmare began with Juan Vallejo Corona's arrest.

The jury arrived at the courthouse Hall of Justice at five minutes to nine. The press, the supporters, and the Corona family awaited them. The bus pulled into the rear parking lot at the east side of the courthouse and stopped in an area surrounded by a twelve-foot-high fence. Newsmen were taking pictures through the mesh fence as the jurors began getting out of the bus. Most of the jurors kept their heads down, but a few did not. Larry glanced at the crowd of people. He recognized many faces—the family, the twelve or fifteen regular press, and the six or eight long-time supporters. He smiled, and that smile of Larry's was photographed and all day long and into the weekend people would speculate about *that smile*.

Larry was one of the most controversial jurors. He was over forty but, with his brightly colored clothes, he had an air of youthfulness—not a come-lately hippie like Matt but . . . less obvious, more subtle, and maybe more genuine. A few years back Larry had quit smoking and drinking and had purchased a ten-speed bicycle and begun to take long rides alone on weekends. And doing this, he met many young people, and he began to eat less rich food and more vegetables and nuts and dried fruits. Old feelings of his forgotten youth surfaced and he re-evaluated his life and went back to doing little things he'd cherished years ago, like making homemade ice cream, enjoying a walk to the local store instead of driving, and not watching TV so much but instead equipping his pickup and going camping with his children.

The jury wasn't called to order until sixteen minutes after nine.

Rick had forgotten to prepare the electric coffee pot the night before.

Ernie began by going over what they'd covered the day before, saying that they'd discussed victim number one in detail, then covered victims two and three and four in a sporadic, superficial way. "So, has anyone thought of anything that they could add to these victims or should we proceed to the other victims?"

Rick raised his hand. Ernie recognized him.

"Why don't we take a vote to see where we stand?" said Rick. "I think we could save a lot of time if we all knew how we felt."

"Right!" said Rogers. "Let's see how we really stand. Otherwise we could be here for months. Hell, it took them five months just to present us with the prosecution's side! It's a good thing the defense never said anything. We could've been here for a year."

"I don't think I agree with that," said Rick. "I think Hawk blew it when he didn't present a case!"

"He had nothing to say!" said Rogers.

"After five months of evidence against his client he had nothing to say?" asked Rick.

"Okay," said Matt, "so he passed the buck. That's no news. Officers and professionals and politicians have been doing that since time began. Who do you think foots the bill in blood for all these wars? It's us, me and you, the people who go out there and die. Big deal, so Hawk didn't put on a case, so the prosecution put on an ass-backward, messed-up case, so . . ." He shrugged. "That's life, we got no one lower to pass the buck to so we might as well shut up, dig in, and go to it." He licked his lips. "So sit back, quiet down, and let's follow those basic rules Ernie laid down yesterday or believe me, we're never going to get anywhere."

Rogers and Rick did as told.

"Well," said Ernie, "thank you, Matt, but how to go on I don't know. Maybe—" Faye raised her hand and so he recognized her.

"Ernie," began Faye, "the Judge told us at the end of his instructions that—oh, I wish I could recall the exact words. But no matter, in essence he told us that we are not partisans or advocates, like the attorneys. That we are the judges. And he stressed the fact that it was rarely good for a juror to express his opinion or to state how he intends to vote at the beginning of deliberations because his sense of pride might be aroused, then he, or she, may be hesitant to change his position even if their position was later shown to be wrong."

She took off her glasses and began polishing them. "I'm sorry. I know I'm not making myself quite clear but do you see what I'm trying to say? I'm trying to say that I don't believe we'll save time by taking a vote before we first go over all the evidence; that it's important not to jump the gun, as the saying goes." Faye smiled and put her glasses on the table. Her last words had surprised her. She'd never heard herself use that corny saying "jump the gun," which so many men used back home in Iowa. She sat back and folded her arms and, squinting, glanced around the table. She would fight for this point. It was important.

Rick began to talk.

Faye cut him off. "You were not recognized!"

He looked at her and began to raise his hand but then didn't.

"Well," said Ernie, "I guess there won't be any vote taken at this point."

Rogers grumbled.

Victor laughed.

Calvin smiled.

And no vote was taken and all twenty-five victims and most of the evidence were talked about but . . . it was difficult for it truly seemed that most of the jurors were anxious to know where everyone else stood before expressing their own views. So, an hour later, after their first morning coffee break, they took their first vote.

Secretly. By written ballot. Using ripped-off pieces of paper from the long rolls of paper on the court reporter's desk. Each juror wrote down his or her verdict and then put the paper into a cardboard box Matt had found in the trash can.

When everyone had voted, Ernie read each slip of paper.

Not guilty.

Innocent.

Guilty.

Not guilty.

Guilty.

Innocent.

And so forth until he'd read off all twelve. They stood at seven for innocent and five for guilty.

There was a lot of heavy breathing, a lot of smiling, and a lot of stretching. And then everyone looked at everyone else, trying to see how the others had voted.

Ernie gave them a ten-minute break and suggested that everyone relax, not work his fellow jurors over the hot coals trying to figure out how he or she voted. These were secret ballots and the reasons for secrecy were obvious and most essential.

They were back at the table in five minutes, ready to go.

Ernie smiled.

Matt laughed.

Rick had his hand up, Faye had her hand up, and Rogers—who had voted for innocent although no one would have guessed it—also had his hand up. Ernie didn't want to call on any of these three because they did more than their share of the talking, so he looked around. Jim and Calvin raised their hands. He recognized Jim.

"Ernie," said Jim, "I'm still bothered by this collective or separate business."

"Oh, God!" said Rogers.

Jim stopped, looked at Rogers, and then continued, "What I mean, Ernie, is I voted innocent and it's beyond me how anyone could have voted Corona guilty. Guilty of what? Count one, count two, or all twenty-five?" He stood up. "There was not one eyewitness, there was never any motive established, and my gosh, the innumerable mistakes and contradictions in the prosecution's first phase, the body-discovery phase, were appalling. Their victims weren't even numbered correctly! Evidence was misplaced. Fingers, which they amputated from the victims for fingerprinting, were lost. Ernie, I'm for going back and working on each victim, one by one, getting each one straightened out before proceeding to the next." Rick sat up and began to wave his arm. Jim noticed but continued. "We all recall how Hawk made the prosecution look like fools in those first two months. Even the Judge was so angered at the prosecution's mistakes and contradictions that every few minutes he'd say that he and counsel would have to go to his inner chambers." Rick was still waving his arm and Rogers was beginning to speak. "Rick!" said Jim. "Put your hand down and let me finish what I'm saying! I can't think with you waving like that."

Calvin nodded. "I agree, it's disturbing and rude to be waving like that."

Rick turned to Calvin, then back to Jim, and there he held . . . halfway between anger and embarrassment, and then he put his hand down and Rogers closed his mouth and the table was heavy with silence for a long moment.

Ernie finally spoke. "Proceed, Jim."

"Thank you," said Jim. "Well, what I had in mind is that we take one of the victims, the one which seems to have the most direct evidence and—"

"That's what I was going to suggest!" snapped Rick. "I'm not against you, Jim. I'm your friend and I was only trying to . . ." Quickly, he broke off, swallowed, and sat back, rocking in his chair with his head down.

Jim said, "I'm sorry I was sharp with you, Rick. I'm your friend too and I'm sure your intentions were to help me, but please, I'd like to do my own talking, my own thinking, and see for myself if I'm right or if I'm wrong. I'm sorry I hurt you. I didn't mean to." Everyone was looking down or away out of respect for Rick's privacy.

Jim continued, "I believe that Sample's grave with the meat receipts is a good place to start. That's one of the few victims where we have something concrete to work with. We have testimony that Corona purchased meat at Del Pero and Brothers on—what was the date, Rick?"

Rick was writing in his small notebook. He looked up. He thought, then said, "May 21st."

Jim smiled. "Thank you, Rick. On May 21st. The clerk personally gave the two receipts to Corona and Corona signed one, or both, and then folded them and put them in his shirt pocket. Then we got testimony that when the deputies unearthed Sample's body on May 25th—several bodies were discovered on the 25th—they found those meat receipts in sample's grave. We have Deputy Sizelove's testimony saying that he was in the hole doing the shoveling and in one of his shovelfuls of dirt he saw the pink papers out of the corner of his eye as he threw the dirt up on the bank. Then we got testimony by the undersheriff that he picked up the pink papers and unfolded them and found Juan Corona's name on them.

They were made out to Corona for the purchase of meat four days before.

"Now, I believe this is incriminating evidence and if we stick to this one grave, then maybe we can figure out if Corona is indeed guilty or innocent. I mean, there's a big difference between us saying, yeah, it looks like he maybe did it, to saying, yes, we're sure he did it and he's guilty beyond any shadow of a doubt." He stopped. "That's all I have to say."

Many hands shot up. Ernie passed over them and said to Calvin, "Cal, you had your hand up a little while ago. Do you still have something you wish to say?"

"No, not really," said Calvin in his deep but soft voice. The table became quiet. Cal's voice had a sincere quality which made people listen respectfully. "I agree with Jim. I voted innocent and it's beside me how anyone could've voted guilty. All trial long, week after week, I shook my head every day as I went home and I told myself, man, why'd they ever bring this thing to trial. Like Jim said . . . with no eyewitnesses and all the mistakes the sheriff's men made I could never figure how they figured to even arrest the man." A few jurors began moving in their seats, anxious to raise their hands and speak. Calmly, Calvin glanced around, guessing that these were the ones who'd voted guilty: Rick, yes, Faye and Rogers, yes, and maybe Matt and Ernie or . . . it was hard to tell. Maybe the quiet ones like Frank and Larry had voted guilty. He quit guessing and sighed, going on, undaunted. "So like Jim was saying I think we should slow down and work on one victim real good. I think we should pile up our ideas, our evidence, like that—what was his name—that little short attorney that came in halfway through the case?"

"Fahey," said Ernie, "Ronald Fahey, chief deputy district attorney from Santa Rosa."

"Thank you," said Calvin. "Remember how we kept hearing that the prosecution had hired a high-powered attorney at forty-five dollars an hour to come in and put their whole mess together?" Calvin laughed and slapped the table top. "Well, I tell you, when that Fahey came in those first few days and got so mad at Hawk that his face turned purple and he got to stuttering so he couldn't hardly talk I said to myself, man, we got here another Sutter County mistake." Many jurors laughed. "And I didn't change my mind about him until right up there to the very end. I mean, Fahey never seemed like no high-powered attorney. In fact, all three of those prosecutors seemed so slow, so dumb, so . . . you know what I mean. Hawk, he's fast with words and he had them knocked down all the time. Even in his final argument Hawk mixed up all their evidence and made them look so ridiculous that I figured there was no case, no way anyone could ever think this man Corona was guilty. But then, after Hawk talked, Fahey came on for the prosecution's—what do you call it?"

"Rebuttal," said Ernie.

"Yeah, that last talk," said Calvin, "and you know, that was the first time that I saw that that little short Fahey really was a high-powered attorney. He talked like he'd never talked before. He explained everything so nice and simple that nothing was confusing anymore and then . . . when we took each piece of their evidence and piled it up in front of us, piece by piece, gun and knives and slips of paper and pictures of blood running out the back of Corona's van, I then said to myself, hey, they got themselves a case. They've been having one all along but it's just always been too mixed up for me to see it.

"So I think what we should do, is do like that Fahey did, and pile up our ideas and our evidence so we can see it. I don't think we should just run around with all these twenty-five dead men all over the place. Up and down the river like Hawk showed us the sheriff's men did." He laughed. "That Hawk, he was so quick." Calvin laughed some more. "But he didn't put on no case and so I think, to be fair and honest to Corona, we should do like Jim said and work on this one grave with the meat receipts and pile up all we got and see where we are, see if Corona's really guilty or really innocent. And not guess." He stopped. He looked around. "I'm sorry I talked so much. It's not like me but I think this is really important, to not guess."

Ernie stood up. "Don't be sorry, man. I think you did a fine job. I think we should do just like you said. Pile it up like Ron Fahey did and see where we are. I voted innocent myself." The jurors looked at Ernie more closely, expecting him to say more about his vote, but he didn't. He went on. "Okay, who's next? Who has something to add to Sample's grave, number E-1-3, meaning the third victim but the first body found on the east side of Highway 99?"

The Sutter County Sheriff's Department had labeled the first two bodies W-1 and W-2, indicating that these graves had been located on the west side of Highway 99, and then, when the subsequent bodies were discovered *east* of 99, the sheriff's men began labeling them E-1, E-2, E-3, and so forth. Then when they'd unearthed so many bodies that it was getting not only shocking but terribly confusing, they added *another* qualifying number, making them W-1-1, W-2-2, E-1-3, E-2-4, E-3-5, E-4-6, E-5-7, E-6-8, E-7-9, E-8-10, E-9-11, and E-10-12—and then the thirteenth body was found on the west side again, so that one was numbered W-3-13, and then all the rest were found on the east side so they went back to E-11-14, E-12-15, E-13-16, all the way to the twenty-fifth victim, which was numbered E-22-25.

Many jurors had their hands up. Ernie called on George, who always seemed to be able to handle things without offending anyone.

"Well," said George in his quick-snappy voice, "I voted innocent too and I have several things to say, but before I do I'd like to ask a couple of questions." He sat up. "That empty hole in the orchard was seen on May 19th, right?" Faye and Ernie nodded, as did Larry and Frank. "It was reported to the police on May 20th, right?"

"Yes," said Faye, "and that same day, May 20th, 1971, the Sheriff's Department investigated and subsequently unearthed that first body."

"Okay, on May 20th the first body was found." He sat back, shaking his head. "And now you're telling me that on May 21st Corona was given those meat receipts and those same receipts were found in a grave on May 25th?" Jim and Faye were nodding. So were Victor and Rick. "Well, tell me, how can we believe any of this?" asked George. "Good God, this would mean that Corona killed another man even after the first body was discovered and deputies were all over the place looking for other graves. How can you figure that this makes any sense? I mean, wow, this is crazy unless Corona was trying to get himself caught or unless . . . yeah, unless someone else, or maybe a whole group, was doing the killings and planting the evidence against Corona." He glanced around. "Really, I don't see where these meat receipts are all that incriminating. So they have Corona's name on them, so what? That doesn't prove he murdered that man or that he was even there when Sample's body was put in the grave.

"Hawk told us that there is a dump in that area, that it's the ranch's dump, and that everyone on the ranch dumps their garbage there. So why couldn't Corona have dumped his receipts, along with his camp garbage, in that dump, and the wind have blown those receipts over to that grave? Ah, you tell me? I voted innocent and I'm a long ways away from being convinced that anyone is guilty in this case. Those deputies didn't even fingerprint those receipts to see who handled them last. How can we convict someone without any solid proof? I can't." And he sat back in his chair and five or six jurors waved their hands.

"Okay," Ernie said. "We'll go around the table like before. Anyone who wants to say something, just speak up." Calvin was to the right of George but he said he'd already spoken. Naomi was next and she coughed, clearing her throat, then said:

"Well, I voted innocent too and I think we're doing good to go back to the most important victims. How else can we ever straighten out this mess they gave us? Like Hawk said, those receipts could have been blown in there by the wind or those receipts could've been put in there by the real killer, or killers, and because they didn't take fingerprints we'll never know." She smiled and glanced around. "Also, how about the body switch? That's really important. Hawk spent an hour in his closing argument showing us how those policemen were digging up bodies so fast that they fouled up the whole thing. Those receipts didn't come out of Sample's grave. If they had, the prosecution would have a good case, like Hawk said. But they didn't. Those meat receipts came out of Smith's grave, the nine-finger man with the beard, and that body was so old it smelled really bad. Those deputies could hardly bring themselves to get down in the hole and keep digging.

"So, what I'm saying is that George is right and I don't see how four-day-old receipts can be in a grave that's months old unless those receipts were planted by the real killers. And I say killers because I don't see how one man could kill so many men. It don't make sense. And besides, Corona is a happily married man. We all saw his wife and beautiful little girls. And these were homosexual crimes." She took off her glasses and looked around the table. "I voted innocent, I want you to know." She blushed.

Jim was next. He said that he'd already spoken, but that in some ways he agreed with Naomi—many things were still in question and they'd have to be cleared up.

Faye was next, and she sat up, not telling how she'd voted, but commenting that, first of all what Hawk or Teja or any of the attorneys said in their closing argument was not evidence. The Judge in his instructions had told them that they were not to consider what the prosecution or defense had said, that they were only to consider what was said under oath by the witnesses and what was marked in evidence.

"And keeping these things in mind," Faye continued, "I'd like to ask, do we have anything in evidence or any testimony under oath that shows us how these receipts could have blown from the dump three or four hundred yards away and landed in this particular grave? Do we have anything in evidence or testimony under oath that demonstrates that there was indeed a body switch? Do we have anything in evidence that in fact these were homosexual murders? Do we have anything in evidence that indicates that fingerprints could have in fact been taken?

"Remember, these meat receipts were underground and they were damp and dirty and I don't see how prints could have been taken. So what I'm saying is that if we stick to the facts in evidence and the testimony under oath instead of getting into the area of speculations that certain attorneys would like us to get sidetracked with, I believe these meat receipts are very incriminating.

"Besides, consider this: Corona was not a careless man, as we well know. He kept all his receipts for the different camp purchases on a nail in the kitchen. He is not the type of man to have discarded receipts with his garbage in the dump. I believe these receipts do place Corona at that grave while the dirt was being shoveled over that poor man's body." She stopped, face hard set, and said no more.

Rogers, who was next, said, "I agree! Corona was unusually neat for a Mexican and he didn't dump his receipts in the dump. He kept them folded in his shirt pocket and he was planning on tacking them up in the kitchen. I say that they fell out of his pocket when he was shoveling dirt over Sample's body. And about this business of a body switch, you tell me how could those cowtown deputies pull a thing like that off? Eh? I know these type of boys and I say with all the mistakes they made all through this whole case they're not smart enough to pull off a body switch. The only one smart enough to pull off a switch is Hawk. That man is smart and slick and I say those deputies, after they'd dug up so many bodies, they just got their numbers mixed up and fouled up their book work. There never was no deliberate switching of old bodies and new bodies because they—oh, hell, you all know what I mean. We've been seeing and hearing their mistakes and screw-ups for five months! They're not smart enough or organized enough to pull a switch and keep quiet about it. They're honest country boys. Only Hawk, the big city slicker, could've dreamed that one up. And that's that." He sat back, putting his cigar in his mouth. "I voted innocent, too. But not because I have any doubts that Corona isn't guilty. I was just afraid we might've convicted him on the first ballot and I don't think that's right. I think we should do all kinds of talking and explaining before we convict a man of murder." He drew on his cigar. "Fair is fair!"

Larry was next, and he said he didn't have anything to say at this point. He was reading his notes. Frank followed, saying he didn't have anything to say either.

Faye, realizing that neither one of them had said how they'd voted, stared at them and figured they agreed with her verdict of guilty.

Calvin saw Faye looking at them and, like her, said to himself that these two quiet ones were probably for guilty along with Faye and Rick and Matt. He shook his head, disagreeing completely.

Next it was Victor's turn. He laughed and pushed his glasses higher up on his nose. "Well, I'm not agreeing with Rogers." He laughed louder. There seemed to be a nervousness in his laugh. "For in my experience it is not unusual for Mexicans to be neat." He turned to Rogers. "My son-in-law is Mexican, Chicano, whatever you want to call him—" Rogers sat up and began to protest. "No, you said your piece!" bellowed Victor. "Now sit on it! I'm talking!" Rogers shut up. Victor tried hard to calm himself, and then continued more easily. "My daughter is married to a Mexican, as I was saying, and that boy is a cop in Sacramento. He works at night and he goes to college in the daytime and he studies so much and knows so much that my daughter has returned to junior college so she can keep up with him." He swallowed. "She told me, 'Daddy, I can't talk to him anymore. We don't have as much in common as when we both went to high school, so I have to go to college at night after work so I can keep up with him and we can have things in common.' And my girl is no dummy. She's smart. She got good grades in school and has to work, to think, to keep up with this Mexican son-in-law of mine. I can't tell you his name. He's an undercover agent. He has long hair. Longer than most of these Chicano boys out there on this Corona picket line. And when he's off duty he's neat, and he's Mexican!" He took off his glasses, rubbing his eyes. No, he wasn't crying. He was simply speaking with much emotion. "But even though I disagree with a lot of things Rogers says, I still did the same thing he did. I voted innocent because I didn't want us convicting Corona on the first ballot." Many chairs were moved and moved again. "I wanted to make sure that we talked more because this is a serious thing we're doing and, like Jim said, we have to be sure beyond any reasonable doubt. After all, we're going to live with our decision not just today but for the rest of our lives." He said no more.

Next in line was Matt, who leaned forward and said, "I voted guilty. And even though Rogers isn't too tactful a speaker, I also basically agree with him. Those deputies couldn't've made that body switch like Hawk claims they did. In fact, I don't even believe they realized the significance of that or many other things until Hawk brought it out in court.

"They were digging, they were running around in peach orchards with a lot of dead bodies, and they were trying to pawn them off on the morticians as fast as they could. Have any of you ever smelled a man that's been dead for three months? I have and, man, I'll tell you, I would have tried getting rid of those bodies quicker than I found them. You can't imagine the putrid smell we humans give off. That's probably why we've survived as a species. No animal in his right mind would want to eat us." Matt roared with laughter. "So picture this, there they were, country boys, too lazy to work so they became cops in a nice little farm area where crimes hardly ever happen, much less murders, and then they find one dead man, then another, and then lo and behold they're digging and working and sweating and passing bodies to those crazy morticians and the simple truth is that they got their numbering screwed up.

"Believe me, it's not common sense that they stopped and figured, 'Hey, wait boys, something is wrong here. We got four-day-old meat receipts with a three-month-old body so we best change this around and say we found these receipts with the freshest body, which happens to be—oh, yeah, Sample's grave, number E-3-5 or whatever his number is.' No siree, these boys were just digging and trying not to puke—excuse me, ladies—and they never used their head for anything more than something to put their hats on.

"Hawk, he's the one that spotted their bookkeeping mistake and built it out of proportion and has been trying to convince us that it was a purposeful, well-thought-out, deliberate, premeditated coverup and no way in common sense can I accept that." He leaned back, stroking his well-groomed beard. "I voted guilty . . . but not because of what we've covered so far but because . . . good God, the case as a whole. All the blood types, all the suspicious places where Corona was seen, and . . . maybe not most important but highly significant, because of the death ledger where he had so many of the victims' names. Man, do you realize we haven't hardly mentioned that ledger?"

Rick was next. "Well," he began, "I voted for guilty, like Matt." Rick was sitting next to Ernie. Matt sat the east end of the table. It was becoming evident to some jurors that the east end of the table was strong for guilty, and the west end, where Calvin sat, was strong for innocent.

"Talking about this theory of the body switch," Rick continued, "I'd like to say that not only do I agree with Matt and Rogers that the deputies didn't do it, but I'd also like to show—through Hawk's own statements—that these bodies ended up in the very same graves they started in. In other words, Hawk outtalked himself and ended up contradicting his own theory." He ripped a sheet out of his large pad of paper. Rick had several books and several pads of paper with him. Although he was a welder, he went to school three nights a week, hoping to become a teacher, and his favorite classes were in psychology, "Here," said Rick. "Look for yourselves. Hawk tried using the recording officer's report, then the morticians' autopsy report, then an imaginary account of the final renumbering report of what he, Hawk, thinks happened. And, between the three reports, he at first tried mixing up two bodies, an unknown body which was old and Sample's which was fresh. Then when that wasn't sufficient juggling he brought in another body—the bearded man, Smith.

"By the way, Naomi, when you spoke you said that Smith was a nine-fingered man with a beard. According to my notes, *Sample* is the nine-fingered man and Smith is the bearded man, and Sample's is not an old body that smelled like you said. Numerous deputies testified that Sample didn't smell and his skin didn't come off in the deputies' hands when they took him out of the grave. Sample's body was fresh. Smith, the bearded man, was old and smelled bad and his flesh came away from his bones."

Naomi was large-eyed. "I didn't say that!" she yelled. "I mean, I don't recall what I said exactly so how can you remember? I talked a long time ago and all these people have talked since I talked, so how can you tell me what I said?"

"I'm keeping notes," said Rick. "I'm keeping three different sets. One for mistakes, one for evidence, and one for victims in relationship to specific evidence. Each time a juror speaks I mark what he or she said and relate it to—"

"Ernie," said Naomi, "is that legal, what he's doing? He's not our judge." She lit a cigarette and opened her bottle of pills. She called them nerve pills, and she'd been taking them for years, but in the past two or three weeks she'd begun taking them more frequently. "Who does he think he is? He's nothing but a kid."

Rick's face became flushed and he stared straight at Naomi, getting up from his chair. Ernie also stood up.

"Sit down, Rick," said Ernie. Then, turning to Naomi, he said, "Now Naomi, I don't approve of his notetaking either, but please, let's not start on each other on a personal level. We're jurors. We have a responsibility that's one of the very foundations of our entire legal system."

He turned to Rick. "Now you, I will not allow any direct remarks made toward any juror about what he or she said, or did not say. Proceed."

And so Rick contented himself with explaining his sketch and passing it around the table, but within moments it was back to him. And it wasn't because the other jurors disagreed with Rick, it was just that they didn't see the need to find Hawk's theory to be incorrect. Correct or incorrect didn't matter. They'd already agreed that Hawk's first premises had been out of the realm of common sense and so why dwell on it any further? There had been no body switch, in their estimation.

Rick felt a little hurt. He'd worked so hard trying to remember Hawk's exact words in relation to this sketch. He'd thought that maybe he'd be the only one able to explain this problem in a logical manner. He shrugged. Oh, well, he thought—at least Hawk looked worse than he did. For Hawk had literally spent hours belaboring his theory that the deputies had been dishonest, and after all that effort the jury had tossed Hawk and his theory out in a matter of minutes.

Rick was amazed. Hawk was educated and intelligent. So how could people like these, just average people except for Faye, who was highly educated, have seen through his theory so easily? Rick was genuinely concerned. This was all turning out to be very different than he had expected.

The jurors quit their deliberations and were stretching, yawning, and moving about when Ed Hehr came with their lunches on an aluminum wagon. But no one was really very interested in lunch. The catering service was the same one used by the Travis military base for airborne lunches, and George and Ernie—ex-Air Force men—were especially tired of these meals, having had them for over twenty years. Cold roast beef sandwiches on stale white bread, cold mashed potatoes, and cold, over-cooked vegetables. The only things halfway good were the milk, the fruit salad, the two cookies, and the little bits of beef if you threw away the bread.

After lunch Ernie said he thought it would be a good idea to proceed with deliberations by a summation on the evidence in connection with the two victims they had so far discussed the most thoroughly—W-1-1, Kenneth Whitacre, and E-1-3, Melford Sample. He then outlined the evidence pertaining to both and asked who would like to do the summations.

Matt Johnson laughed and said it looked like Ernie had just done it.

Nodding her head, Faye agreed.

Ernie laughed too, and said, "Well, I guess I did. How about that?" Then he asked if he'd covered everything they'd discussed or if there was anything else to be added before taking another vote.

No one offered anything. All the jurors seemed anxious for another ballot. Then, as Ernie was handing out the pieces of paper, Victor started laughing and everyone turned to him. He pointed to Frank and Larry, who were talking together, and said: "You should hear what those two were saying. I never saw it that way."

"Well," said Ernie to Larry and Frank, who were usually the quietest jurors, "what is it? I'm sure we all need a good laugh."

"Well," said Larry, "Frank was telling me that when Hawk had the undersheriff on the stand in cross-examination—you remember at the beginning of the trial—Hawk handed him those pink meat receipts and said, 'You show me how you picked up these two receipts when Deputy Sizelove shoveled them up from the grave. Go ahead, you show me how you put your big sticky fingers all over those receipts.' " Larry laughed and many of the jurors joined him. "Remember how Cartoscelli—I think that was the undersheriff's name—was so scared it looked like Hawk was handing him a cobra?" And he laughed again, rocking in his chair. For it was true, the undersheriff, a handsome young man, had leaped back when Hawk handed him the meat receipts. "But anyway, Cartoscelli finally calmed down and said, 'They were folded, Mr. Hawk.' And so Hawk folded the receipts and handed them to Cartoscelli and he took them with his fingertips. He was so nervous, jumping at Hawk's every word, that he could hardly unfold those two pink papers." Larry was trying hard to stop laughing. "Well, the point Frank makes is that for all of his badgering, what Hawk really proved to Frank here was *not* that those papers should have been processed for prints, but that those receipts could never have blown with the wind a couple of hundred yards from that dump. They were folded up when they were discovered in the grave. They were exactly the same as when the Del Pero meat clerk saw Corona fold them and put them in his shirt pocket." Larry turned to Frank. "Did I state your idea all right?"

"Yes," said Frank, smiling and he leaned forward, glancing around. "I have trouble expressing myself but what I would like to say is that I think Mr. Hawk, the defense attorney, did a fine job of proving to me that those receipts had to have fallen out of Corona's shirt pocket while he was covering up that poor man's body. That those receipts prove beyond any reasonable explanation or doubt that Corona was there at this grave, just like those tire tracks, the second set they showed us, prove to my common sense that Corona was at Whitacre's grave, W-1-1.

"Do you recall what Dr. Rooney from Sacramento said? He said, I believe it was in connection with one of these two victims, that they found residues of dirt in the lungs, that one of these men was still alive and breathing when he was buried." Frank stopped, inhaling deeply, then yelled, "These were terrible murders! These men were brutally killed!

"Oh, it was no joke! And Hawk may be a brilliant man, but I think he missed the boat many times, and this business of Hawk belittling that undersheriff is one of those times! We were all on the stand during voir dire. We all know how it feels. I was so scared on the stand. And Hawk should have done his job of defending his client and not been so theatrical in his . . ." Frank stopped. His eyes were wide, but then they returned to normal. "I'm sorry. I got carried away." And he smiled, and said no more, and once again he was a fine, gentle-looking man, seemingly incapable of such an angry outburst.

Frank's idea was passed around and discussed, and then the jury took its second vote at two o'clock, three hours after the first vote. It came in at three for innocent and nine for guilty.

Everyone was shocked. The first vote had been seven for innocent and five for guilty. Four people had changed their votes. Everyone looked at everyone else, trying to read each other's faces. Not that much evidence had been covered between votes, so how come their voting had changed so drastically?

Calvin and Jim looked at each other. They both shook their heads and knew they were still for acquittal, but who else was with them? They glanced around the table. Not Faye, not Rogers, not Larry or Frank or Victor or Matt or Rick . . . well, it had to be Ernie or George or yes, sitting here between them, Naomi.

Cal and Jim shrugged to each other, not knowing that in fact it was George who was still for innocent, and that Naomi and Ernie had voted for guilty, along with Victor and Rogers.

Ernie suggested that they take another ten-minute coffee break.

Outside the courtroom, Richard Hawk was walking about the courthouse. Now and then he'd stop to talk to a newsman or a supporter, but he wouldn't talk long.

He'd never liked waiting for a jury's verdict. Juries were as fickle as women, in his estimation. You could never tell how a jury would interpret the proceedings in the courtroom. He'd won an acquittal a couple of times when he personally hadn't though he'd had much of a chance; and he'd lost a few, though not many, when he thought he had a good case. To win, Hawk would explain, didn't necessarily mean that you got your man off free as a bird. It meant that, sure. But it also meant that if the prosecution was going for a first-degree conviction and thought they could get it and you ended up with a second-degree or a manslaughter conviction, then you had won.

But in this case there were no second-degree or manslaughter convictions possible. These twenty-five murders, Hawk always said, were as premeditated as taking a steer to the slaughter house. These were first-degree murders. All the victims had been from the lower south side of Marysville—the skid-row part of town—across the river from Yuba City. All had been bums, winos, men without homes or addresses, men who could easily be talked into getting in your vehicle to go do a little job to earn enough money for another bottle. All had been men whom no one would miss. And the killer or killers knew this when he or they took these men out to a dark secluded place and killed them, using a knife or a meat-cleaver type of weapon, and then buried them. Time after time. No money motive involved. Just maniacal mass murder. Chopping and slashing and stabbing. Splitting an entire skull. Hacking off a fourth of another skull. Crushing the nose of another into the brain. Shooting one victim in the head after butchering him. Or maybe shooting him first, then butchering him. These were first-degree murders and the jury in this case would have to come in innocent or . . . No, thought Hawk, a verdict of guilty was out of the question. All these months of trial, with all the mistakes the prosecution had committed, couldn't possibly convict a man.

The jury was discussing victim E-22-25, the last body discovered, and they were beginning to realize that as far as the evidence was concerned, the most important graves were W-1-1, E-1-3, and this last one, E-22-25. Hawk had always referred to the last grave as "a bit much" because not only had it been unearthed on June 4, nine days after Corona's arrest on May 25, but it had been loaded with things that could only be explained as either household garbage or planted evidence to incriminate Juan Vallejo Corona. Hawk had always used this grave to show to the public at large that Juan Corona had been arrested first, and then an investigation had been launched to prove him guilty. That Sutter County had not bothered to investigate anyone else, but they had known by the time they got to court that they'd arrested the wrong man. But, Hawk had said, if the county authorities admitted this they'd leave themselves open for the largest lawsuit in U.S. history.

Faye was talking. She was going over some points in connection with the evidence found in grave twenty-five. Some of the articles had already been discussed: the child's white sock, the Bermuda grass, the religious candle holder, the broken mirror, the rolled-up newspaper, and the bank-deposit slips with Juan Corona's name printed on them.

"I'm not going to belabor the bank receipts," Faye said. "I believe, as Jim so well said, that the witness from the bank covered that sufficiently. Corona, when he came to the bank to make deposits, used the blank deposit slips which are there for anyone to use. He kept his personal deposit slips with his name printed on them at home and used them as a scratch pad, and when he finished with them he threw them in his garbage, along with his lawn trimmings, broken things, and old newspapers.

"Now, the article I want to talk about I don't believe was ever made very clear. Certainly not by Mr. Teja or Mr. Fahey. And Hawk, I don't think he was even aware of this—in my estimation—very important point." She took off her glasses. "Remember the day they brought in that little boy who delivered the newspapers? Bart Williams was doing the questioning. The boy was, oh, about eleven years old and very nice-looking and Bart Williams, poor man, kept going around and around with his questions, trying not to badger the boy and yet make his point. Hawk, very rudely, kept yawning and it seemed like Bart Williams would never get his point made.

"Well, I believe Bart did in fact make a very important

point." She leaned forward. "Bart asked the boy if he liked his job. The boy said not really. Bart asked the boy why not. The boy said because he didn't get paid. Williams asked why he didn't get paid. The boy said because it was only to help out his older brother, who had a real paper route. Bart then asked why wasn't this a real route and the boy said because these were free throw-away papers and he didn't get paid. People laughed. Bart didn't. And Bart asked how long did it take him to deliver these free throw-away papers. The boy said a long time, depending on—and the boy didn't finish his sentence. Bart very tactfully then asked if he'd ever found a way to make his route shorter, if he'd ever been reprimanded for doing something wrong.

"Hawk at this point laughed loudly and many of the press also laughed and I don't think they caught the next line, which was that the young man said yes, he had been in trouble. And Bart asked for what reason and the young man said because on some days, when he wanted to get done early with his route, he'd roll the papers two at a time and . . . the rolled paper in grave twenty-five had two issues of the same paper rolled in one. So I believe not only did Bart show us that this boy threw papers on Corona's block, but that he rolled them *two* at a time, like very few boys do, I'm sure, and this places all those articles in evidence from this last grave as very likely having come from Corona's house and his house alone." Faye hesitated. "Did I make my point? Not just the bank slips with Corona's name but these rolled-up papers. And also this religious candle . . . identical to the one in Corona's kitchen. In my estimation this is conclusive. How else can these articles be interpreted other than that

Mr. Corona was there when victim twenty-five was killed and buried?"

Immediately Rogers agreed with Faye that Corona had definitely been there. That in fact Corona had done the killing and burying. Several other jurors also agreed. There seemed to be no other way to look at the evidence. Then George raised his hand and Ernie recognized him.

"Well," said George, "I know this isn't part of the evidence but I'm human, I'm not a machine, and I'd like to say . . . okay, so it looks like this man Corona did these murders but this isn't proof beyond a reasonable doubt that he did them. I mean, there has got to be more." George shook his head. "God, I wish Hawk had put on a case. For five months I listened to the prosecution's case . . . seeing all their mistakes, hearing all of Hawk's promises that he'd do this, and do that, and then when the prosecution finished and Hawk just sat there and said, 'The defense rests' I could've fell out of my chair. I expected Hawk to give us his side of the story. Sure, I know a man is innocent until proven guilty, and sure I know an accused person doesn't have to testify or defend himself. Sure, I heard the Judge say all that, but . . . good God! If I'd been accused of these twenty-five murders there's no way on earth they could've kept me off the stand. It's not fair what Hawk did. Here we have all this prosecution's stuff to discuss and we have nothing to discuss from the defense's point of view. Hell, I'm not smart. How can I contradict what Faye just said? Her stuff was given to her by the prosecution and unless I'm given something by Hawk to argue back with, I can't contradict her." He sighed, then yelled, "I feel cheated! I wanted to find this man innocent, really I did, but how can I?" He hit the table top. "Dammit! That twenty-fifth grave does look awfully incriminating."

Many jurors nodded, even Jim and Calvin. Then Rick raised his hand, and Ernie recognized him.

"Well, I've written out a few points here that might answer a lot of people's questions but before I read this list I'd like to add to what George just said . . . I feel cheated, too, and I resent Hawk for that." His face flushed angrily but then he continued more easily. "In the first few months of the trial I thought Hawk was the good guy in the white hat. He was brilliant, and quick-minded, and he was tearing those cops apart. Teja and Williams were the bad guys. That's how I saw it. You all remember how Hawk was cross-examining those deputies and making them look like fools. The bodies were all mixed up, the evidence was never finger-printed, and Hawk was bringing all their mistakes out into the open.

"I was an alternate juror then—Hicks hadn't broken his arm yet—and I told my wife that I dreamed of becoming a regular so I could help Hawk. He was so brilliant. That's what I honestly thought. Then, I don't know how to explain it, but things started changing in the third month, about the time I became a juror. Hawk was still tearing people apart on cross-examination but . . . somehow it was different. He wasn't refuting the evidence any more. He was just bad-mouthing people. Then came Dr. Ruth Guy, and when Williams and Hawk asked her about her qualifications she said she was one of the forerunners in the study of Rh babies, and I paid close attention.

"You see, my wife . . . our first child was an Rh baby and I already knew quite a bit about the Rh system. The hospital had my wife and me read about it and . . ." He stopped and breathed deeply, looking down for privacy, then went on. "That woman, Dr. Guy, who talked so much nobody could shut her up, was one of the people who saved our child and enabled us, my wife and me"—he hesitated a moment and then continued—"to have another baby, and she was eminently qualified and in *Who's Who* and in *Men and Women of Science* and in lots of blood-bank societies . . . innumerable achievements to do with medicine and science. And I looked at Hawk and saw him belittling her and saw that sidekick of his with the beard—Cray, I believe his name is—laughing along with Hawk and I said to myself, hey, this Hawk isn't the good guy."

Now Rick's voice was hard and heavy. "It's like George said. We're human, we're not machines, and I turned on Hawk at that point. Not meaning that I'm prejudiced toward Corona because of Hawk, but I am saying . . . that I stopped believing wholeheartedly in Hawk's brilliant way of cross-examining, and I saw him for what he really is. In other words, looking back now, I don't trust Hawk and I question him at every turn and I think he didn't put on a case because, one, he thought he had us in his pocket, and two, he didn't have a case to put on, and three, I made a list of things to show why he has no case."

Many jurors were now murmuring. Rick was going too far, too quickly. The only one who agreed with him wholly and openly was Rogers.

Rick then read his list:

1. Four types of blood were found in trunk of Corona's Impala.
2. Three types of blood were found in back of Corona's van and running down behind the bumper.

3. Corona's van was seen near grave twenty-four for over two hours, unexplained.
4. Blood-stained weapons were found in Corona's possession. Home and messhall at Sullivan ranch.
5. Ledger with the names of seven victims was found in Corona's bedroom, and it was not a normal business record.
6. Corona was seen in north river-bottom orchard by numerous people at various times. Seven bodies found here.
7. Blood-stained boots and a shovel were found in the van. Bloody shorts were found under the seat along with 9-mm. cartridges and the bolo machete.
8. A bloody jacket was found in the rafters of Corona's garage.
9. The blue van was seen backed up to an orchard early in the morning near where a body was found.
10. Testimony that Corona was seen driving the blue van.
11. Corona was seen washing the *inside* of the blue van, the yellow van, and the pickup.
12. The fact that Corona was seen picking up four of the known victims and they were never seen again.
13. Two meat receipts with Corona's name on them were found in the grave with the nine-finger man.
14. Blank-deposit slips were found in the twenty-fifth grave with Corona's name on them.

15. Testimony of Mr. Pervis, a prospective victim, that he was asked to go to work by Corona but he refused.
16. Testimony by Jose Raya that he was asked to go to work by Corona at night in a blue pickup.

"So what I'm saying is that if we look at this case as a whole, with these sixteen points as a basis, we have a very conclusive picture. Like a circle, with Corona in the middle. And unless someone can show me differently, I don't see how it doesn't all point consistently to Corona." Rick licked his lips. "Thank you, Ernie." And he sat back, feeling a lot better. That thing about Dr. Ruth Guy had hung heavily on him for many weeks.

Ernie suggested a ten-minute break. Rick objected and said they should take another vote first. Ernie said no. Rick said yes.

"No!" snapped Ernie, standing up, and they took another break.

After the break the jurors didn't hurry back to the tables. Things were heavy. Rick had been very convincing with his sixteen points, and Faye had been very convincing with the two newspapers rolled into one, and Frank had been convincing with the folded meat receipts falling out of Corona's pocket.

At four o'clock they came reluctantly back to the tables, and Ernie made a thirteen-minute summation. First he brought up the grave of the nine-fingered man and asked if anyone had anything to reiterate in relation to the meat receipts, pointing out that as it stood it appeared that in fact the receipts had fallen out of Corona's shirt pocket. Hawk had brought that out.

Second, the bank receipts and rolled newspapers seemed to indicate that all those items found in grave twenty-five had come from Corona's house exclusively.

Third, the points Rick listed pretty well covered the evidence found in Corona's house and messhall, although not all sixteen were that incriminating in Ernie's estimation. And so he asked if anyone had anything to say for or against these points. He himself had a lot to say against most of them. In fact, out of the sixteen points he thought only four or five were conclusive or consistent with the idea of mass murder and, hence, thoroughly incriminating.

Rick shot to his feet and began to speak.

Ernie only stared at him levelly. Matt patted the younger man on the shoulder, and reluctantly Rick sat down. Ernie licked his lips and said that out of the sixteen points one good example of evidence, in his personal estimation, was the four different types of human blood found in Corona's Impala. How could this be refuted? Even if Corona's wife and Corona's children had cut themselves that would only be two types of blood, because children were either their father's type or their mother's type of blood. And another thing, most people were type A or type O. These two types of blood covered 90 per cent of the earth's population. Testimony after testimony had brought this out. So how could one logically explain away four different blood types in the trunk of the family car? God, these four blood types represented the whole spectrum of all human blood types. And as Fahey had said, the only common-sense explanation would be that these four types of blood were consistent with what one would expect to find in the vehicle of a mass murderer.

The next point, continued Ernie, was the three types of human blood in the van and especially in that area between the rear bumper and the under-rear part of the van where a fourteen-inch-wide area of running blood had been found. This certainly was consistent with what one would expect to find in the vehicle of a mass murderer who washed his van out regularly after committing his murders.

Next of Rick's sixteen points was the human blood found on the two knives. This was most consistent, as Ronald Fahey had kept saying over and over again as he piled up the evidence in front of him during his closing argument, with what one would expect to find in connection with mass murder.

Ernie asked Matt to get the two knives that were in evidence and bring them over so they could see them again. Matt had been put in charge of the evidence during their last ten-minute break.

One knife was fourteen inches long with an eight-inch blade, and was heavily constructed like a Bowie knife. The other was ten inches long with a four-inch blade, and was of medium construction, like a deer hunter's knife. Each was stained with specks of different types of human blood, and there were large splashes of blood up against the handle guards.

Ernie described the knives and the blood types and passed them around the table, but many of the jurors didn't want to handle them.

Ernie continued talking, bringing up Corona's rubber boots, which had human blood on them, and the Levi's jacket found in the rafters of Corona's garage at home, which also showed traces of human blood. Then, in summation, he said that in this whole case, what was more incriminating than anything was the blood: so many different types of blood had been found in so many different places.

Rick agreed.

Rogers agreed.

Faye agreed.

Matt had always thought this. In fact, he and Ernie had spoken of it before deliberations had begun.

And at four thirty on Friday afternoon, on their second day of deliberations, their third vote was taken. It came in at one for innocent and eleven for guilty, and this time no one was surprised.

The circle of circumstantial evidence was closing in and Corona, as Rick had said, was always there in the center. Consistently.

Juan Corona's four daughters arrived at the courthouse after school. Their mother, Gloria, asked them if they'd eaten and how school had gone while she opened her purse and brought out a comb and brush. She began fixing the youngest girl's hair as Martha, the oldest, answered her questions. After all four girls were looking their best, Gloria got up to take a walk with them, and one of the TV men asked her if he could photograph them. Gloria lowered her head. She was tired of people taking pictures of them. Candida, Juan's mother, who had been sitting at the next table, got up and told Gloria to tell the man to go away, to tell him they were tired of being made a spectacle. Gloria said no—Mr. Hawk and her son Pedro had told them all to cooperate with the press. What was wrong with Candida—was her personal comfort more important than Juan's freedom? The elderly Doña Corona said she would pretend she had not heard this last remark, and she left to go and talk to her sons. She had four of them here and three more in Mexico and they were good sons, and no daughter-in-law should talk to her like that. She was too tired and she knew no English and she was so confused and yet no one bothered to explain things to her. That was what happened when one got old . . . no one bothered with one anymore.

So Gloria and her daughters posed for the TV reporter from Sacramento, one of the regular newsmen. His long white Anglo face was familiar to the Coronas. He asked if he could have each girl's name and a photograph of each one individually. Gloria, who didn't know much English, asked Martha to interpret what this man had said. Martha was hesitant. Jokingly, Gloria pinched her daughter and told her to explain. Timidly, Martha kept her head down and hugged close to her mother.

"Tell me," said Gloria, smiling at her daughter. Gloria had had her hair fixed and was wearing a lovely dress and pretty high-heeled shoes, and she was always in good spirits when she was with her daughters and they were properly dressed and groomed.

Martha didn't speak to her mother but instead she stepped forward and spoke to the TV man. "I don't want you to use my first name. I don't want my picture taken alone. Please, at school they don't know who I am." She turned to her mother, then back to the man. "Don't tell my mother, please."

The newsman saw, nodded, and stepped back. The impact of this girl's words was devastating. Here he was, only trying to get his story for the day, and here was this small child fighting for her life. He tried not to show his shock. Gloria was asking her daughter what was going on. What had she just told the TV man? Martha began to speak, but hesitantly. The newsman moved forward, distracting Gloria by showing her that his photographer was once more getting them on film. He told her to look this way and that way, but still Gloria asked her daughter what was going on and Martha finally said that she felt sick, that she'd told the TV man that she felt sick and preferred not to have her picture taken alone. Gloria said, "Well, why didn't you tell me? My God, I'm your mother." Gloria now felt less confused, and told her daughter they would go to the restroom, that there they could have privacy.

Inside the courtroom Jim was standing up, tall and handsome, and everyone else was listening to him. Jim had never said how he'd voted, hadn't told the other jurors that indeed he was now the lone holdout for innocent.

"I'm not saying that Corona doesn't look pretty guilty. I'm not saying that I don't personally believe that he wasn't in fact involved with the victim with the meat receipts and the victim with the bank-deposit slips. No, I think those two look pretty conclusive, but . . . still . . ." He shook his head and glanced around. "Tell me, how did one man alone . . . kill and bury so many people? Sure, I know this isn't part of the evidence. I know that. But it's a question I have here"—he patted his heart area—"where it counts, where I'm going to have to live for the rest of my life.

"And another thing, tell me, why didn't Hawk put on a case? Is it as simple as Rick said, that Hawk thought he had us in his pocket? Or that maybe he didn't really have a case to put on? Or, tell me, could it be more complicated and be that Hawk figured that the prosecution's case was so full of holes, so filled with reasonable doubt, that he thought it would be an insult to us and Mr. Corona to even answer their accusations? That he thought by not putting on a case—which indeed he did have well prepared in advance—he would cause us to open our eyes wide and search our souls in such depth that . . ." He stopped. "Hey, don't be shaking your heads at me." He looked around. "You know, I think this head shaking is one of our problems here. At first most of us thought the prosecution had no case and Hawk was brilliant. And then, when the prosecution closed in with so much evidence here toward the end and Hawk then didn't put on a case, we've become emotional. Like Rick said, we feel cheated, we resent Hawk having made all those promises in his opening statement and then not putting on a case and fulfilling his promises.

"We stopped laughing *with* Hawk and his showmanship in the courtroom and began laughing *at* him. Sure, I'm as guilty of this as anyone else. He'd do something funny and I'd laugh at him like I'd laugh at Abbott and Costello. But . . . this isn't the point.

"The point is that we're not supposed to be emotional. We're not to be prejudiced toward the defendant because of what we may personally think of Hawk or anyone else. The Judge told us that in his instructions. That we are not to be swayed by thoughts of Corona's family or children or anyone else. Well, I believe this also covers Corona's attorney, Hawk. Just because Hawk turned sour on us, because he stopped being brilliant after the second month of trial and began to get repetitious and look more like a man trying to impress us with his personal knowledge of medicine in cross-examination instead of a man who was doing his job of refuting the evidence, I don't believe we should turn around and be blind toward his client's defense.

"We have a responsibility here, like Ernie keeps saying. We are a jury. We are twelve average people. The same type of ordinary people that Christ chose for his twelve disciples and . . . I say there is more here than we've covered. That just because Hawk chose to quit, to not give us a case in defense of Juan Corona, is no reason for us to quit. That a man is presumed innocent until proven guilty and that we have to turn every piece of evidence over and over again before we say it definitely points to guilty.

"Don't you remember that diagram Hawk gave us? It said that if two interpretations of the same fact can logically be interpreted and one points to guilty and the other points to innocent, then we are compelled by law to take the one that points toward innocence. That's the law. That's our security that justice will be done to us if we're ever accused of something. And beyond this we have to be convinced of a man's guilt beyond a reasonable doubt . . . to a moral certainty! These are the Judge's words. And I'll tell you, when the Judge read those words I didn't believe I would ever be in the position of having to say these words, and feel them, knowing the impact of their full meaning.

"Okay, let's go over this evidence. Let's see. Yeah, it was said that all this blood is very incriminating. Irrefutable. Okay. Let's take the blood, the blood in the Impala, four types, eh? Well, to start with, who'd been using that car? Does Mrs. Corona drive? Did Juan's brothers ever use the car? Did his workmen use the car? Oh, I wish Hawk had put on a case! I have so many questions! That car was never even fingerprinted. Nothing was ever fingerprinted, and Hawk should have done something. He could have. I can see that, you can see that, so please, I'm asking . . . let's not quit, like he did."

And for the next five minutes Jim hammered at the evidence. He disputed the four types of blood in the car by saying that no one knew who had been using the car. He discounted the blood in the van for the same reason and then asked what van were they talking about, anyway? A blue van, a yellow van, a red van? Juan had a van, Pedro had a van, and this older brother Natividad had a van or a pickup. And which pickup? Whose pickup? There were pickups all over the place. Everyone had a pickup out in that ranch community. And then Jim talked about the two knives. He picked them up and felt their weight and said no way on earth could these little things cut a man's skull in half. He went over to the eight charts showing the wounds.

The charts were three feet by six feet and showed every wound in each of the twenty-five victims. A couple of charts showed the front facial wounds and front chest wounds. A couple more showed the wounds on the sides of the heads. Others showed the backs and tops of heads. Each chart had twenty-five small sheets of paper and on each sheet was a small individual outline representing a victim, on which the doctors who had done the autopsy records had indicated the location of the wounds.

Jim said to look at these wounds, at their length, their depth, and imagine the brute force needed to inflict them—that these knives couldn't have done it, that the specialists from Sacramento and from Washington, D.C., had agreed to that, and he further pointed out that the machete in evidence didn't match the striations found on the skull of victim one. So where was the murder weapon?

"Those specialists never said that machete couldn't have killed the other twenty-four men!" yelled Rogers.

Jim looked at Rogers . . . shook his head, then said, "You can't possibly say that and mean it?"

"Why not!" said Rogers. "Just look at that machete blade! It didn't match Whitacre's skull because it was resharpened. You can't go around chopping up twenty-five different skulls without needing to sharpen your—"

Ernie was trying to talk over the commotion and bring order. Matt got the gavel from the judge's bench and pounded the table. Only then did the room fall silent.

Matt handed Ernie the gavel and said, "And if that doesn't do it we can always resort to the machete."

"Thanks," said Ernie, and he turned to Jim. "Proceed, Jim. It's your turn and yours alone."

Jim continued and once again asked where the murder weapon was. Where was the motive? Where was the common sense that told one that only one man could possibly have done all this killing and burying and still have time left to run a labor crew and be a husband and a father?

So much was missing from this case, Jim said, that he couldn't see how they could get beyond the fact that yeah, Corona looked pretty guilty. But how could they possibly jump to the conclusion that absolutely yes, Corona was guilty beyond any reasonable doubt . . . to a moral certainty?

He stopped. He sighed. And said no more. Rick, Rogers, and George raised their hands, but most of the jurors were quiet, reserved, thoughtful. Jim sat down. Ernie told everyone to put their hands down. They'd go around the table and everyone would get a chance to speak, and George would be first.

"Well," said George, "I'd like to say thanks, Jim. I voted guilty a few minutes ago and I'll tell you, it's going to be a long, trying time before I ever do that again. I mean, I voted guilty because everything pointed toward Corona but now I say, so what if everything points toward him? That isn't proof that he did it." George sat up. "Look at it this way, if I got arrested, or you got arrested, and one and a half years and half a million dollars were spent on trying to pin it on me . . . man, I'd hate to think of what they'd find. They'd find blood for sure. Human blood. Little specks here and there. Think back over the years how many times you and your friends have cut or hurt yourselves. And I mean years. Because these experts, particularly this Mrs. Ruth Guy from Texas—boy, wasn't she something?" He laughed. "Even the Judge couldn't stop her from talking. Hawk was making fun of her and baiting her with a question and she just smiled right back in his face. The Judge told her not to answer that question, that it was entirely out of order, but she just waved the Judge away and said, 'It's all right, Judge. I'm used to teaching little boys.' And she turned to Hawk and kept on talking and talking and even Hawk finally gave up and stopped strutting about like he owned the courtroom.

"Well, anyway, getting back to my point . . . this woman was eminently qualified and if a speck of blood were ten years old, was there even before you moved into your house, she would be able to find it and test it. Now tell me, did Corona buy his car new? Did someone own his van before he got it? Was it his brother's, that other guy's—Natividad's—before it was his? And his house, how long had he lived there? A month? Two years? I don't think we know, and the fact that they didn't take fingerprints really bothers me. That troubles me more than almost anything else. That and the fact that they never turned up an eyewitness.

"Really, think about this, how can a man kill and bury so many people with no one ever seeing anything? That's incredible. And that crew that was with Corona the day that first body was found, Whitacre's body. Why weren't any of them brought in to testify? Damn, I wish Hawk had put on a case. Just to have the man Corona get up there on the stand and say: 'I didn't do it!' That would've been a great help." He shook his head and sat back. "That brother of his, Natividad, who owned the bar, maybe he did it. Hell, I don't know. God, I wish he'd got on the stand."

Calvin was next, and he said: "Well, I voted guilty too and I'll tell you . . . it's going to take a lot of convincing before I vote guilty again. Like Jim said, like George said, sure, everything here seems to point to Mr. Corona, but if a year and a half are spent by the Sheriff's Department to build a case around this one man, then even if he were innocent things would still point to him.

"Now don't get me wrong. I'm not saying he's innocent and he doesn't know anything about all this blood . . . but I am saying where is our solid, convicting proof? Does a man have to prove to us that he didn't do it just because a whole year's worth of investigation says maybe he did do it? Ah? Do you see my question? I say we've got to pile up more evidence, more proof, and answer more of our questions like Jim said . . . which are not just up here, in our heads, but down here, in our hearts and in our souls." He faced Ernie. "Thank you. That's all I have."

Naomi was next. She said, "You know, I think what Jim said is right. Hawk didn't put on a case because he thought he'd be insulting us if he put on a case. Hawk is no stupid man. He must have not put on a case for some very well-thought-out reasons. Really, there's so much here that doesn't meet the eye. Like that twenty-fifth grave and the fact that it wasn't discovered until nine days after Corona was arrested. That's very mysterious, if you ask me. And that white sock that was found in that twenty-fifth grave. I read a book a few years ago written by a doctor, a psychiatrist, not a fiction writer, and in this book one of the main clues they always referred to was a white sock. They explained that a white sock has something to do with homosexual murders."

Shocked, Rick turned and looked at Matt. Matt winked at Rick and motioned for him to keep still.

Naomi never noticed. She seriously believed in what she was saying.

"So I think we should take this white sock in the twenty-fifth grave and combine this fact with what Hawk said. He said that these killings have overtones of homosexual murders. That many of these men had—" She blushed. She lowered her head, and she looked more like a little curly-haired girl than a woman in her sixties. "Well, we are in deliberations so we should use the correct word. You remember they all used that word over and over in court. Right in front of the Judge himself and everything.

"Anyway, Hawk revealed to us that many of these victims had their pants down and several had their penises out and others were only partially dressed and had their shoes untied. So obviously, these were homosexual crimes of some sort. Hawk said that, and added that in Mexico—where homosexuality is looked down on severely—there are two types of homosexual partners, the *pasivo*, meaning passive, and the *activo*, meaning active, and that when a Mexican does the *pasivo*—I think—the passive, the female role, then he turns insane with guilt and anger and is potentially a very dangerous person.

"So, thinking along these lines"—she took off her glasses and glanced around—"I believe we should consider this white sock in the twenty-fifth grave very seriously, a grave mysteriously found nine days after Corona was imprisoned. And we should put this question to ourselves—"

Rick turned away and hid his face so he wouldn't burst out laughing.

"—why didn't the prosecution take that small, single white child's sock and try and find its mate in Corona's home? Ah, you tell me! Even Hawk himself stipulated to the fact that Juan has four little girls and it could've been one of their socks. Remember that?" She glanced upward, nodding in self-agreement. "It was when Fahey first came into the case and he was so mad at Hawk that he stuttered, and I've always been puzzled why Hawk did that. Whose side was Hawk on?" Now many jurors were smiling but Naomi didn't notice. She now had her head down in concentration and she was indeed recalling correctly. Defense attorney Hawk *had* made these statements. "Why did Mr. Hawk do things like this? He would get on the prosecution's side as if to show them that if he were the DA he could do their job better than they were doing it. Remember when Teja couldn't put an article into evidence because he didn't know how to do it and so Hawk winked and took over and did it for Teja, the main prosecutor?" She shook her head. And what she was saying was true. Hawk *had* helped Teja put an article into evidence. "But Hawk was so smart that I always figured that when he put on his case for the defense he'd then turn all these peculiar tricks around and expose to us the real mystery, the real case; which doesn't meet the everyday eye."

She hesitated and Rick and the other jurors who had been smiling were not smiling any longer. Sometimes she spoke with such insight that it caused them to wonder about her more exaggerated statements. Sure, they all realized that in the last two weeks Naomi had begun smoking more and taking more pills, and had been acting very edgy. But, on the other hand, they'd all begun to experience unreal-nervous moments. Especially since Hawk had said: "The defense rests." That had jarred everyone. And so now . . . when a juror made a remark about a white sock being a clue to homosexual murders, it was not as strange as it seemed, considering that twenty-five horrendous killings didn't make any sense either.

"And yes, one more point," Naomi said. "How could a man with a wife and children, lovely children—we all saw them all trial long, sitting there with their big dark eyes and rosy complexions—be a homosexual? Ah? You tell me. How could a family man do these terrible homosexual things with old dirty bums and yet be happily married?" And she made a face of repulsion. "And still another point, tell me, why was this twenty-fifth grave found nine days after Corona's arrest with all the incriminating garbage unless . . . the real killers were trying to frame him?

"I tell you, poor Corona is nothing more than a simple, honest Mexican man . . . you all saw how he sat there like a vegetable all trial long. Not even knowing enough

English to understand the proceedings, much less defend himself.

"Thank you. That's all I have to say at this point."

Hands were waving and Rick and Rogers were bursting to talk but Ernie stood up and said: "All right, I'm going to talk before anyone else talks, so put your hands down." Faye made a resentful face. "Go ahead, make faces," continued Ernie, "but you elected me foreman and I'm going to serve as I see fit for the jury as a whole . . . not for those who seem to be better in the art of rhetoric. We're all going to have a voice while I'm foreman." Rick raised his hand again. "Put your hand down! I'm still talking!" Rick did so.

"Now . . . what I'd like to say is—like Naomi so well said yesterday—I personally think we're doing fine." He dragged out the word "fine." "We're having excellent discussions for guilt and for innocence and I'd like us to keep it this way. Remember, we are here as twelve separate people . . . to give our individual verdict, and I don't want one person jumping on another person because they happen to disagree with each other and their version—or should I say *vision*—of the evidence." He glanced around. Seeing no objection, he continued. "Okay, going on, you're next, Faye. I believe Jim considers that he already had his turn." Jim nodded. "All right, Faye, go ahead and discuss the evidence . . . but not the individuals here who have given their interpretation of the evidence. The evidence itself. Independent of the—"

Faye cut him off. "I understand what you're implying, Ernest Phillips. And I think your implications are well founded for those individuals whom you're hoping will acknowledge them, but I'm not one of those individuals. I always, consistently, address myself to the evidence, not to people, so . . . don't use your rhetoric on me." She was determined, and Ernie understood, smiled, and sat down. "Thank you," said Faye, and she began by saying that she could see once again that their main problem was one of following the Judge's instructions, because he had clearly said that they were not to consider what an attorney had said. Prosecution *or* defense. They were to consider only the statements given to them by witnesses under oath and the articles that were in evidence. Of course there were many unanswered questions in this case, and of course there were many intelligent-sounding theories of how these murders were committed and why these murders were committed, but these were theories and theories were not given under oath on the stand. Also, as Fahey had said, ten psychiatrists could work ten years and they would never come to agreement on a motive. Who could possibly say what was going on in the mind of a man who systematically killed and buried twenty-five men? Historians still couldn't agree on Hitler.

"So I don't believe," she continued slowly, in a calm voice, "we'll ever have all of our questions answered to our heart's content. And I don't believe that's the reason why we're here. We're not here to speculate and theorize about homosexuality; we're not here to speculate if one man could do it or if one man could not do it; we're not here to worry about the past ownership of Corona's vehicles or home. We're here to deal with the evidence submitted and the testimony given. We're here to follow the law as the Judge gave it to us. We all agreed to do this when we were questioned by both the prosecution and the defense before we were selected as jurors.

"So now, keeping this judicial procedure in mind, I'd like to say that even if we did consider the previous ownership of the vehicles and home they still would turn out to be of little or no importance because . . . the oldest death we have—I don't recall the number—is not older than eight months and not less than three months. We have a great deal of medical testimony to that fact, and this means all these murders were probably committed in six months' time, more or less, and so we're not talking about blood specks two years old or five years old or any such time element, and therefore . . . previous ownership is of small consequence. And if it were it would have been in the last six months and . . . don't you think Hawk would have brought it out if it was significant?"

"Yeah!" cut in Rogers. "Hawk's smart, and if he could've dreamed up anything to bring in he would have done it, believe me." Rogers glanced around; everyone was looking at him, so he nodded and sat back. "Continue. I just agree, that's all, I just agree."

Faye lowered her head in concentration, putting her fingertips to her temples. It was almost five o'clock, they'd been at it since nine that morning, and she was tired and Rogers' loud voice gave her a headache. "As I was saying . . . these murders, horrendous and incredible as they are, did happen. They are a reality, and we are never going to make common sense of their type of reality so . . . we should understand this fact, and accept it as we accept all the truly unusual and unexplainable things that happen here and there throughout all history. Then, accepting and understanding that we do not know many things in this case as we do not know in life, we should proceed and consider only the evidence and testimony given under oath and not allow ourselves to be sidetracked by speculation or theory or what the attorneys said or . . . we'll never reach any verdict. Innocent or guilty." She raised her head, putting her hands down, and breathed deeply, trying to recapture her thoughts, her impressions of this long, confusing trial. "Now Corona was seen driving his van and parking it in places where he had no reason to be parking. He wasn't working; he didn't have any crews working; and yet time and again we have sworn testimony that his van, his pickup, was parked here for two hours where later one grave was discovered, was parked there where later five graves were found, was parked late at night where three bodies were unearthed, was coming over the levee early in the morning where later another was found. And this testimony was given by people who knew Corona personally, who knew his van well, by fellow workmen on the Sullivan Ranch, by fellow Mexicans who had no reason to lie or dislike Mr. Corona."

She stopped. Ernie asked if she'd like a glass of water. She nodded, and Jim got up, saying he'd get a pitcher and some glasses. Ernie suggested they take a break, but Faye said no, not on her account, that she would prefer to finish while her thoughts were fresh. Jim returned with the water and Faye drank and then continued with a sense of need and determination.

She said of course she could sympathize with and understand the motive behind Jim's powerful attack on the evidence, that she too would like to destroy this case of circumstantial evidence and find some reasonable explanation that would undo this web of incriminating facts. Could they help her? Could someone show her a way to find this man innocent and set him free and yet know in their soul that they had done so honestly and not just because they were swayed by emotion and the natural human desire of not wanting to condemn another human being?

"Keeping this in mind," she said, "the Judge in his instructions said that everything in life is open to possible or imaginary doubt and that we should not confuse those calibers of doubt with reasonable doubt. And I believe, so help me, that within the realm of reason, common sense, and logic, so many things don't just point to Corona, they engulf him. For instance, not only was Corona seen at these places where graves were later found, not only did meat receipts tie him to one grave, but as Fahey so intelligently asked, what would you expect to find at the place of a mass murderer? Blood, different types of blood? Well, they had found it. What else would you expect to find . . . knowledge that the accused knew some of the victims? Well, they had that, too. They had testimony showing that Corona offered jobs to some of these men and that they had gotten in his van with him and then they were never seen again. And then, for further knowledge that he knew them, they have Corona's own ledger, found in the bedroom of his home, with seven of these men's names in it. Dates and locations."

"He was a labor contractor!" said Naomi. "He had to keep the names of people who worked for him."

"Oh, no, Naomi. Listen and let me help you . . . these names of the deceased were in the middle of an old ledger that didn't have Social Security numbers and amounts of money paid like his regular business ledgers for his work crews. We have the ledger in evidence. Take a look at it and you'll see there, in the middle of an old ledger book that had not been used for several years, since '68 or '67, I believe, that in 1970 there was a listing of . . ." Faye stopped, shaking her head, and then said:

"I think maybe we should all review that green ledger book again. I think we should not let ourselves be swayed by emotion or allow ourselves to be side-tracked by speculation. That's all I have. Thank you." She was tired and she sat back in her chair and breathed deeply. It was five o'clock. They were all exhausted. They'd covered a lot of ground and done a lot of searching within themselves, and put their convictions on paper three different times when voting.

Ernie stood up and suggested they take a break, and during the break anyone who wished to review the ledger could do so. People began getting up and stretching. They'd been deliberating almost nonstop for eight hours.

Many of the jurors stayed behind to go over the ledger. The specific pages in question, the so-called Death List, were pages 50, 51, and 52, in the middle of the book. This ledger, found in Corona's house on the night of his arrest on May 25, 1971, was the piece of evidence that had been argued over so much—by prosecution and defense—before the trial began, and, indirectly, it was why Hawk had been sent to jail just before the trial. The prosecution had wanted more samples of Corona's handwriting. Hawk had said they had all they needed and that the only reason they wanted more was because handwriting specialist Terry Pascoe, with the California department of criminology in Sacramento, had told the prosecution "they were in trouble if they thought this ledger was written by Juan Corona." Then, only days before the trial, they wanted to go to Los Angeles and hire a mercenary, a man who would tell them—for a price—that Corona had written all this.

The prosecution paid little attention to Hawk's accusations and demanded, on legal grounds, that Hawk give them the handwriting samples they requested. The court ruled in their favor but Hawk still refused, and told his client to refuse also. Corona did as told by his attorney. Hawk was found in contempt and sentenced to forty-eight hours in jail, and the story of Juan Corona's lawyer going to jail made headlines across the nation, even though it had been a year and a half since Corona's arrest and interest in the case had diminished.

Eventually Hawk told his client to give the prosecution a sample of his handwriting, and Corona did so in open court; then Bart Williams, District Attorney Teja's assistant, sent the samples to a well-known handwriting expert in Los Angeles, John J. Harris, who later testified that Corona had written the entries on pages 50, 51, and 52. Then Williams went to Sidney Goldblatt, of the U.S. Treasury Department in Washington, D.C., one of the most renowned handwriting experts, and Goldblatt testified that Corona had written the entries on pages 50, 51, and 52. And *then* Williams was able to get Terry Pasco, who had earlier refused to confirm Corona's handwriting in the ledger entries, to testify that in his expert opinion it was well within Corona's range of penmanship to have written everything on the pages in question.

At ten minutes after five the jurors were back at the tables, and Ernie called them to order. Rick suggested they finish going around the table and then take a vote. Several jurors looked at Rick and shook their heads: they were so tired, and here he was raring to go.

Matt raised his hand and said: "Ernie, why don't we do that and see where we all stand, but then call it a day immediately thereafter. Sure, they don't let us out until six but we sure as hell don't have to keep deliberating up to the last minute."

Most of the jurors agreed.

Ernie said okay and asked if Faye had finished before the break. She nodded yes. Rogers, who was next, surprised everyone by saying, "I got nothing to say. It's too late in the day and people will now vote according to how hungry or how tired they are, so I say why talk?"

Victor sat up and said, "Rogers, you know maybe you're not so bad after all."

Several jurors laughed.

Rogers blushed and murmured to himself.

Calvin, Rogers' roommate, shook his head and chuckled to himself.

After Rogers came Larry, who also said he had nothing to say, and neither did Frank or Victor. Then came Matt.

"Well," Matt began, "I have something to say. I say it's a lot easier to find a man innocent than guilty and I think on that last ballot we all felt Corona was guilty. Even the one person who voted not guilty. And I think it kind of upset each one of us individually, so we're all going to back away and sort of look at each other, hoping we can find a personal way out. And listen, I'm not criticizing, or saying this is wrong. Hell, look at the mess they gave us. One side screwed it up and the other side just plain quit. So I'm not blaming or criticizing, believe me, all I'm saying is that the buck stops here with us, the people, like it always has and so we got to be honest with ourselves and what we're doing, and we should realize that of course this is a pretty nasty job we have here, and of course it's doubly nasty because of what the prosecution didn't do and the defense didn't do, but beyond these obvious handicaps we still have a responsibility and, believe me, there's a lot of evidence here." He looked at the others and then added, "We have a lot to do yet, a lot to recall and think about, and considering this trial took five months, I think we're doing well for only being in our second day. Thank you. Naomi was right when she said we're doing fine."

And hearing this, Naomi perked up and said, "Thank you, Matthew, that's very nice of you because I really meant what I said and I'm really trying my best."

Matt winked. "I know you are."

"I think we all are," said Ernie, "it's just that . . . well, hell's bells, we don't know the law. We're not lawyers, all we have is common sense, and I pray to God that's enough." And he then called on Rick, who was next.

Rick leaned forward and said, "I agree with Matt on both of his basic statements. One, it's a lot easier to find a person innocent than guilty. Faye also stated this. She said it's our natural human desire not to want to condemn another fellow human being and I believe she's right. But point two, like Matt said, there's a lot of evidence here." Rick was trying to choose his words well. He knew he was the youngest juror and he was beginning to realize that a few people resented him because of this, and so he was trying hard not to offend anyone, trying to agree with as many other jurors as he possibly could before he spoke his own piece. But it was difficult for him to keep his emotions down because to him Corona seemed so obviously guilty that he couldn't see why all these people were hiding from the truth. ". . . Faye also said there's a lot of evidence. In fact, she said that if anyone could help her to see differently, could help her do away with all this circumstantial evidence that not only points to Corona but engulfs him, to please do so.

"Well, I agree with her, but I don't really see how anyone can show her differently. Not if we honestly do as Fahey suggested, and Hawk suggested, and take the evidence as a whole. That's the key to this whole mixed-up case, to look at this entire case as one large, single picture, to view the individual pieces of evidence not as separate items but as parts of the over-all puzzle, and relate this puzzle to the case as we heard it during the first couple of months and as we heard it during the last few months.

"Look . . . the first few months of the trial were about the bodies. About the graves. And in that first phase the prosecution looked ridiculous. So ridiculous that Teja, the top DA, stopped coming to the trial and sent Williams alone. And every day Hawk would tear up Williams and all the deputies so badly that we felt sorry for Bart Williams and thought the trial was a joke. Like Calvin said, we'd shake our heads and wonder why they'd ever brought this mess to court. Hawk looked brilliant in those days. He was like a hero on TV in cross-examination. We could hardly keep from laughing as Hawk revealed mistake after mistake that those cops had made, but"—Rick sat up tall—"things changed after the body phase. After that the prosecution began, clumsily at first but better toward the end, to bring in the evidence that tied up Corona with those twenty-five dead men. Do you see what I'm trying to say? This case came to us like in two parts. The mixed part which established the graves, and the second part, which I agree was confusing because of its huge amount of witnesses and evidence. But, in this second part Hawk was no longer brilliant. He was just loud. Jim Owen said that. Jim Owen agreed that Hawk just ridiculed everyone after the second month. He no longer destroyed or refuted the evidence. And, in this second part of the case, I believe the prosecution convicted Corona. Slowly, day after day, they fitted the pieces of the puzzle into one larger picture in which Corona was always the man. Really. The prosecution did a good job in the second part, and their witnesses, including the deputies, got better and better as the case developed. Hell, Hawk even started looking bad. How about when he ridiculed that one deputy about 'Don't you know how to make out a report? Don't you people up there in Yuba City even know how a report begins? Ah, does it start with the story for the three little bears or what?' And the deputy looked at Hawk straight in the eye and said, 'Well, Mr. Hawk, if you happen to be investigating the three bears, then I guess your report would start off with the story of the three little bears.'

"The courtroom roared and Hawk turned red. He wasn't in control anymore. You all remember that. Those cow-town deputies weren't scared anymore. They were getting sharp after two months of looking like fools, and Hawk was beginning to look like the fool. Really, I believe this, and I say that since we already agreed that there was no body switch in the first part, that those cops aren't sophisticated enough to pull off a deliberate premeditated lie and much less keep quiet about it, then this second part, with my sixteen points taken as a whole, as one larger picture of the entire case . . . is conclusive.

"My God, this man Corona is absolutely there in the middle all the time, and things just don't point, they *do* engulf him beyond any reasonable doubt.

"The blood, the different types of blood. The ledger, with seven of the victims' names and dates within the six months in which the killings took place. The locations, the places where Corona's pickup and van were seen, time after time, where later graves were found—and Corona was seen at these locations by fellow Mexicans, not by white Americans who might have a racial ax to grind and didn't know Corona personally, but by men who definitely knew and could easily recognize Corona and the different vehicles he drove.

"So what I'm saying is that if we look at the evidence like Faye said and don't get sidetracked with theories of motivation and speculations of 'Could one man do it?' and 'Why didn't Hawk put on a case?' . . . because, one, speculation and theory are in the realms of possible and imaginary doubt, and not in the realm of reasonable doubt; and, two, because the Judge told us to follow the law and the law says that we are to consider only the evidence presented, then I say that we have a very conclusive and convincing picture. Thank you. That's all I have, except to please keep in mind a big, over-all picture. Like a circle of facts. And I think you'll then see that Corona will always end up right there in the middle."

Rick sat back. Ernie stood up and said okay, to please keep in mind what everyone had said. Not just Rick's last words here, but also Jim's and George's and everyone else's. Then he said:

"Let's take a vote and call it quits for the day."

The vote was taken—four for innocent and eight for guilty—and everyone looked at everyone else in complete silence.

They were shocked.

Some expected a full conviction. Others had expected an acquittal.

Victor and Matt smiled and then began to laugh, and the tension in the room began to lessen.

It was five thirty and all the jurors were drained. Naomi was taking her nerve pills, Rick was gulping down aspirins, and Jim and Calvin were at the window, looking out in silence. No one knew where anyone stood and, for the first time, they didn't really care to know. Faye approached Rick.

"Rick," she said, "I'd like to tell you that I think you are a bright young man and I believe you put on a very logical and insightful argument. The prosecution did not put on that bad of a case. Even from the beginning they were doing well even without Fahey. Like you said, Hawk just ridiculed, he didn't refute the evidence in testimony."

"Thank you," said Rick warmly, "thank you. God, here a man killed twenty-five human beings and I sometimes feel like a bad guy for simply speaking the truth. People are so unrealistic. How can they forget the victims? Like all these damn marchers outside that are trying to make this into a noble cause. Hell, Corona is no Cesar Chavez. He was a labor contractor, making his living off other people's sweat." He shook his head. "Just look at the posters they're carrying, they're as unreal as these signs that say 'Have a Happy Day' when some of our GIs are still over in Nam. Dammit, it makes me mad! Some of my friends are still over there."

Faye glanced at the marchers outside on the sidewalk and then touched Rick on the shoulder. "Rick, I admire you for always being upright and truthful, but if people are against you, don't get angry, simply consider the source, and I believe you'll go further and be more convincing."

He nodded. "Maybe. Thank you anyway."

She smiled, stopped touching him, and they parted.

A few minutes later Ed Hehr knocked on the courtroom door and asked if they were done for the day.

"You bet!" yelled George. "Come on in, I want to ask you something. I've been talking to a lot of the jurors and as a whole we don't like the idea of going to a restaurant and then to a hotel. We'd like to go to our rooms first and have a chance to wash up, unwind, and then go eat.

"So why can't we go to a hotel that has its own restaurant? Like the Holiday Inn over on Highway 80. They got good steaks too and we've been working like hell—shooting craps. Ah, do you think that could be arranged? Besides, the noise behind Sambo's where we slept last night was awful." George finally stopped. He was a small wiry man who could eat and drink and yet never seem to put on any extra pounds.

"I'm sold," said Hehr. "You don't have to explain any more. The alternates have clued me in, too. I was just coming in to ask you people before I called the Holiday Inn."

George raised his voice. "Gr-rrr-eat! Go call 'em! And tell them we're hungry and thirsty and ask them if they got any dancing girls!"

Hehr left and went down the hall to inform Gloria and the Corona family that they could now visit with Juan Corona. Gloria, her daughters, and Juan's mother would go in first, and then the rest of the family.

The elderly Doña Corona didn't like it. Why couldn't they all go as a family to see Juan? Was this more treachery? Pedro Corona assured his mother that it was not only treachery but racial as well. Felix Corona, a level-headed businessman, told Pedro that he did not think it was treachery or racial, that it was simply that the cell was small and they were a large family. Pedro replied there were other rooms large enough to accommodate the entire family. Felix shook his head and walked away.

Pedro said yes, of course you can walk away. You live a thousand miles away in Arizona. You weren't here day after day living in this nightmare.

Felix turned and came back toward Pedro. Felix was dark and small, about five foot five, but he had a walk, an air like a very quick, very muscular, powerful fighting rooster, which made one look at him twice. He always wore a dark suit and tie, and he radiated an alert, serious intelligence that always earned him respect. Pedro was dark and almost six feet tall, but he had no such air. Although he was lean and fit and strong, he did not radiate any real self-seriousness. So now, as he faced his younger brother, Felix said:

"*Usted compadre*, you should be more careful in your choice of words. I could say that I was not here because I've been working, sending money for our attorney, but I will not say these words because that would be abusive of me." Felix was using the formal "you"—"*usted*"—because he was telling off his brother in a respectful manner, in the traditional way between brothers *a la cortez*. Then Felix turned and strode away as he said, "Need I say more, dear brother?"

Pedro's eyes blinked and he apologized and lowered his head respectfully. Not only was Felix his older brother, but their father, in his dying days, had said that Felix would be the head of the family. Not Natividad, the oldest. Not Juan, the favorite of their mother. But Felix, the shortest, darkest, toughest of all.

* * *

Juan Corona was unusually happy, stretching a big smile across his wide Mexican face as he received Gloria and his girls and his mother. Gloria had told the girls to give their father a tight hug when they first went in. Each girl did so and then the three other girls sat down. The youngest remained on her father's lap and Juan bounced her up and down as he spoke to his wife and his mother. He and Gloria did not embrace. They spoke of the business of the case. They started each sentence with "Geneva Hawk said this" and "Geneva Hawk said that" (because Geneva spoke Spanish), and Geneva had said that Mr. Hawk had done this and that and all was going very well legally.

Juan asked if anyone had seen the jurors.

Candida's face lit up and she said yes, this morning as the jurors got off the bus they, the family, had seen them all and one juror was seen to have smiled, and everyone in the world knew that a happy man could not have condemning thoughts in his heart. Which juror? asked Juan. Candida didn't know; it had been one of the men and these Americans all looked about the same to her. Gloria said it had been the slender one that always sat in the front row. Juan asked where in the front row. Gloria tried to explain that this juror sat close to the spectators' seats but not real close because those close seats were for the alternate jurors, not the regular jurors, but the more Gloria explained the more confusing it became and finally the juror in question, Larry Gallipeo, was lost among the others and Juan was no longer happy and yet . . . when the deputy, who stood nearby, came and said their time was up, Juan quickly stood up, respectfully, and tried to smile and say thank you, but his smile was so tight, so stretched, that the skin on his high cheekbones looked like it might snap like old sun-dried leather.

The deputy saw, and backed away, and Juan said thank you again and continued to be polite and soft-spoken and smiling, standing there nodding and bowing with such respect, a respect that came from his cultural heritage. A sense of respect coming down from landowner to peasant, from high priest to peasant, from the educated who write and read and do-the-law to the peasant; from those on the side of God and money and knowledge to those on the side of the underdogs, the outsiders, the poor, the sinners from as far back as Original Sin. Needing to be thankful, respectful, nodding and bowing with their eyes lowered to authority's feet.

Juan's mother, Doña Candida Corona Vallejo, stood up and said, authoritatively, that's all, that they would go now, and she came forward and told her son to embrace her, and Juan did so and she hugged him in return, kissing him on the cheek, and then she turned to go, mumbling religious phrases to herself as she walked by the deputy with such an air of power and confidence . . . for she knew who she was without question. She was the matron of her household, she was the Power, the Strength, the Knowledge, the one enshrined with the reflection of the Virgin Mother.

Juan and Gloria embraced, then shook hands, didn't kiss, and then he turned to his daughters, no longer stretching his tight wide smile, and warmly said a few words to them and kissed each one individually and told them to go, that the Mr. Officer had said their time was up and he would see them tomorrow with the grace of God's blessings.

* * *

In the courtroom Ed Hehr knocked on the door and told the jury their bus was ready, and they began filing out. Rick and Calvin were the last to leave because Calvin had asked Rick if he would make a copy of the sixteen points for him to sort of think over during the night. Rick had happily agreed and had sat down to copy the list.

Naomi noticed Rick doing so and told him he had no right to be pushing his ideas on other people, but Cal quickly explained that he had asked Rick for the list.

Naomi said oh, and lit another cigarette and walked away. Then, as the jurors went down the hallway to the elevators, Faye walked with Naomi and told her to calm herself, that they were not advocates, or against each other in any way; the Judge had made that very clear and in his instructions he had said that the jurors were the sole and exclusive judges, that they were the ones who passed final judgment on the value of the evidence and the witnesses, and that surely Naomi should not let a young man like Rick upset her.

Naomi said that Rick, and Hicks before him, had moved about in their chairs all during the trial, making noise with their feet, and they did it just to harass her because she was a poor, lonely, old widow, and that was the truth.

Faye said, "Naomi, I have a son about Rick's age and boys are just noisy by nature. Consider the source and don't let it bother you."

"The source!" yelled Naomi, but she said no more.

It was a cold, wet winter night. The bus was waiting and all around it were deputies and around the deputies were newsmen, supporters, and closest to the door of the bus was the Corona family. The children were in front and behind them were Gloria, Pedro, Felix and his wife, and Candida, and to the side were Hawk, Geneva, Hawk's daughter Cristi, and Eddie Cray, Hawk's assistant.

It was darker than the previous day, and when the jurors emerged the flashbulbs were terribly bright and the pouring rain seemed to freeze in mid-fall as the strobe lights flashed. First flashing from here, then flashing from there. One cameraman backed into another. The one in the rear fell, but was quickly up and getting more shots. The TV crews with their huge shoulder cameras worked from farther back and were able to get some wide-lens shots that gave a truer picture of the whole thing . . . thirty seconds, sixty seconds as the jurors came out to board the bus, and the Coronas with their supporters waved flags, yelled slogans, and cheered their belief in Juan Corona's innocence.

Then it happened as it had the evening before . . . there were the first jurors handing their bags to the bus driver to put in the outside compartment and then they were getting in the bus, and Faye saw it again.

Eddie Cray, there he was—he'd moved up from out of the darkness with his hand down by his side as if no one were supposed to see, and he motioned the Corona children to move up, and they did so as cameras flashed. All four girls were frightened, terrified in their eyes one could see it, and they went to move back away but there was Pedro, their uncle, and he pushed them from behind, bodily moving them a foot or so and telling them to go on, go on, didn't they love their father, didn't they want him to get free? And the girls moved up along with Pedro's three boys and Faye saw it, and she was so angry she felt like going up to Cray and telling him off but she didn't. She lowered her head, closing her eyes to all the world about her that was exploding in flashes of light as bright as day.

Third Day—
Saturday, January 13, 1973

Calvin and Rogers had been up quite a while Saturday morning by the time Ed Hehr started knocking on the jurors' doors at the Holiday Inn at seven. Again Calvin had been doing his calisthenics and again Rogers had lain in bed watching him. Rogers watched Calvin run in place, do twenty-five push-ups, run in place again, do twenty-five more push-ups, and then twists and bends and sit-ups. Finally Rogers said, "Man, I'm tired just watching you."

Calvin looked at Rogers. "I'm sorry if it makes you tired," he said, "but I'm used to doing this every morning."

"Oh," said Rogers, laughing. "I was only joking. What's wrong, can't you take a joke?"

"Sure," said Calvin, "I can take a joke. I just didn't know that you were joking."

"Well, what did you think I could've meant?" Instinctively Rogers' joking mood was changing to nervousness and anger. He got out of bed, stared at Calvin, and said, too loudly, "I was just being friendly!" He was a few inches taller than Calvin and twenty-some pounds heavier. Then he turned, went into the bathroom, and closed the door.

Calvin watched the door close, then breathed deeply, shook his head, and continued his exercises, vigorously working his dark mahogany body into a shiny sweat.

In her room, Naomi was looking through her purse to see how much money she had left. She needed cigarettes, more of her nerve pills, aspirin, and vitamins, and she didn't have enough money. She began talking to herself, saying that it wasn't right that they only paid the jurors five dollars a day plus mileage. It was ridiculous, as outdated as wages of fifty cents an hour. Sure, some of these people that worked for big companies got paid their regular wages besides the five dollars, so they didn't care; but she, a retired widow with no one giving her anything, couldn't live on five dollars. As she came out of her room Naomi ran into Faye and after saying good morning she began telling Faye about the five dollars, and her cigarettes, and her nerve pills. Faye commented that not only did cigarettes cost a lot but they were a stimulant and made one nervous. So if Naomi would quit smoking . . .

Naomi looked at Faye as if she were crazy and said that wasn't the point. The point was that they were in the midst of the largest mass-murder deliberations in all history and she needed her cigarettes and, anyway, the jurors were supposed to be nervous.

Faye said no more.

It was fifteen till eight and time for breakfast.

* * *

After breakfast Naomi approached Mrs. Wallis and said she'd like to talk to her, and the matron invited her into her room.

"Well," said Naomi, "it's about our juror's pay. I need cigarettes and, you know, my pills, and I didn't have a chance to go to the bank before they decided to keep us here and I was wondering if maybe you could"—she hesitated, then spoke quickly—"get me my juror's check early. It's been over a week, and I would certainly appreciate it." Naomi didn't like to talk about money because it made her uncomfortable. All her life she'd had a hard time financially. Her first husband had given her a son and then left her. She came to California from Pennsylvania and raised her son by herself, sometimes holding down two jobs. They were difficult years until she remarried and had a daughter, and things just seemed to be going well when her second husband died.

"I'll see what I can do, Naomi," Mrs. Wallis said. "I'll check on it this morning, but remember"—she smiled soothingly—"it's Saturday and it may be difficult to get you your check today. But I'll do what I can. I promise. Okay?"

"Okay," said Naomi, but her "okay" had come out sounding too low. She coughed, clearing her throat, and said, "I know you'll do what you can. You've been very good to us all these months. Thank you."

As Naomi left the room she still felt blue. Money problems were not her only concern. She'd only left a few cans of food for her cats; her sister, who had come to Vallejo from Napa Valley to take care of the cats, would probably use those few dollars she'd left for whiskey instead of cat food. Naomi went back to her room. She'd washed a few clothes the night before, and now she'd have to pack everything up. Every day the jurors had to pack up because no one knew when they would reach a verdict and be sent home.

It was eight thirty-five, so she'd have to hurry. The bus would be ready to take them to the courthouse in ten minutes.

At eight fifty-five the bus pulled into the rear parking lot of the courthouse, and when some of the jurors saw the Corona supporters and newsmen with cameras everywhere they began to complain.

Matt roared with laughter and said this complaining reminded him of a homely-looking girl who got all dressed up in a short little skirt and then became indignant when men looked at her. Matt and George were in fine spirits. Last night before dinner they'd had a few shots of Sunny Brook whiskey in their room and then for dinner they'd had shrimp cocktails, salads with Roquefort dressing, a New York steak for Matt, and a Maine lobster for George. They'd slept fine, and this morning they'd had an excellent breakfast, and now they were raring to go. And their joviality was contagious, so most of the jurors seemed happy and rested as they stepped off the bus and walked past the newsmen, the cameramen, and the Corona children.

A chanting for Juan Corona began. After having seen the jurors, the Corona family and their supporters were absolutely confident that an acquittal was close at hand. A deputy closed the doors behind the last juror but the chanting did not cease. It increased as the hundreds of demonstrators got in line and began marching around to the front of the courthouse.

Gloria was delighted. She was in front, carrying a large

sign that read "Juan Is Innocent." Behind her were the four children carrying a long sheet of cardboard reading "*Justicia para Juan!*" Behind the girls were some young, hip-looking Chicanos with signs saying "Racist Pigs," "The Sheriff Is the Murderer," "Teja Is Not a Man," and "Teja and Roy Sleep Together." And behind the young Chicanos there were other Mexicans, not so hip-looking, and among these were Pedro and Montes and their families. Felix Corona was not marching. He was over by a tree trying to keep out of the wind. He rolled the collar of his raincoat and stood there shivering as he watched the happy-loud demonstrators . . . Then Gloria, carrying her sign, faltered and Pedro quickly came up and took the huge sign from her and continued leading the marchers, chanting as he moved. Felix stopped watching and turned, going toward the courthouse where it was warm.

Going up the steps, he overheard some young Chicanos saying how they'd slept the night here, on these cold courthouse steps, and how this weekend Corona supporters were coming from as far away as Fresno, Los Angeles, and Ventura—Sunday morning would be something to see. *Chicanos!* From everywhere, united in a righteous cause, for liberty, for justice, for the basic ideals of every American citizen. Felix said nothing and went inside the courthouse.

By nine fifteen the jurors were seated at the two tables listening to Ernie, but not very attentively. Some were drinking their second cup of coffee, some were looking at Ernie and wondering when it would all end, and some, like Matt, were just sitting back and watching. And if one watched carefully one could almost see where the jurors stood as Ernie reviewed the evidence and reconstructed what they'd talked about the day before: some were nodding in agreement, some shaking their heads in disapproval. It was obvious that they were split about eight for guilty and four for innocent.

Since Matt was for guilty, absolutely, he stopped listening to Ernie and began to study the four jurors he figured were for acquittal, trying to evaluate them as persons with individual needs, as people who thought Juan Corona was guilty but could not bring themselves to admit it, vote it, and stick by it.

Matt was very good at evaluating people. In the Marine Corps he'd been the best small-weapons man in his whole regiment. Mortars, machine guns, rifles, and hand grenades had been his speciality, and he'd always done well—meaning he hadn't gotten killed—because of his ability to choose men and position himself in relationship to his men. Whether they were brave or cowardly, gun-ho and stupid, or hesitant and smart, it didn't really matter as long as you, the one in charge, knew who they were and what they would do and positioned yourself accordingly.

Matt nodded to himself and glanced around the table. He quickly decided Calvin and Owen were for innocent, and concluded that the difference in their skin color didn't matter. What mattered was that they were both religious and being religious they considered themselves extra sensitive, extra conscientious, but . . . Matt smiled, pulling at his beard. All through history these people with the security of religion had proven to be the most fanatic and zealous of soldiers once they figured they were in the right. Hell, no group had ever done more killing and slaughtering in the name of truth than the Christians. These do-gooders would jump for guilty and stick to it once they cleansed their conscience and saw that finding Corona guilty was in the name of truth.

Matt grinned as he continued watching the jurors, and decided that George and Naomi might also be for innocent. George, his roommate, was no problem; he was a reasonable man, a good level-headed man. But Naomi, now, she was emotional and she could be a real problem. Especially if Rick, who was so strong for guilty, kept pushing her so much. These two, Rick and Naomi, were the most dangerous of all the jurors. They had actually *wanted* to be jurors—they were so naive they thought being a juror was some great and noble calling. And if Rick didn't shut up, he could force Naomi into a vote for acquittal so irrationally that she would never come around.

Matt sipped his coffee as Ernie continued talking, reviewing, and using his enormous vocabulary, which in Matt's estimation was the first tip-off of a man who had not gone to institutions of higher learning and felt so bad about it that he always used big words.

At ten fifteen Ernie said, "I'm done talking but, before we start around the table, I think we should take a break."

Faye smiled.

Matt grinned.

Victor laughed.

Ernie saw but continued, undaunted. "I think I've briefly covered what we've discussed since deliberations commenced on Thursday, so now I'm suggesting we take a ten-minute break so as to allow the development of our own personal train of thought and hence see what can be added in order to germinate new ideas for further enlightenment as to innocence or guilt."

Matt shook his head and got up. Then everyone

else stood, shaking their heads and stretching. It was their third day of deliberations and they were still only beginning.

At eleven twenty-five, after a lot of talking, the jurors were getting ready to vote. This would be their first vote of the day and they were trying to do it quickly, before their lunches were brought in. Rick was talking, saying that the jury had to stop looking at the evidence as separate items and the murders as twenty-five separate counts, that if they were ever going to get anywhere they had to see this case as a whole, as one continuous flow of evidence, as one continuous assault of murder, as one continuous testimony of witnesses who had seen Corona here where five bodies were found and there where two bodies were found; and add to this the fact that Pervis, the only living witness, whom Corona had tried to pick up to go dig a garbage pit . . .

"That's right!" said Rogers. "When Pervis came into the courtroom to testify Corona almost fell out of his chair! Man, he'd killed and buried so many people he'd forgotten who was dead and who was alive."

Ernie stood up, trying to silence Rogers, but Rogers would not be silenced.

He stood up too and kept yelling, "Dammit! Corona turned white as a sheet! Thought he was seeing people come up from the dead! And I agree that Corona is guilty if one sees it as a whole, like Rick keeps saying." Then, finally, Rogers sat down.

"Okay," said Ernie, "you all heard Rogers, and Rogers is certainly Rogers and if he could just be a little . . . oh, well, I guess what he said is basically true. In fact, I believe a few of us spoke about it the day it happened."

Matt and Faye nodded. "All trial long Corona had sat there immobile, as if he were not even here. Only now and then he'd turn a page of the transcript Hawk would give him but it was obvious to us that he wasn't reading. It was all Hawk's idea. Hell's bells, Corona's eyes would never even move down the page. But that day when Pervis, a little old harmless-looking man, came through that door and Corona turned and saw him . . . man, you would have thought the devil himself had entered. Corona's eyes nearly jumped out of their sockets and he turned sickly pale, and all through Pervis' testimony Corona's feet kept jumping under the table.

"Okay, so what Rogers said is true, but please . . . this is not evidence. So forget it. I repeat, forget it. Now, does anyone else wish to speak before we take a vote?"

Matt raised his hand. Ernie recognized him and sat down. "Well," said Matt, leaning back, "too many people are pushing too much and this pushing, I believe as the young people nowadays say, is turning many of us off. You see, I figure that most of us think Corona is guilty at this point but we're still divided at about eight for guilty and four for innocent and . . . I don't really believe it's going to change, the way we're presently going about it.

"In other words, I don't believe anyone is going to convince anyone of anything if we just keep hammering at each other. Convicting a man or acquitting him is largely an emotional thing. Sure the Judge told us to not be swayed by our emotions, but hell, we're everyday type of people with all different backgrounds. We're not professional jurors. We're not trained in law, or trial, or anything like that.

"So . . . being realistic, I think we should each stop and think to ourselves why we're for innocence or why we're for guilt and then, having done this, we should consider the other person's point of view and respect what that other person says. Whether we think he's right or wrong doesn't matter. It's up to each one of us to talk, and talk, and talk until we feel we've convinced ourselves. Guilt or innocence. Either way. It's each one of us convincing ourselves.

"Hell, no man likes to be told what to do; no one likes to have another man make his decision for him. Yes, I'm for guilty but I'm not going to force my thoughts on anyone else. For I believe as we go over this evidence again and again, becoming more familiar with it each time, the case will speak for itself. Thank you."

Rick, Faye, and George raised their hands. Ernie recognized George.

"I'm still for innocent," said George, "but I think what Matt said is absolutely twenty-twenty because nobody is going to convince me of guilty. Not meaning that I'm unreasonable; just meaning that this case was so long and fouled up that I'm surprised Matt or anyone can say they're for guilty.

"No fingerprints were taken. No one saw Corona do any of the killing or digging or burying. Sure, I've been over these points before, but, I'll tell you, I'll go over them a thousand times more before I see differently. I don't care if we look at it as a whole or separately, this case is still so full of holes and reasonable doubt that . . . damn, how can you people even think of sending a man off to the gas chamber with the type of evidence we got here?"

George sat back. Faye raised her hand, as did Rick and Naomi, and Ernie recognized Faye.

"Well, first of all," said Faye, "I'd like to say that I

believe that what Matt said is the large part of the truth. I do sincerely believe that most, if not all of us, believe Corona is guilty but"—she put on her glasses—"like I said yesterday, it's our natural human tendency not to want to convict anyone. Especially when we never heard the accused testify in his own behalf.

"In other words, what I'm saying—having had several nights to think about it—is that I'm beginning to believe Attorney Hawk was indeed a brilliant man to not have put on a case because . . . look at us, half of our defense for Corona is that Hawk didn't do this and Hawk didn't do that and so therefore we conclude this is reasonable doubt. Do you see what I mean? We've done what the Judge in his instructions warned us not to do. We've replaced reasonable doubt with possible and imaginary doubt, and the law reads that we are to find Corona guilty beyond reasonable doubt, not beyond imaginary and possible doubt."

"I said that yesterday!" said Rick.

"Yes," said Faye, "you did Thank you. But now, to go on . . . since Hawk promised us so much and then didn't give us anything he has tricked us into feeling guilty . . . yes, us, the jurors . . . guilty for not knowing everything and hence, in Hawk's estimation, we could never then come to a verdict." She removed her glasses. "Could someone help me with this concept? How can I express it? Jurors, I believe, have natural complexes. One being the gas chamber, as George mentioned. And another being—oh yes, I have it now. You see, Hawk, being an experienced professional in the courtroom, realized that jurors are amateurs with complexes so he decided to compound our problem.

"Of course that's it! Hawk knew that the Judge would

tell us that the punishment to be rendered by the Court is not to be of our concern but . . . like Matt said, acquitting or convicting a man is largely an emotional state with us amateurs, and Hawk knew this and he decided to add guilt to our existing dread of the 'death penalty' . . ." She closed her eyes in concentration and ran her fingers through her snow-white hair. ". . . Do you know that the death penalty is not currently in existence? That this one fear, or guilt, or worry of ours is not present and so Corona—if in fact we do find him guilty—is not going to die. He is going to simply be put away. And I believe some of us at this table are holding out because of the thought of 'What if we convict him and we were wrong?'

"Well, please think of this. I thought of it last night a few hours after we witnessed that detestable little man, Cray, when he and Corona's brother forced those lovely children toward us as we boarded the bus. I thought, my, what if we let Corona go and he not only returns to killing more old men but he harms his own children?"

Naomi's hand shot up.

Faye turned, "Yes, Naomi?"

"But how can you think that? All through the trial Hawk kept telling us that Corona was hopelessly heterosexual and a happily married man."

"Oh, Naomi," said Faye, "don't you recall that in his instructions the Judge told us to disregard what the attorneys said? To only consider the evidence and testimony that was—"

"Sure, I remember that, but Corona himself . . . he always smiled at his kids when he came into the courtroom. And also, Corona is nice-looking and his clothes are neat—and a killer, to have killed twenty-five men in the manner that these were killed, wouldn't look or act like Corona looks and acts . . . would he?" And Naomi put her hand up to her mouth and her eyes were big. "Oh, God! Why didn't Hawk put on a case?"

"Maybe he had nothing to put on," said Faye. "Or maybe, as I tried to explain a moment ago, it was a trick to make us feel so confused that it would prevent us from ever reaching any conclusion—conviction *or* acquittal." Faye lowered her voice. She had spoken a little too loudly there at the end. "Maybe a hung jury was what Hawk had planned from the beginning, knowing—because, I grant you, Hawk is a smart and learned man—that a hung jury would be all he'd ever possibly get." The room was noisy with moving chairs, coughing, and murmuring. The tension was heavy. Faye continued, "I know my last statement sounded quite cynical but believe me, it comes straight from my . . . please, let us not forget the twenty-five men who were murdered, killed, and the person who did this is indeed capable of—"

A strong knock sounded on the huge main doors.

Naomi and several of the other jurors jumped, but Faye did not. Someone outside the door called out that their lunches were ready. Quickly, the jurors began getting up moving about, and talking among themselves.

Jim, the only juror consistently for acquittal, went over to Faye and congratulated her on an insightful discussion.

Faye smiled and thanked Jim and then added that she didn't know if she could last through the afternoon's session. She was so tired, and these deliberations were too exhausting for an old lady.

"Oh, Faye, you'll work us all under the table, I'm sure." And Jim continued laughing, trying to cheer the older juror. But it was difficult because last night, he hadn't been able to sleep. A man's life *was* on the line, in Jim's estimation, death penalty or not, and he was going to fight for acquittal until it was proven differently to him. Not only beyond a reasonable doubt, and to a moral certainty but . . . more. Much more. Or how could he ever live with himself? And that question—how could he ever live with himself—haunted him because that question meant that he was a selfish man. He was not really worried about Corona as much as he was worried about his own peace of mine, and that was not Christian, that was thinking of his own self first, and he felt bad.

At twelve forty-five the jurors were back in deliberations and immediately decided a vote should be taken before further discussion.

Each juror wrote down his or her verdict on a slip of paper and put the paper in the small cardboard box. When everyone was finished, Ernie stood up and began to read them off: guilty, innocent, innocent . . . the final vote came to seven for guilty and five for innocent.

Rick leaped from his chair. "What's wrong with everybody! We've been over the evidence umpteen times!" He was so mad the cords of his neck were bulging. "Tell me"—he tried to calm himself—"how can any one of you vote for innocent? Tell me, show me, hell, I'll change my vote if you can show me, but . . . you can't if we stick to the facts, the evidence, and quit all this imaginary speculation which some of you—"

Ernie tried to quiet Rick, but Rogers was urging him on.

Matt, who was sitting at the east end of the table behind Rick, stood up, placed his heavy hands on Rick's shoulders, and in one swift motion lowered him into his chair.

But Rick was still talking, saying that it was her, her type of thinking that was so scatter-brained that it—

Naomi looked at Faye, wondering if Rick was referring to Faye or to herself.

Faye didn't look at Naomi, she simply lowered her head. She knew who Rick was referring to.

Matt told Rick that this was the very thing he'd been talking about this morning. What was wrong with him? Did he want to blow this thing sky-high?

Rick said he was sick of how everyone kept feeling so sorry for Corona—hell, how about those twenty-five dead men? Everyone was forgetting about them just like they forgot about the crimes they committed overseas while they sat here at home in peace. Maybe they should start calling the victims by name. And he shouted, "Mr. Sample! Mr. Whitacre! Mr. Donald Smith! Let's quit all this number crap and be realistic! This is a murder trial! Men, harmless old men, have been hacked, chopped, and stabbed! Killed in premeditated cold blood! Twenty-five men! And like Hawk said, there are probably a lot more buried out there!"

Rogers was up again. "I agree completely! Hell, this man is guilty and we should think about those dead men!"

Frank said to himself that he agreed with them, but didn't like the way they were talking, so he pushed his chair away from the table and covered his ears, not hearing any more.

Larry also pushed his chair away from the table.

Naomi looked from person to person very attentively.

At first Ernie was red-faced and angry, but now, thinking that maybe it was for the best to get everything aired out once and for all, he just stood there, waiting it out; as he looked from juror to juror he decided that they were doing fine. Frank, Larry, Victor, George, and Calvin had all pushed their chairs back and now the talkers were kind of left alone and things were beginning to quiet down by themselves.

Ernie turned toward the judge's bench, picked up the gavel, and tapped the table top. "Okay, we'll adjourn for fifteen minutes."

Quickly the nontalkers got up, most of them leaving the room.

The talkers noticed, and Matt and Victor laughed. Then Victor said: "Keep talking, nobody is listening." And he laughed again.

The talkers glanced at each other and then left the table.

Ernie came over to Rick and softly said, "Man, you fuck up like this again and you've had it." He looked around, then leaned in closer. Eye to eye. "Buddy, I'm not going to put up with this kind of childish crap. Do you hear me! Kindergarten crap! A man, if he's a man, doesn't cause outbursts like that. Especially toward women. What are you, some snot-nose kid that can't stomach a little disagreement, needs everyone agreeing with him, or don't you have the guts to be a gentleman?" Ernie breathed heavily, looked around the room again, and then added, "Rick, I expect more out of you. Dammit, man, I voted innocent on that last vote myself." Rick looked at Ernie in bewilderment. "You don't believe me, well, friend, you got a lot of growing up to do. And I suggest you do that growing up now, this minute, during this fifteen-minute break and do like Matt was saying this morning. Hell, Matt here knew you were going to break down before you even knew it yourself. A man doesn't fight wars all over the globe and live . . . if he can't first evaluate situations.

"Now, stop, and think, and collect your senses." Ernie licked his lips. "Man, I'll promise you one thing. I'm not changing my vote because of your yelling. You're going to have to do a lot of convincing, a lot of smooth talking, so I suggest you just quit worrying about a certain woman, and you all worry about me, yours truly." And then Ernie growled like the ex-sergeant he was, saying, "And if you don't think I can back up what I say, remember this, buddy, I fell into a fox hole with five live Germans in my day and not one came out alive." And there Ernie held . . . a long time, breathing, eyeing, saying no more; then finally he turned and walked away.

Matt, who had been watching from a respectful distance, now came over and patted Rick on the shoulder. "Rick, I've always considered the biggest fool of all is the man who gives advice. Because, one, those who need the advice won't take it and, two, those who will take it don't really need it." Matt laughed, putting an arm around Rick and drawing him close. They were about the same height but Matt was a good forty pounds thicker. "Anyway, going against my own advice about advice, do you recall how Hawk always kept saying that reasonable doubt was like love, you either got it or you don't? Well, maybe like love, you best start using sugar and honey to reach your goal instead of muscle and brains. Remember, Rick, ultimately we're all going to have to live with our decision the rest of our lives and that, my friend, is more of an emotional commitment than a brain or muscle trip." He slapped Rick on the back. "Come on, let's get some coffee and think sugar and honey, and forget all this muscle and brains. How about that?"

* * *

The jurors were not deliberating when Ed Hehr entered the courtroom at about three thirty to tell them that Judge Patton wanted to know if they would like to take tomorrow, Sunday, off or if they preferred to deliberate straight through. Several of the male jurors mentioned the Super Bowl; others said they were tired, and a couple asked about church. Hehr smiled and said it was all up to them. Ernie asked for those in favor of having the day off to raise their hands, and they all did.

"Great," said Hehr, and he left.

At four twenty, the jurors were back at the tables. They were going to go around once more and then take a vote and call it a day. George was the first, and he said:

"I'll tell you, this isn't evidence, I know that, but how could one man do so much killing and never even get hurt? Ah, you tell me! I say there's just too much that we don't know. Good God, I still can't really believe this case!"

Calvin, who was next, sat forward and said in his deep slow voice, "Well, you know I've been thinking, especially since things got hot back there"—he chuckled to himself—"that maybe I personally should try to do what Matt suggested for us all to do. So I said to myself, Cal, why is it that you're for what you are? You know, innocent or guilty. And the first thing that came to my mind were those children, those four little girls, but then I remembered that the Judge told us that we are not to be swayed by emotion and right after that I recalled what Faye said on the bus last night going home, that those men were using those kids, that those men didn't care about those children and they didn't care about Corona himself. That if one loved and cared about one's children one wouldn't be pushing them like that.

"Of course, Faye was mad, I know that but still she made sense, and after that, well, things kind of turned around inside my head. I mean, how can I say it, all this time I'd always been thinking, Cal, you got to look at how little we know. You got to look at how much more you'd like to know, but today after Matt said what he said and Faye said what she said about what if Corona is guilty and we let him go and he goes back not just to hurting old men but his own children . . . well, that hit me. That really did, because I'd never dreamed of seeing it that way. And so I said to myself, man, maybe I should look at it like how much we *do* know. Not how much we don't know. Because I think this 'don't knowing' leads one to guessing, to wondering, to speculation, and to that there imaginary doubt; where I think this 'knowing,' this considering what one does know, leads one to reasonable thinking and then to that there reasonable doubt and *not* that unreasonable doubt."

He stopped, glanced around, then asked, "Do you see what I mean? I'm not educated but I do want to make myself clear, and I'm saying if we stick to what we know instead of jumping the rails, then we know a lot. See what I mean? It's like my wife with all her cooking and baking. She don't figure how much she don't know when she wants to cook up something new, she all figures how much she does know and then . . . well, she's the best cook around. So I figure if we just turn things around inside our heads"—he was using his large dark hands to explain himself—"to work with what we do know and do like that little prosecutor did when he piled up the evidence and put it all together, then we got something. We really do. Like that human blood in the van, four types, like the human blood on the rubber boots, the human blood on the Levi's jacket, the run of human blood, fourteen inches wide, coming out the back of the van. And then pile up on top of that the people that saw Corona out on the ranch and keep in mind that they were Mexicans, his own people, and I'll tell you . . . I bet they know a whole lot more than they said in court but they didn't want to testify against their own.

"Man, you could see it in their faces. They didn't want to be on the stand." Calvin hesitated and then added, "So to finish up, I suggest we do like Matt said, we stop, we think, we sit here a while, or stretch, or whatever, and don't talk, but think personal and be honest with ourselves before we open our mouths because really"—he looked around—"we shouldn't be feeling bad about what we got here because we got a murderer, a killer, and those are beautiful children and I wouldn't push mine up like that. Thank you."

Hands shot up.

Ernie stood up and said, "Put your hands down. I agree with Cal, I think we should all take a ten-minute break of thoughtful silence. Not a rest or a coffee break, but a few moments of personal meditation and search our souls." He glanced around. "Does anyone disgree?"

No one did. In fact, almost everyone nodded in agreement.

"Good," said Ernie. "It's four thirty-five. Let's be back at these tables at four forty-five and finish this thing up by five. Man, I'm tired, and today I hardly did any talking."

All the jurors laughed.

* * *

When the jurors came back to the tables things moved quickly. Most of them didn't seem to have much to say, not even Rick or Faye or Rogers. It seemed as though Calvin's words—having come after such a loud, unexpected outburst—had settled a lot of things within the souls of most of the individual jurors.

Ernie asked if they were ready to vote. Most people nodded and Ernie was getting ready to get the roll of paper from the court reporter's desk when Naomi said:

"Wait. I got one thing to say. If Corona is so guilty, then why didn't the sheriff himself ever testify? Ah, why didn't the sheriff come and tell us that he knows Corona is guilty?"

Everyone looked at Naomi. Victor and Matt, almost in unison, pushed back their chairs and lowered their heads, trying not to laugh. Frank and Larry looked at each other. Rogers yelled:

"Because that's not evidence! That would be hearsay! Dammit, why don't you ask why God doesn't come down here and tell us everything about everybody, then we don't even need the jury system and we can all go home!"

"—I wasn't talking to you, you deaf, loud-mouth, old—"

"—what'd you say? Did you call me—"

"—you can hear! I bet you didn't hear half the evidence and half of that didn't register and you think he's guilty because you hate Mexicans!"

"—why you old bag, I heard the evidence and that's—"

"—not ashamed of my age, and you were always looking at Hawk's daughter all trial long. Dirty old man."

Matt was laughing.

Victor was laughing.

Rick was red-faced, bursting to speak, but he didn't say one word.

Faye and Jim were shaking their heads.

Frank was covering his ears.

Ernie, trying to keep calm, was tapping the table with the gavel.

Finally things quieted down and Ernie said, "All right, let's take a vote and call it a day. Good God, has this been one hell of a day!"

And so the vote was taken: nine for guilty and three for innocent, and no one seemed surprised. In fact, many of the jurors had expected the vote to be more like ten guilty and two for acquittal, the two being Jim and Naomi.

They got up and began to stretch. Victor was still laughing. Like Frank and Larry, Victor had hardly said a thing all day but, unlike Frank and Larry, who were getting upset by all these emotional outbursts, Victor thought the whole thing was getting so ridiculous that it was fun. He had no problems sleeping at night. The ones who were taking it so personally were the ones who were not sleeping, who kept dreaming about evidence, the Corona family, attorneys, witnesses, and judges all night long.

It was the end of their third day and, although they didn't know it, they'd be at it for four more days and the worst was yet to come.

Getting on the bus was the same for the jurors as it had been the two previous nights. Pedro Corona and Eddie Cray lined the children up—four of Juan's and three of Pedro's—by the door of the bus and then, as the jurors began boarding, the two men ordered the children forward. But this time, as Faye got on the bus she paused and looked Cray straight in the eye and Cray, consciously or unconsciously, realized what her look meant, and he moved back toward Richard and Geneva Hawk. Hawk never noticed. He'd been having his picture taken by a TV crew.

Riding back to the Holiday Inn the jurors were quiet and tired. Mrs. Wallis sat down by Naomi and told her she had a surprise for her—she'd been able to get her paycheck after all. Naomi was happy. Now she'd be able to get cigarettes and nerve pills, and be able to endure another day of Rogers and Rick and all this shouting.

"You know," she said to Mrs. Wallis, "I've been on two juries before but none were ever like this. My God, the things that are happening in these deliberations. If I told you, you wouldn't believe me."

"Well, don't tell me," Mrs Wallis said, smiling. "After all, your deliberations are supposed to be in strictest confidence."

Naomi smiled. "You're a good girl. You've been most helpful and courteous to us all these months . . . My, just look outside. It's dark and cold and looks like it might rain. When this trial began, it was like summer-time. Do you know that when I first started driving here from Vallejo with Larry and Frank it was so warm in the mornings that sometimes we'd keep our windows half open? Now just look at it. Last Thursday when we drove over the hill from Vallejo the cattle on the hillsides had white snow on their brown backs. Can you believe that, snow, here in California?"

"I believe it," said George Wallis. "The papers say this is the worst winter in forty years."

"How about that? The worst winter. We're not supposed to read the papers, you know."

"Yes, I know. Excuse me, Naomi." And the young brown-haired police woman got up and went over to Faye. Naomi watched her and mumbled something under her breath to the effect of "I don't care. She and Faye think they're so educated." Naomi opened the envelope the matron had given her and began to think about her cats—maybe she should send some money to her sister so her sister could buy some more cat food.

It was Saturday night and tomorrow the jurors would have the day off, so they loosened up at dinner. The men talked about Sunday's Super Bowl game, the Washington Redskins, an old forgotten team, against the world champion Dolphins of Miami, a sensational new team. The men made bets among themselves and expounded on their knowledge of football. The atmosphere at the dinner table was exuberant and jolly.

Faye said to Naomi, "Let's not sit down at this end of the table, like we always do. Let's sit with Matt and George."

And George, hearing his name, yelled, "Come over here and join us. We're the party end of the table. Ernie and those guys at that end are too old and serious. Come on, Naomi!"

Happily, Naomi went to George and Faye to Matt, and each man pulled out the chair for his respective lady and used great charm to seat her.

George and Matt had already had a couple of drinks in their room, so they were very loose and their loose-party style was quickly becoming contagious. Many of the jurors were smiling and talking football, and for the first time since they had begun deliberating they seemed to be outside the realities of the murder trial.

The alternate jurors—one young man and two older men, one of whom was black—were at a small table a few feet away from Matt and George. At the other end of the jurors' table, just a few feet from Ernie and Calvin, sat the three bailiffs and the matron. No one in the dining room could approach the jury without passing by the bailiffs.

In the cocktail lounge off the dining room Judge Patton and two young writers were having a drink. Often those involved in the case were in the dining room or bar of the Holiday Inn while the jurors were having dinner.

When the waitress came to take the jurors' orders, Matt said tonight they wanted cocktails before dinner. The waitress said she didn't know anything about that—weren't they the jury group? Matt said yes, and she replied that she didn't believe they were allowed to have drinks. Matt said to ask the bailiff—dammit, they weren't kids, and if the county wouldn't pay, they'd pay themselves.

The waitress went over to the officers' table. Ed Hehr was off duty that night and the lieutenant in charge for the evening told the waitress to go ahead, that the Judge had authorized one cocktail per juror.

While the waitress was talking to the deputy, Matt told everyone on his side of the table to order a Manhattan whether they wanted it or not, and he'd drink all of them. George told his side to order martinis and he'd do the same.

When the waitress came back everyone at the long table was in on the secret and even those who weren't drinking ordered drinks anyway.

When it came time to order dinner, Matt was looser than ever, and he noticed that Naomi kept saying everything was so expensive that she didn't know what to order.

"Let me order for you girls," said Matt, who had three Manhattans in front of him. "Okay?"

Reluctantly, Naomi agreed.

Faye said, "Fine. I like surprises."

"Great," said Matt, and with a flair he ordered a salad with Roquefort dressing, shrimp cocktail, and filet mignon with lobster for the women and New York steak with lobster for himself and George.

"But that's so terribly expensive," said Naomi.

"Well," said Matt, "Sutter County is paying."

"But I could never order this expensive a dinner myself," said Naomi.

"Look," said Matt, "be realistic. I bet they paid those expert witnesses a thousand dollars a day. They've blown over half a million on this screwed-up case. This is chicken feed. And hell, we're doing all the work."

"But what if everyone in the country spent the taxpayers' money like we're doing?" said Naomi. "That wouldn't be right, would it?"

"Of course it's right," said George, with his three drinks in front of him. "Here, Naomi, have one of my martinis. Relax and enjoy yourself. Believe me, we're the cheapest part of this whole damn trial."

"You think so?" asked Naomi.

"Naomi," said Faye, "I think the boys are right. Remember what you were saying this morning . . . five dollars a day is as outdated as fifty cents an hour. Relax. It's all right for us to have a nice dinner."

"But I just don't feel right about wasting money. My father always taught us back in Pennsylvania—"

"We're not wasting, we've earned ours," said Matt. "It's

those generals and politicians who waste. Believe me, I know. Millions just on straw dogs around the globe alone."

"Matt is twenty-twenty," said George. "What do you think the President is eating tonight, Hamburger? Come on, take a drink."

George handed Naomi one of his martinis and they toasted; George drank his but Naomi didn't touch hers, and when her steak and lobster came she found the steak too thick and too juicy, so they had to take the filet back and cut it in half, butterflying it out flat, and cook it extra well done for her.

Matt shook his head in disbelief when it was brought back to the table.

Then the long night began and because they had the next day off many of the jurors stayed up late and talked among themselves while others were so uptight that, even if they had not had Sunday off, they wouldn't have been able to sleep anyway and so these spoke also. And strangely enough, in relationship to their stands on a verdict they made odd couples.

George, who was rooming with Matt, was for innocent while Matt was for guilty.

Jim, who was the only juror who had always voted for innocent, roomed with Rick, who had always voted for guilty.

Victor, who had voted for innocent on the first ballot because he was afraid they might all find Corona guilty on the first ballot, was with Ernie, the foreman, who had vacillated between guilty and innocent more than any other juror.

Like Victor, Rogers, who had voted for acquittal on

the first ballot because he'd been afraid they'd convict Corona before they even discussed all the evidence, was with Calvin, who had voted more times for innocent than anyone else except Jim and George.

Of the men, Frank and Larry were the only roommates who believed the same way—guilty—and interestingly enough they were also the softest-spoken and mildest-mannered members of the jury.

Then, of course, Naomi and Faye made an odd couple, but they were not roommates since each had a separate room.

It was a long night and the longest discussion pertaining to the trial was the one between Jim and Rick, and at the end of their talk Jim said, "Okay, thank you, Rick, I'll now think on it and in the morning if I still have any questions I'll ask you. Goodnight."

But Jim did not go to sleep. He lay there, eyes open, staring in the darkness; then in the early morning hours he opened his Bible, turned on his bed lamp, making sure he didn't disturb Rick—who had not slept well either—and began to read. Quietly. Trying to be honest and find some peace of mind.

Fourth Day—
Sunday, January 14, 1973

Sunday morning many of the male jurors wanted to sleep late, skip breakfast, and have an early lunch so they could be back in time to watch the Super Bowl kickoff. The lieutenant in charge of the crew of sheriff's deputies said that was fine, and so the only ones who had breakfast were Naomi and Faye. They went with Mrs. Wallis. Faye and Mrs. Wallis had bacon, eggs, and rolls, but Naomi ate nothing. She didn't feel very good after all the rich food they'd had the night before.

Mrs. Wallis talked about her experiences in Europe, where she had been in military security. She had enjoyed the service very much, and now she enjoyed her work as a police woman. Faye talked about her son, who'd also been in the service in Europe.

Naomi didn't talk much, and after breakfast she asked Mrs. Wallis if she could send out for some more of her nerve pills, because they didn't have her brand at the Holiday Inn.

"Well, of course, Naomi," said Mrs. Wallis with a smile, "we're here to do all we can for you."

The three women returned to their rooms. The men were in a room the hotel had set up as a lounge for them. Jim and Calvin were reading their Bibles. Matt, Ernie, George, Rick, and Rogers were playing poker. Larry was exercising and Frank and Victor were watching him. It was almost noon and everyone was fairly loose. The emotional outbursts of the previous day's deliberations were far in the background.

Only the three alternate jurors were not at ease. They were restless and becoming angry. They'd listened to all the evidence for five months right along with the rest of the jury, and now they couldn't deliberate or even associate with the regular jurors. One alternate, the black man, stayed in bed all day Sunday, not saying a word. The other two played checkers in their room, but they didn't have much to say to each other. The first day of deliberations all three had talked a little about the case and then taken a vote, and on the first ballot they'd all found Corona guilty of all twenty-five counts of murder. They couldn't understand why it was taking the jury so long, and it was truly getting on their nerves.

Surprisingly, none of the jurors really got into watching the Super Bowl. Even Victor, who had played college ball and was an avid football fan, wasn't able to concentrate on the game. As soon as he started watching the TV set, some question, some flash of forgotten evidence, or some fragment of testimony would crowd into his mind and he'd have to get up to walk around. By half-time most of the jurors had quit even pretending to be involved with the game. Rick and Jim went to their room. Slowly, almost unconsciously, they began to talk about the case, and then Jim told Rick that what really bothered him—he'd only come to realize it this morning—was not the actual evidence but . . .

"Rick, don't laugh at this, but one thing that bothers me is that Corona doesn't look like a killer," Jim said, smiling. "I mean, sure, I realize this is absurd, because what is a killer supposed to look like? Two heads, fangs in his mouth, and all those things out of the horror movies? Sure, I realize my opinion here has no merit but, Rick, we're dealing with a man's life, his family, and it especially bothers me to imagine how his wife and little girls will live the rest of their lives if we convict him.

"I did some praying today. Calvin and I did some talking, trying to resolve within ourselves the problem of this case and, Rick, we both agreed that even though we don't like it, we do honestly think the man is guilty. Especially in regard to those two graves where those slips of paper were found with his name on the paper, but . . . I still can't bridge within my soul from thinking he's guilty to saying and voting that, yes, he's guilty beyond any reasonable doubt to a moral certainty.

"Do you see what I mean? The way our system works it's really hard for us, a jury, to convict any man. What Faye said yesterday is no small matter, she was right when she said we're amateurs, and even though we're not supposed to worry about the court's punishment, we do. It's much easier to vote a person guilty with the death penalty off than if it were in effect. I'm sorry to admit this weakness in me but it's the truth, God help me.

"Oh, I wish I could come to a conclusion today, and feel well enough to get a good night's sleep."

And so Rick and Jim talked over the evidence in the quiet of a peaceful afternoon and, in the lounge, the other jurors paced about, not really watching the Super Bowl.

That evening, as the jurors were walking with the sheriff's deputies from their rooms to the dining room, three forms suddenly jumped out of a garden and yelled, "Daddy, we love you!"

Then the deputies stopped to check who it was, and the jurors also stopped. It was Jim Owen's three teenage daughters.

Jim smiled and said, "Thank you. I love you too."

And the girls, dressed in their Sunday clothes and looking very lovely, ran off through the garden area to the family car, where Mrs. Owen was waiting for them.

George, who was walking alongside Naomi, approached Jim and said, "Tell me, Jim, if you were being accused of those twenty-five murders would you have your daughters, those beautiful girls we just saw there, come to the trial like the Coronas have done with Juan's daughters all these months?"

Jim shook his head. "No. It would have hurt me too much just to see them."

"You mean, if you were guilty," said Naomi. "Not if you were innocent."

"No. I mean if I were innocent or guilty I wouldn't want them there in court."

"I agree," said George, "I got kids and I wouldn't want them around either. My wife, yes, but not the kids."

"I have a girl and a boy," said Naomi, "and I guess

you're right but . . . do you really think Hawk is using Corona's four girls like Faye said? Oh, that's awful just to think of. And Hawk always seemed so nice. Always smiling, always putting on a show. It would have been a boring trial if it hadn't been for Hawk."

"I'll go along with that," said Jim. "Hawk's a real entertainer. I still laugh every time I think of him."

"I don't," said George. "Not after he didn't put on a case. Dammit!" And George shook his head. "Nobody could have kept me off the stand if I was innocent. Nobody."

"Right," said one of the alternate jurors, who were walking behind the twelve regular jurors. "That's what we've been saying among ourselves. In a crime this terrible, only a guilty man, or an insane man, could just sit there for five months, listening to all the evidence, and then not say anything."

"Do you three men think he's guilty?" asked Naomi.

"Well," smiled the alternate who was doing the talking, "I'll put it this way: after the first day we've had nothing to talk about. We all came to agreement on a verdict right away the first day."

"Oh," said Naomi, "and what did you agree on?"

"Naomi," said the man, "we can't tell you that. You got to come to your own conclusion—but, please, hurry it up. It's terrible being locked up in a little ten-by-twelve room all day long while you people get to walk around, drink coffee, and look over all the evidence. I feel like a fifth-rate citizen. I'll go to jail before I ever get stuck with an alternate juror's job again. Man, this is for the birds."

Near the hotel's registration desk, the jurors passed the racks of newspapers, and Matt saw the headlines: "Juan Corona Has Heart Attack." The alternate juror behind Matt also saw the headline, but neither man said anything as they all proceeded to the large main dining area.

Once again Faye and Naomi sat with Matt and George, and they tried to be as relaxed as they'd been the night before but it didn't come off. Tonight everyone seemed tired, quiet, and very tense. At the other end of the table Ernie was talking to Cal and Victor, saying that lately he'd been thinking a lot about this word "peer" and that the law said that one was to get a speedy trial by a jury of his peers, and he wondered if anybody on this jury could truly be called Juan Corona's peer. There were no Mexicans, no labor contractors, there was no one on this jury who knew anything about ranch work, no one who knew if so much killing and burying could be done without the killer ever being seen. And then Ernie asked Cal if he were being accused of murder wouldn't he want some Negroes on the jury, someone who had had the same experiences he'd had or at least knew something about the type of life he'd lived?

Calvin nodded. "Yes, I can see your point. People that have worn one's shoes can understand one's way through a life a whole lot better."

"Exactly," said Ernie, "and none of us came from Mexico, following the crops, without speaking English, and so in no way are we qualified as Corona's peers."

"Ernie," said Victor, "you're taking the word 'peer' too literally and, besides, I was born locally and I've worked in the fields, I speak Spanish, I've worked with Mexicans, and Mexicans are basically no different than any other people. There are smart ones, dumb ones, good ones, lazy ones—no, not many lazy ones. That's a myth. They work like the dickens out in those fields in the hot sun where most people would have a stroke. And besides, murder is murder in any culture, so I don't see how this peer thing is really so important."

"Well," said Ernie, "I think it is. Tell me, Vic, knowing the fields like you say you do, could a man do all this killing and burying—I mean, hell's bells, to have dug so many graves and locate the people to put in them in a six-month period like they said, is a fulltime job."

"Isn't the ground pretty soft on a river bank?" asked Cal.

"Okay," said Ernie, "it probably is in a flat valley like they say that Sullivan Ranch is in. Okay, so let's say the graves didn't take long to dig, let's say that, but why didn't someone see Corona doing some of these things? My God, like George says, I sometimes don't believe any of this case."

Victor then said that orchards were pretty lonely places except at harvest time; the rest of the year they were left unattended except for a few scattered work crews during the pruning months.

Ernie asked more questions.

Victor said he couldn't answer all of Ernie's questions fully, that all he could do was mention a few things he happened to know.

Then Cal said, "Ernie, about that question you asked me, about wanting blacks on my jury if I was accused of murder. I'll tell you . . . maybe I wouldn't. I mean, it all depends on the black man himself. Some black people, like some white people I've known, I wouldn't want at all."

And Calvin looked at Ernie, realizing that Ernie was from West Virginia, and he said no more. Victor said he hoped to God they were doing the right thing and, dammit, how he resented Hawk not having put on a case. There were innumerable things Hawk could've done, said Ernie, and, saying this, he once more thought about Duran, the foreman on the Sullivan Ranch, and how Duran had located several of the gravesites for the Sheriff's Department, and he decided that, yes, he definitely would like to go up there after this trial and sort of nose around. There were so many things he'd like to have asked some of the witnesses who'd been on the stand.

Then Ernie started to talk about how the judicial system was outdated from the jury's point of view—that, hell, so much more could be done with a jury than just have them sitting there like mummies all trial long. Cal and Victor agreed, and Larry and Frank, who were sitting nearby, also agreed. Jury members, because they weren't professionals, were treated like the least important people in the courtroom when, hell, they were the ones who ultimately made the final decision. Why weren't they allowed to ask a question now and then through the Judge? Why couldn't they write down what they believed the attorneys had neglected to ask and submit these questions to the Judge and have the Judge ask the question? Why didn't the system make some use of their collective mind? Dammit, this case had certainly not turned out to be the great trial of the century, as so many papers had said it would be.

Nine miles east of Fairfield, Juan Corona was resting under sedation in the Vacaville Medical Center. Friday night, after he'd been returned from Fairfield, he'd begun to complain of chest pains. By eleven o'clock that night the pain had intensified so much that the doctor on duty had been called in and rumors began circulating that Juan Corona was suffering a heart attack.

Saturday morning many newspapers and television and radio newscasters reported that Corona had suffered another heart attack, the third since his arrest, and quoted Hawk as saying that as soon as the verdict for acquittal came in he'd sue Sutter County for false arrest and ruination of Corona's health, and take the county for its total worth: three hundred million dollars.

On Sunday many papers retracted or qualified their earlier stories: Juan Corona had not had what in layman's terms was called a heart attack; he had had a "coronary insufficiency," a narrowing of the coronary arteries, best explained as a lack of oxygen to the heart muscle. Blood tests and electrocardiograms had shown that he did not have any "detectable myocardial damage"—that is, that he had not actually had a heart attack. All Corona needed was modified bed rest, medication for high blood pressure, and mild tranquilizers for his nerves.

And so all Sunday Corona rested, half awake, half asleep. His wife and family attended a special mass in Juan's behalf and then, in the afternoon, went to a rally with speeches and food and general celebration. Everyone was sure that the jury was going for an acquittal. Even the prosecution was talking at best in terms of a hung jury, because it had been such a long and complicated case.

The rally for Juan Corona went well and while the speeches were going on Juan's mother, Doña Corona, fingered her rosary and, with eyes half closed, kept saying Hail Marys and asking God to please help their cause and see that justice was done.

It was six hundred and ten days since the first of the

twenty-five bodies had been found in a peach orchard north of Yuba City on lovely spring day, and now . . . it was winter, and spring was once again only two months away, and everyone was so exhausted they were instinctively turning to God. The ultimate concept of justice.

Fifth Day—
Monday, January 15, 1973

On Monday deliberations began about ten minutes earlier than they had on the previous days, and in the first five minutes the jurors decided to take a vote to find out where they stood. They thought they might all be in agreement after the day's rest and, if so, there would be no point in deliberating any further.

At nine fifteen Ernie began to read the ballots.

Guilty.

Guilty.

Guilty.

Guilty.

Guilty.

Guilty.

Guilty.

By now all the jurors were looking around at each other. Maybe it was going to be a verdict. Ernie hesitated. It definitely looked as if they were going for a verdict of guilty. Ernie picked up the next piece of torn-off paper:

Guilty.

Rick glanced at Faye and then at Matt. Matt shook his head. Ernie read again:

Guilty.

Rogers laughed and Rick turned to him and Ernie then read:

Innocent.

Rick threw up his arms and yelled, but Ernie continued:

Guilty.

Innocent.

They stood at ten for guilty and two for innocent.

In the uproar the jurors were talking and shouting, wanting to know who was holding out, and why?

Emotions were running high. In less than thirty minutes, after two nights and one whole day of rest, here they were again . . . all the talkers screaming to talk at the same time, the nontalkers watching in disgust and indignation.

Calvin raised his hand.

Ernie stood up and yelled for everyone to shut up and called on Calvin.

"Look," said Calvin, "everybody knows that people can sing together because they're singing the same song." The talkers stopped and looked at him. He'd come at them from such an unexpected angle. "But when people talk, they normally tell different things, so only one person can talk at a time. Please . . . are we going to sing, or are we going to talk? Because if all this talking at the same time keeps up, then I think we might as well have fun and sing."

Victor laughed and raised his hand. Ernie recognized him. "I agree," said Victor, "and I like the way Calvin put it. The next time everyone starts talking at the same time I'm going to start singing!"

"Me, too," agreed Matt, "singing and clapping my hands!"

And so the talkers quieted down and the deliberations continued, and, as they went around the table, starting with George and going to Calvin, no one had anything to say. Not one word. Until they got to Naomi.

"I've been thinking," Naomi said, "and I have an idea . . . I suggest we go backward for a while." Several jurors smiled, lifting their eyebrows. She noticed but continued confidently. "By backward, I mean we should make out a list of reasons why Corona *isn't* guilty. Do you see what I'm driving at? This is a circumstantial case, and Hawk always said a circumstantial case is like a chain of evidence and every link in that chain has to connect to the other and . . . really, if we look at it like this and stick to the chain idea, then I think we'll see that there is reasonable doubt all through this case and the chain is broken." She hesitated, clearing her throat. "Here, I've already made out my list of doubts. I have more than twenty of them. Four more than Rick's sixteen points and—" Nervously, Naomi stole a glance at Rick, and when she saw him smiling she lost her composure. "Ernie, you're the foreman! You tell that kid to stop that! How can anyone say anything when he's always smiling? Oh, it's not fair! All men and one woman and . . ." She reached for her purse to get her nerve pills.

"Please," said Faye, "*two* women and ten men. Here, let me see your list and see if I can't help you."

"I don't need your help! I can talk for myself! Look, I

already have my doubts written out. If you want to help, then why don't you—who's so educated and everyone listens to—write out your own list of doubts?" Naomi put her purse down. Her hands were trembling. ". . . and don't tell me you don't have any doubts. You do. All of you do! All trial long that's all we gossiped about even when we weren't supposed to be talking about the trial yet. We'd all say how awful a job Sutter County was doing. We all agreed that the prosecution didn't even have a case. And like Calvin said, we'd all go home shaking our heads and wonder how they even dared bring this mess to trial. So don't kid me, we all got doubts!"

"All right," said Faye, "I agree with you and so I'll write out my doubts, but . . . I'll also write out my thoughts which are for conviction."

"Okay!" Naomi was at her purse again, trying to get her pills. She got her cigarettes instead. "Do it! List your doubts! See . . ." She turned to everyone. ". . . Faye has doubts too. She just admitted it!" And she began to laugh, but her face twisted and she ended up coughing instead.

Everyone was watching her. Ernie stood up and suggested they take a fifteen-minute break.

At ten they were back at the tables and Faye was reading her list of doubts, written in blue ink on stationery from the Holiday Inn.

EVIDENCE NOT PROVING GUILT

1. Saliva test on cup did not show defendant's type "O" blood.
2. Cigarette butt in Sample's grave, E-1-3,

was "O" while Sample was "A" and it was not shown that Corona was a smoker.

3. Testimony by Mrs. Vallejo who rented a house from Corona almost proved to be an alibi—when Corona went out to fix the screen—but ultimately contradicted and confused other statements.
4. It was not proven to whom the clothing (with blood) in the cabin behind the ranch mess-hall belonged.
5. Evidence of tire track at Whitacre's grave, E-1-1, couldn't conclusively be proved to be Corona's and Corona's alone.
6. Blood on gun didn't match victim's blood who was shot.
7. Striations on machete didn't match skull of victim that was tested for striations.
8. Footprints at gravesites were vague.
9. Fingerprints were never taken.

After reading her list, Faye took off her glasses and said, "Now, before we discuss these points, I'd like to add that I'm sure any one of us could add more to this list of doubts . . . for example the number mix-up which Hawk always called the body switch. Or the fact that no one ever saw Corona doing any killing or burying. Or, maybe most important of all, no motive was ever established. But the reason I didn't include these is because I tried to stick to specific points and not get into generalities which . . . are so tempting for speculation.

"Do I make myself clear? Could someone help me before I read my list of evidence that points toward conviction?" Naomi raised her hand. "Yes, Naomi."

"Well, I think we should continue along this train of thought. We should all write out our doubts and then take a vote before we start all that other type of thinking. I think too many people here are just afraid to vote or even think in terms of innocent."

"Afraid?" said Faye. "Afraid of what? It's Corona's *supporters* who are outside this building by the hundreds. I believe you have your statement—"

"—ass backward!" said Rogers. "Hell, it's easy to find a man innocent. Look what they did with that Angela Davis and those Hell's Angels last month."

Ernie stood up, trying to silence Rogers.

"—Angela Davis and those Hell's Angels were guilty as sure as I'm sitting here but those juries were just afraid," continued Rogers. "It takes guts nowadays to find a guilty man guilty."

Ernie was tapping the table with the judge's gavel.

"Hell!" yelled Rogers. "We're showing ourselves to have real guts with all those supporters marching around and all these papers all this time writing about this case like they've been doing."

"You weren't supposed to be reading the papers!" said Naomi. "That's not right! The Judge told us every day that we weren't supposed to read the papers or watch TV! How can you expect to know the evidence if you got it all mixed up in your head with what you read in the papers and saw on TV? Answer me that! Explain to me how you know the difference between fact and gossip!" Naomi was really mad. "You can't, can you?" She turned to Ernie. "This is grounds for a mistrial, isn't it? He admitted he read the papers."

"Look," said Matt, cutting in before Ernie could answer, "I read three different papers every day."

"What?" said Victor. He was shocked. Five or six other jurors were also shocked.

"Oh, hell," said Matt, glancing around, "I did it all trial long and I'm sure half of us here did it too. So what?" Matt noticed that Frank was nodding in agreement. "Come on, let's all settle down. Dammit, Ernie, the next one who bursts out like that, give him or her the foreman's job and see how they like it. Eh, Rogers, you want to be foreman?"

"I never said that."

"Then why don't you stop interrupting everyone? Look at Rick here. He's red in the face, just bursting to talk, but he's been real cool all morning long."

Everyone looked at Rick and it was true, there he sat—stiff, rigid, and red-faced. He seemed to have aged since deliberations had begun last Thursday.

Jim raised his hand and Ernie recognized him.

"Well," said Jim, "I voted guilty this morning myself." Naomi's eyes grew huge. "I'm sorry, Naomi, but all day yesterday I wrestled within myself, trying to be honest and see why I was so strong for innocent, and I'll tell you . . . the main reason was because I don't want to convict any man of anything unless . . . like the laws says, exactly those words, I know for a fact, not beyond possible or imaginary doubt, but beyond reasonable doubt, reasonable thinking and figuring, and to a moral certainty that he's guilty.

"You know . . ." Jim blushed. "I don't mean to sound preachy but these words of the law are really well thought out, you know what I mean? After days of dealing with them, they seem to even get better."

"Jim . . ." said Naomi in a low voice. She was so shocked she didn't even notice her gravelly voice. "I thought you were always with me. Even that time the vote came in eleven for guilty and one for innocent and I was the only holdout."

"Naomi," Jim said in a kind, compassionate manner, "that wasn't you that voted for innocent, that was me."

"Oh, no." Naomi shook her head, and her eyes were large and frightened. "I've never voted for guilty except one time when it was eight to four, or nine to three. I don't remember which, but, for sure, I was the holdout when it was eleven to one. You still meant to be with me, Jim, but you weren't. You were afraid."

"I was afraid?" asked Jim. "Why do you use that word again? Please, Naomi, let me tell you what happened to me yesterday, and maybe that will help you."

"No," said Naomi, "I don't want to hear about anything that points toward guilty until we first write out all our doubts and find all the things that point toward innocent. Fair is fair, and it's not fair how you're all against me."

"I'm not against you," said Jim, "but please, I'd like to tell you what happened to me yesterday."

Naomi nodded, and Jim talked for quite a while about the turmoil of his conscience and how he had worried about the Corona children. But then he had realized that Ed Cray and Juan's brother Pedro seemed less concerned with the feelings of these children than he himself was, so he decided that, as Faye had said, maybe he should consider: "What if Corona is indeed guilty but they don't convict him and so he goes back to not only hurting poor old men but his own family?"

Naomi was staring at Jim.

Jim saw and said, "Naomi, I know how you feel. Believe me, this has been one of the most taxing weeks of my life. It's been awful. Night and day. But last night I finally came to a solid conclusion within myself and for the first time I was able to sleep. I slept all night. I had no problem with my conscience and today, clear as a bell, I could see and understand, and so I voted guilty for the first time and I feel no remorse or complications within me whatsoever."

Rick began to speak, to agree, to say that he had helped Jim so maybe he could help Naomi.

Matt kicked Rick under the table, hard. And then winked at Rick with a twinkle in his eye.

In pain and surprise Rick pulled his leg away, but he said nothing.

Jim continued, now sounding as sincere for guilt as he had been all along for innocence. He then concluded by telling Naomi about the two "almost" eyewitnesses: a black man named Byron Shannon, and a white man named Pervis.

"Shannon was not a smart man," said Jim, "and we could all tell by his appearance that the poor man had lived a hard life of drinking, not eating, and not sleeping properly." Byron Shannon was an old-looking black man, and he had been on the witness stand a long time, day after day. The prosecution had wanted him to tell about the two or three times he had seen Juan Corona come to the skid-row part of town and ask different men—who were later found dead in the orchards north of town—if they'd like to go and do a little work for him. But Shannon had trouble explaining himself in court because the prosecution kept asking him to go to the big mockup map of the lower end of Marysville and show the jury where he and his friends had been sipping wine when Corona had come by in his pickup or van. It became obvious that Shannon didn't know how to read maps, and so the more the prosecution sent him to the mockup board the more he became disoriented until, finally, he was chewing his tongue rapidly and putting all the stop signs on one corner and confusing north with east and west with south.

Hawk had torn into the prosecution for badgering the poor old man.

But prosecutor Bart Williams had ignored Hawk and continued until, finally, many of the jurors had become apprehensive.

Jim reminded the other jurors that even with all that confusion, throughout all those hours on the witness stand Shannon had never changed his basic story. "Sure, he was so confused that he kept scratching his head and chewing his tongue, but I'm sure that if we had been physically taken to those streets of Marysville, across the river from Yuba City, Shannon could have taken us to each and every place where he'd seen Corona come by and offer these men the work of digging a garbage pit. And remember this, we have testimony—I forget by who—that Corona never hired non-Mexicans for his regular work crews and so why, I ask you, was he offering these old men work? And why were these same men later found dead just north of Yuba City where Juan Corona had a work camp and he could come and go on that property as he wished?

"Sure, we could say this is all just a coincidence, but then tell me—where does coincidence stop being just coincidence? Honestly, if we think, really think, and remain reasonable, I think these things connect Corona to these murdered men beyond any reasonable doubt." He turned to Naomi. "Naomi, believe me, I tried to do everything I could to find this man innocent but Sunday, as I lay there in bed thinking by myself, going over the trial in my mind, I came to the realization that Corona is always there . . . in the middle of it all . . . so help me, to a moral certainty."

"But Jim," said Naomi, "maybe you were just tired on Sunday. Maybe if you write out your doubts you'll be able to see the larger truths of this whole—"

Rogers moved noisily in his chair. Naomi turned and saw but still she continued.

"Please, we have to be fair and just. We can't say a man is guilty because he's there in the middle. We have to have proof, you know, like real mysteries do, and in all the mysteries I've ever read it is always explained that—" Several jurors pushed their chairs back, mumbling to themselves. Naomi turned to Ernie. "You're the foreman, so tell these people to stop interrupting me. It's not fair."

"I agree," said Calvin. "It's rude, and not fair, and it isn't going to get us anywhere."

Naomi smiled. "Thank you, Calvin." And she then continued, saying that she couldn't see how they could be convicting a man without knowing the motive. "Motives are always very important. In every book I've ever read one never has the grasp of the whole picture, you know, the real mystery, until one finds out the motive. Also, I've never heard of a case where the police made so many mistakes unless they arrested the wrong man. So I say, thinking along these lines, why couldn't it be that Juan's older brother, Natividad, who owned that bar, be the real murderer?"

"Then why didn't Juan get on the stand and say so?" yelled Rogers.

"Maybe because Juan loves his brother!" yelled Naomi. "Maybe because they're from Mexico and Mexicans are close family people!" She was mad and Rogers was mad and they were yelling at each other. "Ha!" continued Naomi. "Did you ask a dumb question! Don't you know you're not supposed to speculate!"

Victor and Matt burst out laughing.

Rogers threw his cigar down. He was boiling. "I only speculated after you started speculating!"

Rick held . . . bursting to speak but not saying one single word.

Ernie stood up and things finally quieted down. "All right," he said. "Returning to Jim, do you have anything else to say?"

"Well," said Jim, "not really . . . only, Naomi, what I meant to say was not so much something about the evidence but something about here, inside me, and inside you, and inside each of us. You see, I believe—like Matt said yesterday—that convicting a man or not convicting a man is largely an emotional thing. We're human, and no matter how much the Judge told us not to let ourselves be swayed by our emotions we already are swayed.

"Do you see what I mean? We arrived here in this courtroom already swayed because none of us are professionals. All of us are just everyday people. Oh, I swear this week has been terrible. I've never done so much thinking in all my life."

Larry nodded. "Me too. It's been awful."

"Then why have you two voted for guilty?" asked Naomi, looking from Larry to Jim and then back to Larry.

"Because I think it's right," said Jim.

"Yeah," said Larry, "and what helped me to see that it's right was to stop thinking that all this happened here in his courtroom, but instead realize that it all happened north of Yuba City. Somewhere out in those orchards along the banks of the Feather River. Men, old harmless men, were murdered. Really, they were."

"And Corona is big and strong!" yelled Rogers.

"Yeah," said Rick, "and there was already a big dump at the ranch, and so there was no reason why Corona should be trying to hire old men to go out to the ranch to dig another garbage pit!"

"Right!" said Rogers. "And we all saw how he almost fell out of his chair when Pervis came into the room!"

Victor laughed and slapped his leg and Matt said, "I'm sure glad you spoke up, Rick. Another second of silence and I'm sure you would have passed out."

Everyone laughed, even Naomi, and then, finally, Rick himself.

Ernie said that a lot of truths had been voiced. Yes, Corona's work crews had been made up of Mexicans, not white men like he'd tried to pick up on skid row. They had that in evidence by the work logs, and those logs had Social Security numbers and the amount of hours worked alongside each name, but in the so-called Death List there were no Social Security numbers or hours. Just names, or nicknames, and locations. Also, three experts had testified that those names were written by Juan Corona, and among those names were seven or more of the deceased men.

Jim raised his hand and Ernie recognized him.

"I know I've taken way too much of everyone's time," said Jim, "but I want to repeat that inside me I've come to a solid conclusion and . . . oh, I don't know how to best say it except, like I said, I voted guilty for the first time this morning and it was no easy task, believe me, but I hope we can proceed from here on like good, honest people and not get on each other's nerves."

Calvin cut in. "I agree. Let's all talk one person at a time and not be rude."

"Good idea," said Ernie, and another vote was taken and once more the tally was ten for guilty and two for acquittal, and everyone looked at Naomi.

"Well, I never got to read my doubts," Naomi yelled. "Everyone began telling their own doubts and suddenly all their doubts turned into points of evidence for conviction."

"Well, read your doubts," said Ernie. "Come on, we're all quiet and orderly."

"Okay. I'll read them but remember, I'm not the only one voting for innocent. Someone else is with me." Her face brightened. She glanced around, almost youthful with excitement. "Come on, holdout, don't hold out on me, who are you? I need you more than ever."

Reluctantly, George raised his hand but didn't bother to look up, he was so tired.

"George!" said Naomi. "I should have known it was you. You got doubts too, eh?"

George nodded. "You bet, I got lots and lots and lots of them. Ten fingers times twenty-five bodies plus Corona's prints, too." He sat up and looked around. "Why didn't they take fingerprints? Ah, answer me that?"

"Because these bodies were old and half decayed!" said Rogers. "What did you expect, for Corona's fingerprints to be all over the dead men's bodies? Hell, they were caked with mud. And these country boys don't know nothing. I say, be happy with the evidence we got! Hell, there were bodies everywhere! No police department could've done better. My boy is a policeman and he told me—"

"How'd you ever get on this jury?" asked Victor.

"Yeah," said George, "how'd you do it?"

"Same as you," said Rogers. "I was voir dired! Fair and square."

"Hawk sure made a mistake," said Naomi.

"Okay, okay," said Ernie, "quiet down. My God! Now, please, to go on. Naomi, will you please read your doubts aloud?"

". . . well, the first one I have asks a very important question," said Naomi, and then she paused, realizing that everyone was looking at her. She turned to Ernie. "Ernie, could you please read them for me?"

"Sure," said Ernie. He stood up, took Naomi's list, looked it over, and then began: "Point one, meat receipts could have blown over from the garbage dump. Point two, blue van coming over levee in early morning suggested to the carpenter that Corona was either digging a grave or buying a body because later a grave was found in this area. But at the end of this trial the blue van was claimed by Pedro, Juan Corona's brother, and so it logically follows that maybe Juan Corona wasn't driving the blue van that day and therefore, maybe, Pedro or Natividad are the real killers. Point three, bloody shorts and bolo machete found under van seat could have belonged to still another Corona brother or anyone else on that Sullivan Ranch. Point four, why didn't the sheriff testify in court? Point five, why did the saliva test on the cup show the wrong blood type for Corona? And along this train of thought, if Dr. Ruth Guy could make one mistake in testing blood on a cup then why couldn't she—"

Ernie stopped and looked at Naomi and Naomi, not liking his look, jumped up and said:

"Give me my notes! You don't read them right! You're making fun of them! That woman tested all the blood and she could've made mistakes on all of it! You wear blinders just like that kid! You don't know half of the things I'm referring to! You and that bully kid and Rogers all just look straight ahead and never see the facts all around you that everybody knows about except us, the jury!"

Enraged, Rick was getting up.

Naomi saw him coming toward her and cringed back in her chair as if she were afraid he might hit her.

Ernie winked at Rick and smiled at Naomi, and Rick sat down.

"Don't wink at me," said Naomi. "I'm no fool. I bet you don't even know that Raya was cut up in the Guadalajara Bar and that bar was owned by Juan's older brother, Natividad, and Natividad left the country to go back to Mexico when he found out Jose Raya had not died and was going to sue him for a lot of money. Also I bet you don't even know that Natividad was an admitted homosexual and these are homosexual murders!"

The jurors were startled. None of them knew about the bar incident in such detail. In court all that had come out was that Juan Corona had offered a job to Jose Raya on the street outside the Guadalajara Bar. Granted, while Raya was on the witness stand the jurors had seen that his cheek was chopped up and mutilated, and his left eye was twisted and his lips seemed to be torn up, but it had not come out in court that he had received those injuries on the same night Juan had offered him a job which he had turned down. Also, it had not been revealed that this brutal attack had occurred in the restroom of Natividad's bar, or that Juan and Natividad had been prime suspects.

The other jurors stared at Naomi.

Finally Victor leaned forward and asked Naomi how she knew all this.

"Really," continued Victor, "I want to know how you know about this? I don't remember hearing this in court."

"I read it in a detective magazine months before court ever started."

"But," continued Victor, "they asked us during the voir dire if we'd read about the Corona case before they accepted us as jurors."

"Yes," said Naomi, "they asked if we knew anything about the Juan Corona case which would prejudice us but they never asked"—she smiled—"if we knew anything about his brother Natividad. Now, I'll tell you, in the magazine it said his brother was a homosexual, and Hawk said these are homosexual murders and so it only makes sense . . . ha, I see by the way you're looking at me, Victor, now you're getting reasonable doubt, too!"

"No," said Victor quietly, "I'm just beginning to agree with Rick. I think you're crazy."

"What!" yelled Naomi. "Repeat that, if you're a man!"

"I heard him way over here," said Rogers. "He said he thinks you're—"

Victor leaped to his feet. "Shut your mouth, Rogers!"

Rogers did. Then, becoming self-conscious, Victor licked his lips and said, "Excuse me, but I got to go to the toilet." And quickly he left the room.

Naomi was still talking, saying the whole trouble was that everyone was scared. Then she pointed to Frank. "Look at him, he never says anything. He just sits there and votes guilty every time. That's not deliberating. That's just being stubborn and prejudiced from the beginning."

Naomi got up and went over to Frank. "Isn't it true, Frank, you just don't like me or anyone? All these months we've ridden together in the car you've never talked to me once. Your probably hate me so much you vote guilty just to be spiteful to me."

Frank looked at Naomi but he said nothing.

Naomi waited.

Frank took a deep breath and looked away.

Naomi screamed, "Talk to me! Don't turn away from me! Don't you have the guts to face the truth?"

Slowly Frank got up, staring at Naomi all the while, eye to eye, and it was becoming evident that this nice little white-haired man was not small and weakly built after all. His neck was large, his hands—he'd been a toolmaker all his life—were huge and callused, and his chest was growing larger and larger as she stood there seething with anger. Finally he spoke. "I've talked! You just don't listen!" Naomi backed away. "I talked about those tire tracks on our first day, which show that Corona's vehicle was there at that first grave. That and those two rolled-up papers, and those folded meat receipts, and bank receipts, put him at graves beyond any human doubt. Then on top of that, all this human blood and all the places where he was seen is more than enough for any sane person to see that Corona is guilty. Hawk might be a smart man, but he missed the boat! He made fun of the evidence but he never refuted one piece! There, I've talked! Now will you leave me alone."

Then Frank left the table, mumbling to himself, "Oh, you are a vicious woman. A very mean vicious woman." And he went to the very last row of chairs in the courtroom, as far as he could get from everybody . . . there he sat down and lowered his white head into the callused palms of his huge hands, and the entire room was heavy with silence.

* * *

Deliberations had ceased. After they had all returned to the tables they decided unanimously that, as a jury, they had come to a deadlock and maybe this constituted a hung jury and they should inform the court before deliberating any longer.

They were so tired, and their nerves were so on edge, that when lunch was brought in no one was able to eat. Ernie approached Matt, who was standing alone, and asked him what he thought about Rogers, Frank, and Rick, who were so tight, and most especially what did he think about Naomi.

"I don't know," replied Matt, "but I'll tell you, if we go on a few more days we'll get a conviction on paper. These guys for acquittal got nothing to work with."

"In other words," Ernie said, "if we keep deliberating we can get these people to change their vote but not their minds?"

"Exactly," said Matt.

"But Matt . . . is that right?"

"Right?" smiled Matt. "Hell, Ernie, have any of the jobs we've done as professional soldiers been right?"

"I'd like to think they were," said Ernie.

"Okay, well, maybe then this is right, too. Hell, we all know the man is guilty. It's just that the prosecution was outclassed. They're cow-town lawyers and Hawk is a big-city attorney. Ernie, Hawk had the case won for the first three months, we know that. But then he blew it. He overplayed his hand to the point that half of these people started seeing through him. So don't ask me about right and wrong. Hell, it's all a game of hired attorneys, like it was hired guns a hundred years ago, and like it's hired armies now, and so"—he shrugged—"if this trial had lasted three months we'd all be fighting for an acquittal but, my friend, the reality of this screwed-up situation is that this trial lasted five months and now we're fighting for a conviction and that's that. No right or wrong involved. Only chance, and luck, and timing, and hell, don't ask me about justice or truth. Ernie, you are the foreman and you'll have to make up your own mind: should we call it a hung jury, or should we go on and get those other two votes and convict the man? I don't care, I'll go either way with you."

"Matt, it just can't be that simple."

"Okay, it's not that simple."

Ernie shook his head. "God, I don't know. I guess we'll take a vote to see if we should go on deliberating or see the Judge and ask him to tell us what constitutes a hung jury." He breathed deeply and then shook his head again. "I now see why Hawk didn't put on a case. It's like Faye explained, we're conscientious amateurs and Hawk compounded our natural fears of not wanting to convict anyone."

"And maybe," smiled Matt, "that's the way it should be."

At one thirty-five that afternoon, the defense and prosecution teams were summoned to the Judge's chambers, and both sides were boiling to fight. Hawk was in a happy mood, sure that the jury had heard about Corona's heart attack and would now realize why he had not put Corona on the witness stand. The prosecution was hoping the jury had not heard about Corona's condition, and hoped they wouldn't. As Judge Richard E. Patton spoke, both sides, defense and prosecution, eyed each other with hate and vengeance.

After a good deal of discussion, much of it acrimonious, all parties agreed that the jury would have to be transported to the Vacaville Medical Center in order to convene the court to settle the jury's latest question.

Hawk was jubilant—there was no way the jury could keep from being affected by the sight of the stricken Juan Corona.

Ernie told the other jurors that the bailiff had told him they would have to go to the medical center in Vacaville for the court to be convened.

The jurors began to speculate as to what had happened. Maybe Corona had had another heart attack; several jurors recalled reading something about Corona having an attack right after he was arrested.

Knowingly, Matt smiled and said, "Well, tell me, wouldn't you have a heart attack if you were arrested for twenty-five murders?"

The jurors were not really deliberating anymore. They were sitting around the tables drinking coffee and talking informally.

"But if you committed twenty-five murders," said George, "wouldn't you have to be insane? And, if you're insane, then you wouldn't get upset enough to have a heart attack."

Matt laughed.

George continued, "Listen to me, Matt, any way you cut it, I still don't feel solid enough to vote guilty. I'll grant you maybe I'm wrong, the man is probably guilty; everything points to that but, hell, it doesn't point to him beyond all reasonable doubt. So dammit! Don't laugh at me!"

"What is reasonable doubt?" asked Faye.

George looked at Faye a long time, and then shrugged.

"I don't know how to define it, Faye, but I know my doubts aren't just imaginary. I got *real doubts*!"

"Yes," said Faye, "but consider this—"

"Reasonable doubt is a doubt that any reasonable person has," said Naomi.

"Oh, no," said Faye, "here, let me try to help you understand this concept . . ."

"Help me?" yelled Naomi. "Always wanting to help everyone as if they're little kids or imbeciles. I hate that! It's worse than Rogers' screaming! And I swear if you offer to help me one more time I'm going—"

"Now, now," said Ernie, "we've not even in deliberations. My, what's gotten into us all?" He laughed. "Get up. Stretch your legs. Go to the toilet. Get ready to go."

The bailiff had told them that a bus would be ready to take them to the Vacaville Medical Center in twenty minutes.

The bus, with the jury and two armed deputies, drove to Vacaville slowly, surrounded by an escort of police vehicles. Behind the bus there was a caravan of Corona supporters. The number of supporters was growing daily . . . as the wait for the jury's decision intensified and received more and more front-page publicity across the state, the nation, and abroad.

The jurors were quiet, looking out of their windows at the rain and the wet-shiny asphalt and, in the distance, the small green hills which came stepping down from the north, through Fairfield and Vacaville, into the flat lands of the Sacramento River delta. The Sacramento River was wide here but it was not large when it came down from Sutter County and flowed slowly through the capital, turning in a westerly direction toward the San Francisco Bay.

The bus stopped at the tall gates of the Vacaville Medical Center, waited until the gates were opened, then proceeded into an area completely enclosed in a meshed-wire fence.

Uniformed guards boarded the bus, took the deputies' guns, and searched the bus and the jurors. One guard stayed aboard as the bus continued past several four-story buildings with barred windows.

Between the buildings were huge piles of trash—paper, plastic cups, cardboard boxes—and Larry, who had hardly spoken all day, asked the guard, "What's that?" The guard said it had all been thrown there by the inmates; it was their way of blowing off steam. But then, every day, other inmates had to go out and clean it up . . . it was no real problem or threat to security. Larry nodded and said nothing more.

Then the bus stopped and the jury was taken out and marched single-file through the rain, past a lawn and garden area, to one of the buildings.

The court was to be held in the lounge of the medical facility, which was spacious and had highly polished floors. On all the walls there were paintings by various prisoners, a surprising number of them done in bright, cheerful colors.

When the bailiff called the jury to come in, one could hear, could feel, could almost smell and taste, the nervous expectation in the large room. The jurors filed in one at a time and took their seats across from where the Corona family and the press were sitting.

All was silent.

Then the prosecution and defense teams entered. Juan Vallejo Corona was wearing a dark suit just as he always did, but his face was pale and his step very uncertain.

It was a long walk to the defense table, and the room was in hushed silence as Corona moved slowly across the room. Eddie Cray began to put his arm around Corona as if to support him. Ron Fahey, turning red in the face, moved angrily to keep Cray from helping Corona.

The bailiff called for everyone to stand, that the Judge was entering. Court was now in session.

The jurors saw Hawk smiling and they didn't know what to think, especially since they were nearly unanimous for conviction. The three prosecutors were looking quiet and solemn.

"Well," began Judge Patton, "there are present all counsel, defendant, and members of the regular jury together with the three alternates, and also let the record show that there are some fifty or sixty members of the press and of the public present." The Judge then turned to the jurors and, clearing his throat, said, "Mr. Phillips, I understand, sir, that you are the foreman and you have some communications to make to the court."

Ernie, looking directly at the Judge, absolutely looking at no one else in the room, stood up slowly with his face set, his jaw protruding, and said, "That is correct, sir, Your Honor."

"Will you state it, sir," said the Judge.

"Yes, sir," said Ernie, licking his lips, putting his hands behind his back, standing "at rest" in military fashion. "We have reached what appears"—the room was silent; no one was even breathing—"to be an impasse, sir. We can't decide one way or the other on guilt or innocence, and what"—the room began to hum with people whispering—"we want to know is, does this constitute a hung jury?"

The room rumbled with low voices.

The Corona family, especially the women, were asking Geneva Hawk, what did this mean? Geneva smiled, trying to tell them without speaking aloud.

The Coronas were thrilled. They figured they had won. The case was hung now and so, naturally, they assumed they were now very close to an acquittal.

"Be seated, sir," the Judge said, and as Ernie sat down he glanced around and saw all those happy faces and was struck with this chilling feeling—that God, these people thought the jury was going for an acquittal, and his mind reeled, trying to comprehend. And he realized it was not just the Corona family who were so happy but the press, the defense, everyone in the room except the prosecution, who looked beat, defeated, destroyed—and then it flashed through Ernie's mind that maybe all these people knew something that he and the other jurors didn't know and . . . good God, maybe this man, Corona, *was* innocent. Maybe there was so much, so many facts outside the court that everyone knew of except the jury, that it was like Naomi said—this whole trial was a farce and everyone knew it except the jury. And so he, Ernie, now looked at Corona, the accused, and he so wished that Corona would stand up and speak, if only to say "I'm innocent!" And Ernie took a deep breath and focused all his being on Juan Vallejo Corona, who sat there so calmly, so unemotionally, so totally unreal.

The Judge was saying, ". . . before responding directly to your inquiry I'd like to take this matter up with counsel in the adjoining room.

"You will remain seated and I will ask the defendant and counsel to confer with the court."

Ernie watched the Judge and the attorneys leave and he could feel the blood pulsing in his hands as he gripped his chair. They were going behind closed doors as they'd been doing all trial long, and Ernie felt cheated, betrayed, and so he gripped his chair and at this moment he felt like quitting, like getting up and walking out and telling all these professionals to stick it up their ass.

It was an outrage! Here they were, the jury, the "sole judges of the facts," and they knew nothing!

And all around in the lounge everyone was laughing and whispering and acting so very happy. Some members of the press tried to leave the room but the doors were bolted. Other newsmen took this opportunity to interview the Corona family.

After a quarter of an hour, everyone returned from the consultation with the Judge, and Ed Hehr again called the court to order.

Then the Judge coughed, cleared his throat, and said, "Mr. Phillips, the court wishes to put a question to you." Ernie stood up and all the room was silent. "Please don't respond until I tell you to give me an answer. Will you inform the court as to the numerical division of the jury; that is, whether they are six-six, ten-two, eleven-one, whatever it may be.

"However, I want to caution you under no circumstances will you indicate how the jury stands—that is, whether for acquittal or conviction; just the numerical division only.

"Now, will you please give me that numerical division?"

"Yes, sir," said Ernie, his mind reeling, knowing the last

two votes had come in ten to two and again ten to two but then . . . with these new feelings he now had about the jury not knowing everything and being cheated and kept in the dark and then combining these feelings with the average of what they'd been voting off and on for the last few days, Ernie Phillips now said, to his own surprise, "Eight-four, sir." And his jaw trembled as he heard his own words.

"Eight-four?" repeated the Judge.

Shocked with disbelief, Rick moved in his chair. Rogers grumbled aloud. Faye shook her head.

"Yes, sir," said Ernie, and now all the jurors were moving uneasily in their chairs as Ernie, their foreman, stood there before the court, swallowing, looking very upset.

"Well," said Judge Patton, "as we are all mindful of the fact that this has been a long trial, not only insofar as the court days are concerned but also in the number of witnesses who have testified and number of exhibits which have been admitted into evidence, I would ask that the jury resume their deliberations in this matter, emphasizing, however, that the court in no manner or form whatsoever wishes to coerce this jury into returning a verdict or is even desirous as to a verdict, if any, to be returned by the jury, pointing out to you that it is your duty as jurors to consult with one another and to deliberate with a view to reaching an agreement if you can do so without violence to your individual judgment.

"In other words, you should not surrender your honest convictions concerning the effect or weight of evidence for the mere purpose of returning a verdict or solely because of the opinion of the other jurors.

"And I would again emphasize that in your further

deliberations no juror should change any vote or any opinion merely as an accommodation to any other jurors, but should do so only if convinced that his previous opinion or vote is erroneous.

"And I would therefore ask that this jury resume their deliberations without indicating any particular time for those further deliberations. And I would also suggest that no further additional word in this regard might be sent to the court until noon tomorrow and, with those instructions from the court, then the jury will return to their deliberations in this matter.

"The jury is excused."

"Thank you, Your Honor," said Ernie, and he let out his breath. He'd scarcely been breathing since he'd said that the jury was split eight-four. He now filed out with his fellow jurors, and he could feel the heavy vibrations of disgust that were being directed toward him.

On the way to the bus, Rick was the first to ask Ernie why he had said eight-four when the vote was ten-two.

Ernie told Rick to quiet down, that there were deputies aboard, not to mention the bus driver and the alternates, and that their deliberations had to be kept private.

Rick was bursting, and he was not alone; most of the jurors were with him.

It was a long, heavy trip back to the courthouse.

Back in Fairfield, as the jurors were going into the courtroom and the bailiff was closing the doors, Rick began to question Ernie again but Ernie cut him off, yelling:

"I said eight-four because I thought the Judge wanted an average of what we'd been voting!"

"The Judge didn't ask that!" Rick retorted. "He wanted to know where we now stood! There's all the difference in the world between eight-four and ten-two. Hell, with ten-two he would never have accepted us as a hung jury. He would have told us to go on. But at eight-four he could have maybe thought we were really at a deadlock and we aren't! We're getting closer all the time!"

"Well, if you're so sure that we were not at a deadlock, why didn't you speak up before we went out to Vacaville?"

"I didn't speak up," said Rick, as he wheeled around and rammed his fist out, pointing his finger, "because of her! Her! Her! No one can talk without her going batty with her damn nerve pills!"

Naomi was huge-eyed with shock. He'd almost poked her in the face.

Matt and Victor moved toward Rick.

Rick turned. "How'd she ever get on this jury?" he said quietly to himself, walking out of the room. "She's . . . oh, God! Truth, justice, it's all a joke!"

Naomi, still in shock, was beginning to tremble.

Matt put his arm around her and said, "Come on, you and I will go over there by ourselves and sit a while." And he turned her around and, as he walked her over toward the spectators' section of the courtroom, over his shoulder he asked Victor to bring Naomi a glass of water.

A few minutes later, Naomi was talking and Matt was holding her hand, listening attentively. Naomi was telling him about the white sock that had been found in the twenty-fifth grave, the grave that had not been found until nine days after Corona's arrest. "Good God," she said, "this grave had so much incriminating evidence in it that it's enough to lead one to think that maybe Corona was framed."

Matt said, "Yes, this is true, but also it could lead one to think that Corona was burying so many people, it had become so commonplace to him, that he simply decided, well, why not just take out my family garbage along with this body and bury them both?"

"But then," said Naomi, "if that's true, why did Hawk say that the small white sock could have belonged to Corona's little girls? Oh, Matt, what was Hawk doing? Wasn't he supposed to be defending Corona? And why did Hawk say in his closing argument that there might still be more bodies out there with more of Corona's things?

"Oh, I thought Hawk was brilliant. Such a showman, like on TV. Those prosecutors were dull in comparison, but there Hawk incriminated Corona two times."

"Well, yes, I agree," said Matt. "Hawk outclassed them all through the trial and maybe those things just popped out of his mouth because he had no case. I'll tell you, Naomi, I'm sure if Hawk had any case at all, he'd have won. He's a good attorney."

"Hey, that makes sense," said Naomi. "Hawk's good, and they're dumb, so yes, of course. If he'd had a case he'd have won easily." She held there in thought, suspended. Then she said, "Matt, then you do think Corona is guilty?"

Matt nodded. "Right."

Naomi nodded. "But then tell me . . . why is everyone so afraid?"

"Why do you say that, Naomi?" Matt was still holding her hand, trying to help her relax. "I'm not afraid. I'll sure as hell assure you of that."

"Well, not you," smiled Naomi, "but some of these people sure are. Did you notice how angry Frank became with me when I asked him to talk, to deliberate . . . oh, that man is frightened, I tell you. And take Calvin, over there, see him holding his Bible, he's definitely afraid.

"By the way, have you ever noticed how at the dinner table Ernie is always telling Calvin how much he likes black people?"

"No," said Matt. "I sit at the other end of the table at meal times."

"Oh, that's right," said Naomi. "Well, I'll tell you, Ernie is always telling Cal how he had a black friend here in the service and how he had a black friend there in the service. Do you see what I mean? It's not what meets the eye. It's not that Ernie likes black persons. It's that Ernie is so conscious of Negroes, niggers, that he has to keep talking about it all the time . . . trying to convince himself.

"Do you see what I'm driving at?" Matt shook his head. "Well, listen, if a person really did have black friends, you know, with personal acceptance of each other beyond racism, then they wouldn't be talking about it all the time, would they?" And Naomi nodded, gripping Matt's hand. "Ernie is a southerner. He's just like my husband that left me. He lies. He exaggerates. He says things like 'Isn't she cute as a bug's ear,' and you know bugs don't have ears."

Matt felt like laughing but he held it back.

Naomi continued, "And he hates niggers, only he's hiding from it." She smiled a tight little smile. "Look at that nigger now, don't tell me Calvin isn't scared half to death. And look at Frank, he's terrified of his own shadow because he doesn't like anyone. And Rick's scared too.

Everyone on this jury is so conservative that they're afraid, I tell you, terrified to even think that maybe an innocent man was arrested and we're convicting him because of money and . . . Did you know Hawk will sue them for three hundred million dollars if he wins this case?

"Oh, it's all so wrong, I tell you. I don't know what to do. It's like I was trying to explain to you about Ernie . . . he talks so much about liking blacks that you know he considers them niggers.

"See what I mean? It's the opposite of what one hears, and sees, and thinks. Like this case has so much evidence pointing to Corona that it isn't like it seems. Get what I mean? This man, Juan Corona, didn't do it. His brother, Natividad, did it. Hawk tried to bring it out in court but the Judge and prosecution wouldn't let him.

"The Judge is afraid too. He can't let himself believe, to even think, that this legal system, which he's been a part of for all his life, could be wrong. You know what I mean? You saw how he became so mad when the prosecution wasn't doing so good and Hawks"—when Naomi became excited and spoke faster, she always added an "s" to Hawk's name—"was walking all over them. Judge Patton would object for the prosecution. He was helping them because they weren't representing their case well and he can't afford for them to look bad in his system.

"Oh, these are homosexual murders, I just know it, and you look at Corona's lovely wife and beautiful children and you just know he isn't homosexual. It was his brother who owned the bar that was homosexual and . . . remember how Williams said in his opening statement that one victim had his penis cut off and placed on his chest? Ah, remember that, Matt?"

"No," said Matt, looking startled. "I don't remember anything about any penis being cut off. Who said that?"

"Williams, for the prosecution, in his opening statement."

"Williams?"

"Yes, Williams."

"Williams said that?"

"Oh, quit that, Matt, maybe it was Teja, or Hawks, or . . . oh no, I'm sure it was Bart Williams in his opening statement."

Matt let go of Naomi's hand and said, "A penis was cut off and placed on the dead man's chest, ah?"

"Yes, that's right."

"Oh," said Matt, and he nodded his head up and down and didn't say anything for a long time because he was sure no such statement had been made in court. Then he said, "Naomi, why don't you and I go have a cup of coffee and a doughnut, how about that?"

He was really worried about Naomi now, and so he got up, bowing like a gentleman escorting his lady. Naomi's eyes lit up and she said: "Oh, Matt, you are a fine man. I feel so much better after talking to you."

Matt laughed. "That's what all the young girls say. I got to fight them off all the time."

"Oh, you are a card. I like you."

"Well, let's not overdo it," said Matt. "I am a married man."

Naomi laughed and big Matt, who had been a Marine for thirty years but looked more like a hippie than an ex-Marine, escorted her to the jury room, where the coffee was, and as he passed the other jurors at the two tables he winked and gave them a hand signal that all was well.

At the coffee table Naomi saw George, her fellow

holdout, and rushed up to him. George welcomed her with a smile and began nodding his head in agreement as she spoke rapidly to him.

Matt took a cup of coffee and went back to the courtroom, joining Ernie, Rick, Victor, and Calvin, who were sitting at the tables.

"Ernie," said Matt, "I think you should know this. I'm not spreading gossip, or trying to cause friction or bad feeling between jurors, but . . . I am answering in part the question we were talking about earlier: can the minds of certain jurors take any more of this deliberating? Well, the point is, I just listened to Naomi for over half an hour and I believe she's cracking. Listen to me closely. She's saying we're all scared. She says Calvin here is—excuse the expression—a terrified nigger. That Frank is scared. That—"

Calvin got up. "It's hard to believe she'd use words like that." He shook his head. "But I guess she's right. I live in an all-black neighborhood and I'm scared many nights and . . . to find this man guilty isn't going to endear me to a lot of people I know."

"No," said Matt, "she says you're scared to find him *innocent*."

"Oh?" said Cal.

"She says the Judge is scared too. That he's even afraid to think that Corona might be innocent. But that's not half of it . . . now she's added to that story about the white sock—you know, how white socks are evidence of homosexual murders? Well, now she says a penis was cut off one of the victims and placed on his chest."

Rick laughed.

Calvin shook his head.

Rogers, who had joined them, said he didn't remember

anything about any penis being cut off but maybe it was true because there sure had been a lot of penises and dead men.

Rick howled with laughter, then suddenly began to cough and choke and rub his forehead; he opened his bottle of aspirins and tossed a handful into his mouth. He was truly upset because he definitely knew that no such statement about a penis had ever been made.

Quietly, Ernie and Matt looked at each other as Rogers kept talking.

"Dammit!" said Ernie. "No penis was cut off! Good God, pretty soon we'll have ten Naomis here."

"Possibly," said Matt, "so I suggest that we go real easy. Do you hear me, Rick?"

"But dammit!" said Rick. "None of the victims had his penis cut off. So what are we going to do, let her argue for an acquittal with evidence that's nonexistent?"

"What do you suggest?" said Ernie. "That we not allow her to talk? Ah, do you think you and I or anyone else has the right to tell a person on a jury that what they believe to be true isn't true but what we believe to be true is true?"

"It's easy to call another man's religion or beliefs false and superstitious," said Matt.

"Listen," continued Ernie, "and listen carefully—no one, and I mean no one, is going to ridicule another person's sense of reality while I'm foreman." He leaned in closer. "I've been where this woman is and I think every one of us has been there if we're truthful. Don't smile at me. I'm serious. I was there in that German concentration camp. Believe me, the human mind can only take so much and that's that and, I'll tell you, Rick, don't kid yourself for a minute, your outbursts are just as much a sign of breaking as are her hallucinations into realms of evidence never submitted.

"Grow up and think, and be understanding and have compassion. Because believe me, you're not doing so well, considering your health, your age, and your education." Rick was turning red-faced under Ernie's attack. "Don't turn colors on me, buddy. I already told you once about landing in a hole with five Germans and not one walked out alive."

Rick shook his head and left the group.

Ernie stopped breathing so heavily and turned to Matt. "Matt, what do you think? Are we going to be able to continue? Because if you don't think so, then hell, I'm just about ready to call it quits."

"Look," said Matt, "one big advantage we've got now is that Jim, a man that no one can help but trust and like, is now for guilty as strong as he had been for innocent. So hell, let's pass the buck and get him to bring Naomi around."

Ernie smiled. "Okay, sounds good, but what about George? He's still for innocent."

"Look," said Matt, "do you want a conviction or not?"

"Dammit, man! That's not what I asked and you know it. Shit, I don't care if we bring in a verdict or not. Like the Judge said, I'm not trying to coerce or force people out of their individual opinions. Hell, I might vote for innocent myself in our next vote. But what I am trying to do as foreman is at least put us at ease enough so we, as a jury of twelve individuals, can continue talking, deliberating, and exchanging opinions. Do I make myself clear?"

Matt smiled. "Sure, Mister Foreman."

"Okay, then, please saunter over and tell Jim what you told us and advise him that it would be of great benefit to us all if he used his persuasive powers on Naomi. Especially at our breaks, not just during deliberations."

"Well," said Matt, "like the young people say, right on!"

Ernie laughed. "Okay, you old hippie, maybe after this whole mess is over I'll join you when you go to Santa Cruz and do all that mingling that you're always bragging about."

"Only way to fly, but hell, I wish I could've known about it thirty years sooner."

Ernie and Matt laughed, and then Matt crossed the room to speak to Jim.

Twenty minutes later the jury took a vote, and it came to nine for guilty and three for innocent.

Rick got up from his chair, staring at Ernie. He was sure that Ernie had voted for acquittal just to keep him from fighting with George and Naomi.

Ernie saw the young man's stare; he stared back but said nothing.

Matt motioned for Rick to sit down.

Rick looked at Matt, and then slowly sat down.

"Okay," said Ernie, "it's getting near the end of the day, so what do we want to do? Go on deliberating and try another vote or call it a day as far as formalized deliberations and break up in groups and just kind of talk things over among ourselves?"

"I'm for quitting!" yelled Rick, rubbing his forehead.

Victor laughed. "Hey, we're really coming along here, aren't we?"

"Yeah," said Matt, "a few more days and Rick will be as mild as a well-trained sheep dog."

A few jurors laughed, but most did not. It was almost

five o'clock and this was their fifth day and they were exhausted.

Suddenly George spoke up. "You know, I bet the press has made a bet on how long we'll deliberate. You know, like in the service men do that when they're sitting around with time on their hands. So I say, why don't we make a wager of some sort on the press?" Everyone, including Faye and Rick and Frank and Larry, started laughing. George always seemed to have a joke when one was needed. "I got it, we could bet five bucks apiece on their number."

"How would we check to find out their correct number afterward?" asked Larry.

"Ah, hell, that's easy. I'll make it up and win the bet," said George.

The tension began to diminish as the jurors started to laugh and discuss the press, guessing what they were doing, what they were thinking, and how many stations and papers they represented and how much it was costing for all the news media to be out there waiting for them, the jurors.

Then Matt said to George: "It makes one feel important, doesn't it?"

"Oh, yeah!" said George. "Like a gorgeous movie star!"

And by now the atmosphere of the courtroom was loose and happy; even Naomi was more relaxed.

Ernie sat back and was very grateful that there were some good level-headed men like Matt and George on this jury . . . yes, it had been he who had changed his vote back to innocent and he wondered if he had done it because of Rick or if he had done it because of what he had seen at the Vacaville hospital. And thinking about this, he recalled all those happy faces of the Corona family and the press and general audience and he felt very unsure.

That night as the jurors got on the bus the Corona children did not come close. Ed Hehr and another bailiff stood by the door of the bus, between the boarding jurors and the Corona family. Faye noticed this and felt good about it. That evening at dinner, even though it had been the longest and most difficult of days, Faye and Naomi sat with George and Matt and surprisingly once again the jury enjoyed a light, loose, happy meal.

As they were going back to their rooms Calvin came up to Ernie and said, "It was you who changed back from guilty to innocent, wasn't it?"

Ernie froze, mouth open, but then closed his mouth and said, "Yes, it was me." And as he spoke he realized his heart was pounding as if he'd done something wrong.

"Well," said Calvin, "it's okay. Don't worry about it. After all, it's like Hawk said—it's better for a hundred guilty men to go free than to lock up one innocent man." And Calvin's voice, as always, was low and quiet and calm. "Sleep on it, pray a little, and see how you feel tomorrow. Maybe you'll think of something new and bring us all back around to voting Corona completely innocent."

Ernie nodded. "Thank you, Cal, I appreciate your support."

Sixth Day—
Tuesday, January 16, 1973

Tuesday morning started out easy and kind of quiet. Everyone had gone to bed early the night before.

At nine twenty the jurors were seated at the two tables, and they immediately decided to take a vote. Quickly, they wrote their verdicts on pieces of paper. The result was nine for guilty and three for innocent.

Matt laughed and raised his hand.

Ernie said to wait a minute, and suggested they take a little break, talk among themselves, and then come back and start from the beginning.

Chairs scraped on the floor and there was some coughing.

Undaunted, Ernie said that as far as he was concerned they'd have to discuss all the evidence for and against conviction and acquittal from start to finish. In other words, they would have to start all over again.

Jurors began mumbling resentfully and looking at Naomi and George.

"Listen," said Ernie, standing up, "you might as well stop looking at George and Naomi. The vote was nine to three. That means someone else also voted for acquittal. That must mean that there is still a lot of reasonable doubt in this case."

"Who, if they're reasonable, can still see doubt?" asked Rick.

"Yeah," said Rogers, "if they got a mind?"

"That's not your concern or anyone else's. Your concern is to deliberate, to exchange opinions, and let the evidence speak for itself." And there Ernie held, sticking out his bulldog jaw. "No, let's take a small break and do some soul-searching, like Cal recommended the other day. And meditate on soft-selling. And also . . . I won't tolerate anyone looking at certain people a certain way anymore. Each of us is entitled to his or her personal evaluation of this given evidence. Remember, yesterday the Judge said that it is our duty as jurors to consult with one another, to deliberate, to try to reach a unanimous verdict, but only if we can do so without violence to our individual judgment.

"So believe me, this is not going to be an easy day. We're not going to have the majority running roughshod over the minority. Not while I'm foreman. So settle down, take a break, and prepare yourselves, individually, to resume deliberations in an orderly and gentlemanly fashion."

Matt laughed. "You know, Ernie, you're beginning to sound better every day. I think if this deliberation goes on for another thirty days or so we'll all be wanting to run you for President of the United States." He laughed again. "I'm not joking—incredibly, we're all getting pretty good."

"I agree," said Faye, "like Naomi said at the beginning of these deliberations, I think we're doing fine."

"We are," said Victor. "I mean, we've got so mad at each other I'm surprised we haven't used that gun and machete."

"The gun's not loaded," said George. "I already checked."

Everyone laughed.

"Okay," said Ernie, "let us proceed, and take our break and then we will each speak and the evidence will tell the true story by itself." And so Ernie then tapped the gavel on the table top.

Outside, the Corona supporters numbered well over two hundred and they were marching around, carrying signs and chanting. It wasn't raining but it was an overcast day and it looked as if it might rain at any moment.

In the basement cafeteria some newsmen were playing cards, drinking coffee, talking about nothing, while others lay on the floor with their raincoats rolled under their heads and read paperback books. The atmosphere was quiet but tense.

Once more the jury was discussing the first body that had been discovered, Mr. Whitacre. This gravesite, as testimony had it, had first been seen as a hole by Mr. Kagehiro, a Japanese farmer, on the far side of his peach orchard just north of Yuba City early in the morning of May 24, 1971. He'd seen the hole, thought it strange, but then dismissed it as perhaps having been made by the state agriculture department for soil testing. Kagehiro worked all day pruning trees and then, on his way home that evening, he passed by the hole and noticed that it had been filled in. He was puzzled. The state people wouldn't refill the hole the same day, and also, now that he thought about it more, the hole had been too big for soil testing: it was about the size of a grave. At home he told his wife about it and they decided to report it. They did, but no one came out to investigate it that night. The next morning Kagehiro went in person to the police, who got in touch with the Sheriff's Department because the location was outside the city limits. Deputy Sheriff Sizelove went to the site and he and Kagehiro dug slowly into the loose ground until they hit something. Carefully, they dug some more, and there appeared a foot, a shoe, a man's leg.

They stopped.

Deputy Sizelove called the sheriff's office and reported that they'd found a body. Undersheriff Cartoscelli came out with two other deputies, and carefully they unearthed the body. When one of the deputies saw the victim's huge buck teeth he said: "You know, I think I saw that man yesterday walking along the road west of here."

But it was hard to tell because the body was so chopped and hacked up around the head and chest, and the man's forearms were shattered. It seemed as though the victim, big and heavy-boned, had put up quite a fight for his life.

The sheriff's deputies questioned Kagehiro, but he said he'd seen nothing, no one at all, and he'd been working out here all day yesterday with Juan Corona and his work crew. No one else had been out here. Only workmen and people like that, and he couldn't figure why anyone would bury a body in his orchard.

The local newspaper ran a small article on the dead

man, emphasizing the type and number of wounds, but not playing up the story very much. Then the next day the Sheriff's Department got a call from a policeman in Marysville, across the river, who told them that the victim in an assault the year before at the Guadalajara Bar in Marysville had had wounds very similar to those sustained by the body they had just unearthed, and that Natividad Corona, the owner of the bar, and his brother Juan had been prime suspects in that case.

This information was interesting to the Sutter County Sheriff's Department because they knew, as the Marysville policeman knew, that murder by stabbing or shooting was not uncommon, but murder by hacking, slashing, chopping, and complete mutilation was very unusual. Also, they recalled that Kagehiro had told them that Juan Corona had been working in the orchard where the dead man was found.

The next day—Tuesday, May 25, 1971—Ray Duran, the foreman of the nearby Sullivan Ranch, told the Sutter County authorities that a workman had found an indentation in the ground in one of the orchards on the ranch. Another body was dug up there, and it also had dozens of deep penetrating wounds around the head and chest. An official search for gravesites was begun, and by dusk five more bodies had been found, all with the same kinds of chopping, hacking, slashing wounds.

Floodlights with generators were brought in and the search continued as newsmen from out of town began to arrive. At about midnight Sutter County Sheriff Roy Whiteaker and District Attorney Dave Teja met to try to piece together the evidence they had accumulated since the first body had been discovered the day before.

A ninth body had been unearthed only minutes earlier.

The whole thing was becoming so incredible, so monstrous, that the town would surely be in a panic by tomorrow morning if something wasn't done quickly. Newsmen continued to arrive, and Yuba City was swarming with rumors. By morning the world would know about these nine—or maybe more—dead men. Someone had to be arrested.

Sheriff Whiteaker and District Attorney Teja decided to zero in on Juan Corona. He was the labor contractor for the ranches where the bodies were being found and, in addition to the information from the Marysville police, a few other things were beginning to implicate him.

The jurors were talking about the testimony that Whitacre, the first victim, had been seen walking along the road the day before his body was discovered. They wondered if perhaps Juan Corona had also seen Whitacre as he was driving his work crew back to the labor camp at the Sullivan Ranch.

Faye brought up Mrs. Vallejo's testimony that Corona had fixed the screen door on the house she was renting from him.

Naomi said to remember that Corona had rented Mrs. Vallejo the house for only sixty dollars a month, which was real cheap rent and which showed that Corona had a good heart.

Another juror said that maybe sixty was all he could get, maybe the whole neighborhood was low-rent.

Someone else said not to forget that Mrs. Vallejo hadn't been able to recall exactly *which* day Corona had fixed the screen door—maybe it had been the day before or the day after, and maybe on this day Corona had dropped off his men—all Mexicans—and had come back and picked up Whitacre, driven him to the orchard, and killed him.

Several jurors objected to all these "maybe's."

Another juror shook his head and said half to himself that this whole thing seemed so incredible . . . to dig the hole in that peach orchard first and then go looking for someone to kill and put in it.

Everyone quieted down, and then they all agreed that, yes, this was an incredible and terrifying story and, to keep this in mind, maybe they should all glance through those charts of the drawings of the bodies with the wounds indicated in pencil, but no one got up to look at the charts. Instead they continued talking, now about the second set of tire-track casts that the man from Washington, D.C., had testified matched the type of tires on Corona's vehicle.

They discussed the possibility of other vehicles on the Kagehiro property having the same tire treads, and someone asked if those tires were standard equipment on Corona's type of vehicle.

Another juror asked what were the possibilities of another vehicle with the same tire-tread markings as Corona's coming and going without being noticed? Corona worked there, he could come and go without being noticed, but what were the odds, the percentages, that someone else could drive up to that open hole and kill and bury Whitacre, and not be seen?

Was it possible? . . . Of course.

But weren't they now talking about possibilities and speculations, about possible doubt, which all of life was open to . . . and not about reasonable doubt?

Yes, this was the question, were they being reasonable or were they going beyond reasonable doubt into imaginary doubt, possible doubt, into realms of life where nothing could ever be answered for certain?

They agreed.

They decided to stay in the realm of reasonableness, common sense, and stick with the facts as they'd been presented during the trial.

And so they continued, with Ernie leading them, and the time passed in a very orderly fashion. Then they began to discuss Corona's machete, which had not matched up with the striations on Whitacre's skull.

This part of the discussion became heavy.

Rogers again said that there was no proof that the big knife hadn't been used to kill the rest of the twenty-four victims.

Faye said that this was speculation and to stop it.*

Immediately, someone else said to go on, go on, that this case did not rest on any one piece of evidence but on the over-all gist of all the evidence. And so it was quickly decided to go on, to continue at the fast pace at which they were going so they could see everything as a whole, as one large picture created by all the evidence. For they'd already agreed, more or less, that whoever killed one of these men had killed all of them, because of the similarities of the wounds, the proximity of graves, and the six-month time span. They also figured that, good God, it was hard enough to imagine one man doing all

*The defense had claimed in court that since the skull striations did not match the machete, it therefore could not have been the murder weapon. After the trial Dr. Rooney, the head pathologist from Sacramento, said he had explained to the prosecution several times that even if the machete was the murder weapon it would not match up with the striations on Whitacre's skull because a human skull is heavy and hard, and each blow would change the edge of the weapon's blade. Dr. Rooney said the prosecution never seemed to understand this point.

this killing, but it was utterly impossible to imagine two guys going around doing this at the same time, in the same area, in the same way, without one killer knowing about the other or in fact being his partner.

And so they continued with this first grave. They once again discussed Corona's alibi of going to fix a screen door, and finally decided the alibi didn't hold up . . . Mrs. Vallejo hadn't been able to pin it to the exact day and, besides, it had been obvious that she was trying to help Corona. Also, they figured that if Hawk had had that alibi wrapped up, he would have put on a case.

They talked about the crew of workmen that Corona had with him and wondered why Hawk hadn't brought them to testify either.

The discussion became heated.

Some of the jurors asked yet again why Hawk hadn't put on a case and again they talked about Hawk's credibility and his reasons for doing what he did.

Others immediately countered by saying that they were not even supposed to be discussing the attorneys, that they were only supposed to consider the evidence and the testimony that had been given under oath. Still others said maybe this was true but they were still twelve human beings, twelve individual people, and they'd each come to this courtroom with their life's experiences and they did have opinions and, yes, the lawyers were definitely an issue.

Things quieted down again and it was evident that only one person, Naomi, still believed in Hawk, while seven believed in Williams and ten believed in Fahey—well, didn't so much believe in him as respected him—and three more or less respected and believed in Teja.

Then the issue of why Hawk had not put Corona on

the witness stand arose, and Ernie reminded them that a man need not testify in his own behalf, that the burden of proof rested entirely on the prosecution, and they should go on to the other phases of this case. Ernie also said that if this case had rested solely on the first victim, Corona would not have been arrested and they would not even be here—the prosecution had admitted that. And so, after a little more discussion of victim one, they took a quick vote, which came in at ten to two, but instead of stopping as they had after each earlier vote they continued right along to victims two and three, and things were rolling as they'd never rolled before. Quickly, from point to point. Now no single point of disagreement was large enough to stop them.

They were a group of people who knew each other, and even if they didn't always agree with each other, at least that they were now respectful and orderly and able to move along from disagreement to disagreement, still able to feel, to sense, a unity among themselves.

Then they came to the issue of the meat receipts found with the third body and Jim raised his hand and was recognized. He stood up and spoke at length about these Del Pero Meat Company receipts, which the clerk had seen Juan fold up and put in his shirt pocket and which had later been found—still folded—in Sample's grave.

Rogers then restated his belief that there had been no body switch, in spite of Hawk's attempt to convince them that there had been, and Rogers reminded them that Corona was an orderly man who kept all his other receipts hooked on a nail in the messhall.

Jim agreed and continued, saying that, for him, this was where the camel's back broke, and no longer was it an imaginary belief that Corona was guilty, but a reasonable one. It made sense. In fact, it seemed to him as if Corona had almost been asking to be caught here at this grave, and then again at that last grave. For truly, as Naomi had said, that twenty-fifth grave was so full of evidence that it almost seemed as if someone had been trying to frame Corona.

Well, said Rick, maybe that someone was Corona himself. Perhaps he was tired of killing. Perhaps he wished to be caught.

A quiet mumbling started, but Jim continued over it, saying maybe so, but what this twenty-fifth grave showed to him was that the whole case against Corona went from "maybe guilty" to that position of guilt "beyond reasonable doubt and to a moral certainty," and that twenty-fifth grave was just "a bit much," as Hawk himself had said—because it was convicting. Absolutely. If you then thought about all the human blood found in Corona's van and on his rubber boots and his jacket, and about the human blood in the trunk of his car . . . Jim asked everyone just to think about their own cars, their own boots, their jackets, and then add to this the two hunting knives with human blood up to their guards . . . and it was not only reasonable, it was more than reasonable, to believe . . . to be morally certain that Corona was indeed guilty and to feel morally obligated to see him put away so he would stop all this killing.

Then they took a break. It was almost noon and they'd covered a lot this morning, and emotions hadn't exploded.

During the break Naomi stayed with George, who was sipping coffee and not saying anything; he approached Jim, who was talking to Faye. Jim said he'd slept well again last night, that making a decision had been difficult . . . oh, by far the most difficult thing he'd ever done in his life to date, but that once that decision had been made, it felt good. He had no regrets.

George nodded, said nothing, and walked over to Matt, Ernie, and Victor.

Naomi kept following George.

Matt was saying that doctor after doctor had testified that most of these men's stomachs had been empty at the time of their death and that there was no way a man could get an erection at their age with an empty stomach and the type of wino life that they'd apparently lived.

George asked why this was important.

Ernie explained that they'd been talking about motive and, through common sense, they'd ruled out the homosexual motive that Hawk had tried to establish.

Victor added that it was like Fahey had said—ten psychiatrists could work ten years and never agree about what went on in the mind of anyone who had killed and buried so many men.

Matt suggested it was a real case of Dr. Jekyll and Mr. Hyde.

Rogers came up and loudly asked who was Dr. Jekyll and who was Mr. Hyde? Hawk or Corona?

Everyone laughed.

Rogers looked from one to the other and lit a new cigar and kept right on talking. He'd quit smoking for a couple of years, keeping a promise he'd made earlier to his wife, but since the trial had begun he'd started smoking again. Most of the jurors found out about his promise to his wife the second day of deliberations when they arrived at the courthouse. Rogers had been smoking a cigar but when the cameramen began taking the jurors' pictures as they got off the bus Rogers hid his cigar and looked like a bad little boy. Victor had noticed it and asked what the trouble was and Rogers had said, "I don't want my wife to see me smoking on the TV. Oh, she'd be mad." After that it had become a joke at break time when Rogers lit up a cigar to say, "Watch out! There's your wife!" And he'd fall for it every time, hiding his cigar.

After the break another vote was taken: eleven to one. Naomi looked at George with huge frightened eyes.

Rick smiled.

Naomi pushed back her chair and glanced around and would have seen Rick's smile if Matt had not kicked him under the table; instead she saw Rick staring at Matt and looking half hurt, half mad.

There was a long, heavy silence.

Then Naomi said, "George, you've left me. First Jim and now you. That's not right. You still have doubts. Oh, God, even Faye here still has doubts. She admitted it when she wrote them down."

"Naomi," said Faye, "I wrote down not doubts but specific points which didn't point toward guilt."

"And what do you call those? Those are doubts!"

"No, Naomi, listen to me," said Faye, carefully, "they are points that don't prove he's guilty. There are . . . let me see, yes, nine points but, my God, I have twenty to thirty points that point toward conviction beyond any reasonable doubt."

"Reasonable doubt, hooee! You have doubts, you have points that don't point toward guilty, and you're a reasonable person and so, being reasonable, then these too are reasonable doubts!"

"Naomi, let me help you understand—"

"Don't you dare say 'let me help you' to me!" yelled Naomi, standing up. "God, I've come to hate that expression! You use it in such a high-and-mighty-sounding fashion!" Naomi turned to Jim. "Jim, please, help me. Am I wrong? You tell me. You're a fine man. I saw your daughters come to see you the other night and yell 'Hi, Daddy, we love you.'

"Oh, I've worked so hard all my life. I even worked extra to give my daughter dancing lessons. I used to take her to her lessons along with this boy, he was a Mexican boy, and they both took lessons together and I was so happy seeing my daughter getting what I never got.

"I was born in Reading, Pennsylvania. My children are big now. Doing good for themselves. Especially my daughter. She married well and has a high-class executive secretary's job in San Francisco. That poor boy who she took dancing lessons with got into trouble. He was so nice but he's in jail now, I believe. Oh, we must be so careful with what we're doing here. He was a nice Mexican boy but he went to jail. My daughter didn't. She got ahead in life. She and her husband are building a big gorgeous house on a hilltop in Napa Valley. All below are vineyards. Wine vineyards. And they're so beautiful in the springtime, all green, and then again in the fall with red and orange and all those colors in between.

"I've been on three juries before and I've never felt like I feel now. I'm feeling so alone. My daughter never seems to have time to come see me. Your daughters, Jim, had time to come and see you."

"Naomi," said Jim, "my daughters aren't married yet. I imagine once they're married they won't have time either. Please, I'm sure your daughter is just too busy right now with their house being built. You said she works in San

Francisco—does that mean she commutes to Napa Valley daily?" Naomi nodded. "Well then, my, that's a long drive. She had a full day. Driving, working, and trying to arrange her house on weekends. After their house is built they'll have more time and I'm sure she'll show her love . . . because, Naomi, you're a fine woman. I like you. And I'm sure your daughter loves you most dearly."

Naomi smiled radiantly. "Oh, Jim, you are a fine man. But tell me, why are you voting for guilty?"

"Well, specifically those meat receipts—"

"But Hawk said they could have blown over from the dump."

Again chairs were being scraped and heads were shaking.

"Well, Naomi," Jim continued, "let me ask you this . . . which is more reasonable? Here, come over and look at this mockup map. Now, is it more reasonable that those receipts, folded up as they were, like Hawk pointed out to us when he cross-examined the undersheriff—that they blew from here, the garbage dump, along the ground or in the air, and got through all these trees, this orchard, and landed in this grave area two hundred yards away as the man who was burying Sample's body shoveled dirt into the grave? . . . Or is it, Naomi, more reasonable that these receipts, which the clerk at the meat company saw Corona fold and put in his shirt pocket, simply fell out of Corona's pocket as he was working with his shovel, bent over, putting dirt in the grave?"

The room was silent. Everyone was attentive, admiring Jim's patience and perseverance This point had been gone over more than a dozen times and here was Jim, saying it all so quietly, so thoughtfully, all over again.

"Now, the key here, Naomi," Jim went on, "are the words, 'what is most reasonable.' Add to this what Hawk said: if two conclusions point equally reasonably, one toward innocence and one toward guilt, we must then under the law take the one that points toward innocence.

"A few days back this always got me mixed up. It gave me a pain in my head and heart, just trying to understand but Naomi"—Jim smiled—"I've slept fine these last two nights and I now see it as clear as a bell. Reasonably speaking, the only story that makes sense here is that Corona put the receipts in his pocket and they fell out of his pocket at that grave." And Jim breathed an exhausted sigh, then smiled. "Did that help, Naomi?"

Naomi nodded. "Okay. Okay. But how did they fall out? I don't see how they could have fallen out. Look, let me put a folded paper in your pocket, you act like you're throwing dirt in a grave and let's see if they fall out."

"Christ!" yelled Rick. "We'd have to do it over and over again and use real shovels and real dirt to get any approximation of the actual—'

"Don't shout at me! Get up on the table and pretend to dig! I tell you, Corona would have had to be upside down!"

Suddenly Rick began to laugh and he gripped his forehead and said, "I need some more aspirins. God, I hate aspirins and yet here I am chewing them by the handful. I never got this strung out in combat."

There was a knock at the door. It was time for lunch, and everyone got up, shaking their heads and walking around. Naomi went to the bathroom. She was trembling.

Faye followed her.

It was getting bad.

At one o'clock the jurors were back at the two tables, and after Ernie talked for a while it was decided that, no, they would not deliberate any longer and, no, they were not a hung jury or at a deadlock, but they definitely did need instructions on the phrase "beyond reasonable doubt."

Ernie called in the bailiff—Ed Hehr—and told him this. Hehr noticed that the jurors were not sitting together as they usually were. They were scattered all over the room: two here in the official jury-panel chairs, three there in the audience chairs, one over there—Rick—swiveling in the judge's chair, others pacing around and looking tired, angry, and exhausted. Hehr smiled and said, "I hope everything is okay," but no one answered him and so he shrugged and left to give their message to the Judge.

A little later Ed Hehr informed the jurors that court would be held in the courtroom as usual, and asked them to move to the jury room in back so the press and public and attorneys could come in.

"Is Juan all right?" asked Naomi.

"I can't answer that question," said Hehr.

"We never get to know anything," complained Naomi. "It's not fair."

Ed Hehr said nothing and the jurors went to the jury room as the doors of the courtroom were opened to the public. Sixty newspaper and television reporters, twenty members of the immediate Corona family, and two hundred supporters were vying for the eighty-two seats. The sheriff's deputies and four local policemen were helping line the people up, and checking everyone who entered the courtroom. Security was tight.

No one heard the shouting but the jurors.

"And listen this time!" Rick was screaming to Naomi.

"Dammit! It's so simple if you just follow the Judge's definition and don't go daydreaming all over the place!" Rick stopped, realizing he'd been shaking his fist in Naomi's face, and he took out his bottle of aspirins and shook five into his hand. "Okay, okay, so I blew it. I blew it! Man, who wouldn't!" He tossed the aspirins, one by one, into his mouth.

Naomi watched in bewilderment and then went to her purse for her own pills.

"Mr. Phillips," began Judge Patton, once the court was in session, "as the foreman I believe you had some request of the court, sir?"

"Yes, sir," said Ernie, standing up. "We, the jury, would like to have the instructions pertaining to reasonable doubt reread by the court, sir."

"Thank you," said the Judge.

Ernie continued, "And with due apologies for having to call this whole entire court into session."

"No apology is necessary. And in response to your request, the court will reread the following instruction, Mr. Phillips.

" 'A defendant in a criminal action is presumed to be innocent until the contrary is proved, and in case of a reasonable doubt whether his guilt is satisfactorily shown, he is entitled to an acquittal. This presumption places upon the State the burden of proving him guilty beyond a reasonable doubt. Reasonable doubt is defined as follows: It is not a mere possible doubt, because everything relating to human affairs, and depending on moral evidence, is open to some possible or imaginary doubt. It is that state of the case which, after the entire comparison and consideration of all the evidence, leaves the minds of the jurors in that condition that they cannot say they feel an abiding conviction, to a moral certainty, of the truth of the charge.' " The Judge stopped, glancing around the courtroom at all the people, and said, "May I ask you again, Mr. Foreman, and again I caution you do not tell me how the vote stands, whether for acquittal or guilt, but only give me the numerical division." The room was silent. "How does the jury now stand, sir? Will you give me the numerical division only?"

Ernie licked his lips nervously. "Eleven to one, sir."

A hush, a quiet roar of wild whispering came sweeping across the room.

The Judge, trying to maintain order, quickly said, "Again, then, I will remind this jury that it is your duty as jurors to consult with one another and to deliberate with a view to reaching an agreement if you can do so without violence to your individual judgment. Each of you must decide the case for yourselves but—"

At that point, two reporters leaped up and ran for the doors. A bailiff tried to stop them, whispering, "No, keep your seats," but they pushed by him, swinging out the doors.

Three others jumped up.

The Judge stopped speaking and said, "Mr. Bailiff! Those doors are closed!"

But the three reporters bolted under the officer's outstretched arms.

The Judge bellowed, "Strike that instruction! I will reread this last matter to you, ladies and gentlemen of the jury!" He was so angry he was chewing his tongue. "It is your duty as jurors to consult with one another and to deliberate with a view to reaching an agreement if you can do so without violence to your individual judgment."

Other newsmen were trying to get out, and another bailiff came to block the door, so no one else could leave. The Judge continued reading. The courtroom quieted down.

"In other words, you should not surrender your honest conviction concerning the effect or weight of evidence for the mere purposes of returning a verdict or solely because of the opinion of the other jurors." The Judge looked around. "The regular jurors will be taken to the jury room to resume their deliberations. The alternate jurors will likewise be removed to the room in which they have been held.

"Mr. Bailiff, you will please remove the jurors and the alternates from the courtroom."

Then, as Judge Patton came off the bench and disappeared into his chambers, the courtroom exploded with "Viva Juan Corona! Viva Juan Corona! Viva Juan Corona!" The Corona family and supporters were chanting joyously, and Hawk was smiling, laughing.

All this time Juan Corona sat still, looking down, with his legs crossed under the table and his hands together in his lap. He seemed to be far away in his thoughts. His supporters were calling to him, his wife and children were calling to him, but he was not there. Later, when his wife and children visited him and Gloria asked him how he felt, he slowly, softly said, "Okay. Not too bad. I only hope . . . the eleven are *for* me and not the other way around." Then he added, "It frightens me, sometimes, when Mr. Hawk is so happy with how everything goes." He shook his head. "But he's the lawyer so I guess he should know."

* * *

As soon as the court was cleared the jurors began to discuss the Judge's definition of "reasonable doubt," their understanding of "circumstantial evidence versus direct evidence," and the concept of "burden of proof." They now knew this was the heart of their dilemma—not so much the actual evidence as the interpretation of the evidence in relation to how the Judge had read the law and how they as jurors had agreed, as far back as when they were being questioned in voir dire, to follow the law and the interpretation of the evidence as explained by the Judge.

It was heavy and it was getting heavier by the moment. This was the area in which the key that could resolve their entire dilemma was hidden, but there was all this legal terminology that . . . oh, they were having such a difficult time trying to decipher the legal terminology of the Judge's instructions.

Rick had taken notes on the Judge's definition of reasonable doubt and was reading from them:

"Reasonable doubt is not a mere possible doubt because everything related to human affairs is open to possible or imaginary doubt. It is that state of the case which, after the entire comparison of all the evidence . . . note here, the Judge said *all* the evidence, not separate or individual pieces of evidence . . . leaves the minds of the jurors in the condition that they cannot say they feel an abiding conviction to a moral certainty."

Rick was trying to keep calm, and explain this thing once and for all, so clearly, so simply, and so thoroughly that no one could help but understand it completely. "Now," he said, "I realize that this definition here at the end is hard to understand because it uses a negative to show a positive. It says, I repeat, that reasonable doubt leaves the minds of the jurors in that state in which they cannot feel an abiding conviction to a moral certainty. But the key here is the word 'reasonable,' not possible or imaginary. For, before this negative was given, the Judge had said that reasonable doubt is not a mere . . . why they used the word 'mere' here, I can't understand. Because, what is being said in essence is that everything in life is open to a state of possible and imaginary doubt but if we are reasonable, staying within a reasonable state of mind, then it is possible to believe, to have twelve people agree on a reasonable conclusion, and that this then is a state of mind beyond reasonable doubt." Rick smiled, rocking in his chair, and then shook his head as if he were very embarrassed. "I'm having trouble, I know, but what I'm trying to say, simply, is that we then have no more doubts that are reasonable. We only have doubts that are possible, or imaginary, or in the realm of speculation, and we're not supposed to go that far because if we did no one could ever agree on anything, and also because we're supposed to follow the law, the Judge's instructions, and be reasonable.

"Oh, God . . . I've got a headache." And he gripped his forehead. "It was so clear and then I lost it." He fell back. "Dammit all!"

Faye raised her hand, and Ernie recognized her. "Well," said Faye, "I'd like to add to what Rick said. I think he did a wonderful job but . . . this time as the Judge spoke I didn't take notes and I concentrated on just listening.

"Now, to begin with, the Judge, before he read the definition of reasonable doubt, said something to the effect that a defendant in a criminal action is presumed to be innocent until the contrary is proven, and then he said that if reasonable doubt is satisfactorily shown, then the defendant is entitled to an acquittal." She looked around. "Then the Judge said that this presumption of innocence places upon the State—meaning Williams, Fahey, and Teja—the burden of proving Corona guilty beyond a reasonable doubt." She licked her lips. "Then the Judge, at this point, began reading the legal definition of reasonable doubt and he began by saying that reasonable doubt is not a mere possible doubt because everything related to human life, and depending on one's moral evidence, is open to some possible or imaginary doubt."

Faye put on her glasses again and sat back, glancing around. She seemed quite relaxed as she tried to think, to concentrate, and make sure that everyone got her point. "Now then, at this point I would like to talk about this first part of what the Judge said because, as Rick pointed out, the second part of the instruction the Judge read was not only redundant of this first part but it was in fact, as Rick said, a negative statement. And as a teacher I'll tell you, to use a negative to try to define something is like saying a horse is a horse because it's not an elephant and, I'll tell you, not only does this tend to mislead, but it's not proper. Oh, I'd like to give those men who wrote these legal books a piece of my mind."

Matt and Victor laughed, and quite a few others joined in.

Faye smiled. "Oh, well, the point I want to make here—and mind you, if anyone can help me, please feel free to do so—is that the essence of our dilemma is cleared up very well in this first part, without needing to go into this misworded latter part, and I repeat it as follows:

"Point one, a defendant is presumed innocent until the contrary is proven. Point two, this presumption of innocence places upon the prosecution, not the defense, the entire burden of proving him, the defendant, guilty beyond any reasonable doubt. Point three, beyond reasonable doubt is that state of mind in which the questions of life can be understood, and answered, and agreed upon by twelve reasonable people to the point at which reasonable doubts no longer exist. Now point four—and notice that I'm trying to make all my points in positive statements—pertains to moral certainty, but before we can comprehend this we must accept and understand that all life relating to human affairs is open to some possible or imaginary doubt and . . . oh, well, for point four the law says that we are to feel an abiding conviction to a moral certainty beyond any reasonable doubt but note, *not* beyond any possible or imaginary doubt." She blushed. "Oh, there I did it. I used a negative at the end. But no matter, the essence of what I said, systematically broken down into four parts, with each one following the other in a straight line of logic and all being positives, I believe has helped clarify most of our problem." She leaned forward. "Now, will someone help me? Will someone please elaborate on what I've said and clarify these concepts even more?"

Many people had their hands up. Faye began to call on one of the jurors but Ernie stood up and said: "All right, I think Faye did a fine job, I think Rick did a fine job, so please let's continue like this and not let ourselves become emotional. Okay, George, I think your hand was up first. What do you wish to say or add or elaborate on this same subject of reasonable doubt?"

"Well," said George, "I guess what this all boils down to is that we should use common sense, reasonable common sense, and if we find a man guilty beyond all common-sense questions or reasonable doubts, well, then, that man is guilty by the law."

"Right!" agreed Rogers. "And we've got here everything telling us Corona's guilty by every stretch of reasonable common sense."

Larry's hand was up, and Ernie recognized him. "Well," said Larry, "one thing no one has covered, not even the Judge in his instructions—I took notes too—is what exactly are we supposed to be considering when we take it through these, ah, four points, like Faye put it.

"By this I mean that we're supposed to be talking only about the things accepted into evidence and the testimony told under oath and we're not supposed to be even considering what the attorneys said or what was tossed in here and there as insinuation and speculation.

"In other words, what I'm saying is that if we follow the law and work only with the facts, the evidence, the testimony under oath, and do all this not with possible thinking, not with imaginary thinking, but only with common-sense reasonable thinking, then it's quite easy to see how all these things we've been shown all these months point right toward conviction beyond any reasonable thinking."

"Right!" said Rogers again. "That's exactly what I've been saying since we began here last week."

"Rogers," said Larry, "I sure wish you'd wait your turn."

"I was only helping you."

"I don't need your help any more than Faye or Matt or Jim or anyone else here needs your help," said Larry. He was a small, slender man but he was angry and he looked very determined. "Sure, I'm not educated like Faye, I'll admit that, and sure, I'm not big and strong like Matt and I'm not a good talker like Jim, but, believe me, I'm trying my best . . . good God, I'm trying my best and nobody is going to help me or push me. It's my vote and my decision that I'm going to have to live with the rest of my life!"

"Well, I never meant that you—"

"Shut up!"

"Well, okay," said Rogers, "I'll shut up and you'll never hear from me again."

Victor started laughing. "And we'll tell your wife about your cigars if you don't keep your promise."

Rogers flushed red.

Victor lowered his head, trying to keep from laughing.

"Well," continued Larry, trying to calm himself, "that's all I really wanted to say . . . that not only are we supposed to deliberate reasonably to a verdict beyond any reasonable doubt but we have to keep in mind the things we should deliberate on. Thank you." He looked very tired.

Several jurors had their hands up. Ernie ignored them and said, "How about you, Calvin or Frank? You two have been pretty quiet today."

"Well," said Cal, "all I can say is, if we pile up our evidence like that Fahey did there in the end, then I think we can see that there really is a case here. A strong case. Dozens and dozens of facts and evidence that point toward a verdict beyond any reasonableness. I voted innocent a lot of times there at the beginning but since Monday morning I've been for guilty . . . poor man . . . but I don't see any other reasonable answer." And Calvin said no more and just looked down, shaking his head.

"Frank," said Ernie, "you have anything to say?"

"No," said Frank. "Not really." And he never even looked up. He seemed as tired as Larry.

"All right," continued Ernie, "so what should we do now, take another vote or define these legal terms to some further degree?"

No one responded. A few began to raise their hands but then didn't. So after a moment, Ernie suggested a vote be taken and it was, quickly, and it came in eleven to one.

Everyone turned to Naomi, who said defensively:

"Well, we never deliberated. All we did was talk about the words 'reasonable doubt,' and the Judge didn't say for us to just come back here and talk about his instructions. After he read to us the definition of reasonable doubt he also said that it was our duty as jurors to consult with one another, to deliberate, and that each of us must decide the case for ourself. He said that. I remember. And all we've been doing is repeating back and forth his definition of reasonable doubt and I can't see what that has to do with our duty of deliberating on the evidence."

"God!" exploded Rick. "It's got everything to do with how we deliberate on the evidence. It tells us how to do it legally within the law and it stops us from going off daydreaming all over the place!" He stood up.

Matt told him to sit down.

Naomi insisted that she wanted to deliberate, that she wanted to discuss the case with open eyes, and not just fall into this narrow hole of not seeing all the other facts which were everywhere.

Rick was shouting.

Naomi was shouting.

Matt pushed Rick into his chair.

Naomi was crying.

Jim was trying to console Naomi but she was telling him that he wasn't with her, that he was with them and that she couldn't see how Jim could be with them because of those receipts he always talked about because they could have blown or, if not blown, then they could have been planted there, and she knew about these kind of things because of the detective magazines she'd read years back when police stories weren't censored and one could follow all the inside facts in an orderly manner. Then she was saying that this whole case was not even a real mystery or even a real murder case like in the magazines because all the clues were mixed up and they didn't follow each other like they did in the police magazines or even like the clues on her last jury case where she'd been a juror and two boys had broken into this place to steal some things but only the skinny boy got inside because the fat boy couldn't get all the way through the window and had gotten stuck—and the cops had caught both boys but the skinny one had been acquitted and the fat one, who never even got inside, was convicted.

That had been crazy and this whole case here was so confusing, so mixed up, that there was reasonable doubt everywhere and, if anyone couldn't see it, then they were either crazy or . . . or, please couldn't they see that if one had any kind of doubt it had to be a reasonable doubt because they were all reasonable people? Look at Faye, she was educated and she had her doubts too but she didn't want to admit it because she didn't like Hawk, and the whole reason everyone was so ready to convict Corona was because they felt cheated because Hawk hadn't put on a case after he'd made all these promises which he'd never kept . . . and that was the truth, they were being emotional, because honestly, the prosecution had not proven every link of their chain of circumstantial evidence and therefore . . . oh, God, if they'd just follow the law and not get emotional and angry at Hawk . . .

yeah, now she saw the problem . . . she saw it clearly. They, all of them, were too conservative and Hawk and his daughter with her short mini skirts had simply rubbed them all the wrong way all trial long. Ha! She saw it now! And she began to laugh short tight little laughs.

Ernie called for a break but Naomi continued, talking now about the white sock in the twenty-fifth grave, which was a clue to homosexual murders, and about the penis which had been cut off one victim and placed on his chest. Then she quit talking and followed George to the jury-panel chairs, and she was very quiet. Ernie and Matt and Victor watched her. Larry and Frank watched her. She was nodding, agreeing, as she listened to George.

Then Jim passed them and Naomi got up, leaving George in the middle of a sentence, and approached Jim and said:

"Jim, don't just walk by me without saying a word! Please, I'll change my vote. Just don't hate me. I'll change my vote so you can go home to your wife."

"Naomi," said Jim, soothingly, "I don't hate you. I like you. Now, calm down, and think. This is a murder trial and you can't change your vote unless you've changed your mind."

"Why not? That's what you all want me to do so you can go home to your wives. Here, I'll vote guilty right now."

Matt and a few other jurors who heard what Naomi was saying shook their heads and walked away. Matt, for one, was getting tired of babying her. He'd done it half a dozen times now and he wasn't about to do it again. Larry said to Frank that it was amazing how Naomi sometimes made so much sense and then other times made no sense. Frank agreed.

Jim was saying softly, "Naomi, now listen to me. If you vote guilty the way you're talking right now, I for one will not accept your vote. We're dealing with a man's life. This is no easy matter, and you are not going to change your vote out of convenience.

"Look, Naomi, it was an agonizing ordeal for me to change my vote from innocent to guilty, and you're not going to take an easy way out and say you're changing your vote because you're tired or because you want to please us.

"That's not right. You're ridiculing the emotional turmoil each of us suffered."

"But I want to change my vote," said Naomi, and she turned to Ernie, who had walked over to them. "Ernie, I can change my vote, can't I?"

Ernie smiled. "Yes, Naomi, you can change your vote, but only if you change your opinion and have conviction in your vote."

"I want to send a message to the Judge," said Naomi. "I want to ask him a question without calling back the whole court."

"What do you want to ask the Judge?" asked Ernie, a worried frown on his face.

"I'll write it out. The Judge will understand." She went to the reporter's desk and got paper and a pencil. She began to write but she was having difficulty. Finally, however, she handed the paper to Ernie.

He read what she had written and then smiled. "Naomi, you can't ask the Judge if you can change your vote but keep your own opinions." He laughed lightly.

"Now come on, Naomi, let's you and I sit down and talk reasonably."

"No! And give me back my note! I'll write another one. I don't want to talk to you reasonably. Every time we talk and you tell me to be reasonable, I get the short end of the stick!

"Ha! I'm reasonable, I've been reasonable all my life, so any doubt I have has to be a reasonable doubt."

And she wrote out two more notes for the Judge and Ernie read them and each time shook his head and said no.

"Why not?" Naomi asked.

"Well, because it's not worded correctly."

"Worded correctly! This is no English grammar class! This is a murder trial!"

"Exactly, and, believe me, we all know that, Naomi, and . . ."

"Two women and ten men and that other woman so educated, so smart, she's worse than all the men!"

"Naomi, please, let's me and you go and sit down together."

"No! Leave me alone!" And she went to the restroom.

Ernie called Ed Hehr and told him they had a juror whom they didn't believe was in a state of mind to deliberate any longer. That, in short, one juror was close to a nervous breakdown and that he, as foreman, wished the Judge to know about it. Ed Hehr left and then came back quickly to tell Ernie that the Judge had said that there was nothing he could do or say. Legally speaking, it was up to the jury to handle the situation. But the Judge did suggest that they take some time off to relax. And he reminded them to keep in mind that it had been a long trial and they'd come a long way in the last few days and that they should make every effort to continue toward a unanimous agreement.*

So Ernie told the jurors that the Judge had said he could not help them but had suggested they take a break, relax, and then continue deliberating toward a unanimous verdict.

The jurors nodded, and then decided that maybe they should quit for the day and tomorrow they could continue, or maybe tomorrow they'd just sit around relaxing the whole day.

They'd play it by ear.

It was five twenty-five and their bus would not be ready for half an hour and many of the jurors were pacing around the courtroom. They were worried about Naomi and her story about a white sock being a clue to homosexual murders and also . . . they were worried about this story of a penis being cut off and put on a victim's chest.†

But not all the jurors were worried. Some were resting, and Victor even fell asleep.

Victor had not had any problem making his decision. As he put it, after the third month of the trial he could see through Hawk, and once that happened he could also see that Bart Williams, even though he talked slow and let Hawk run all over him, was making point after point, day after day, week after week, and there was nothing Hawk could do about it except be loud and ridiculing. In

*Months after the trial Judge Patton told the author that Ed Hehr had never communicated any such request to him. Ernie Phillips insisted that the incident had occurred as stated here.

†Months after the trial the author learned that there had been a murder in Solano County three or four years before the Corona case in which a penis had been cut off and placed on the victim's chest. The case had been the subject of articles in several detective-story magazines.

fact, Victor had voted for innocent on the first ballot only because he'd thought—like Rogers—that they might all convict Corona in the first vote, and it had been such a long case that Victor figured they should talk things over for two or three days and cover all the evidence. And so Victor had had no trouble sleeping.

Tuesday night was a difficult night for most of the jurors. They were tired and tense and disturbed.

The talk around the courthouse was that they had a hung jury and that Corona was going to go free because Sutter County would never pay for another trial. So the bailiffs were beginning to talk and to show their disgust, and the jurors became aware of this—they not only saw it but they heard it.

That Tuesday night in the juror's lounge Ernie happened to overhear a deputy discussing the case with Rogers. Ernie reminded the deputy of his sworn oath. Rogers ignored Ernie but the deputy moved away. Ernie then decided to keep moving around and make sure the bailiffs weren't talking to the jurors. In the men's room he found three jurors talking to a bailiff. He felt like asking what they'd been talking about—he thought he'd heard Angela Davis' name mentioned—but decided not to because, hell, he couldn't be everywhere at once, and if he pushed too much all the jurors might turn against him and their deliberations could start going backward.

Seventh Day—
Wednesday, January 17, 1973

Wednesday the jurors decided they would rest all morning and not deliberate, and, having decided this, they began to loosen up and talk with ease. They were able to say things today that would have caused violent outbursts the day before. Sitting around and drinking coffee, Matt laughed and said:

"Man, do those newspapermen and TV guys have it all backward. Last night on TV they said we're eleven for innocent and one for guilty. Have they ever got it screwed up." Matt laughed, and no one even jumped on him about the fact that jurors were not supposed to be watching TV.

Faye then asked, "I wonder where they get their information?"

"From Hawk," said Rogers. "Who else but a city slicker would have the whole world thinking like that?"

"Well, wherever," said Rick, "I'll never believe anything I read in the papers again."

"But it's me," said Naomi, "it's me that's the holdout for innocent. It's not you guys." She looked at Ernie. "Ernie, you're going to have to face those newsmen out there."

"Naomi," said Ernie, "we don't have to explain ourselves to the news media. We're the jury."

"Yes you are, you're going to have to face Hawk and the TV men and tell them the truth. It's me, not you people, it's me!" She got her pills. "Oh, God! Nobody will ever know what I've suffered, but I'll tell you, come hell or high water I'm not changing my vote!"

"Good morning," said George in a cheerful voice, "it's ten past nine and here we are with your happy-jury hour brought to you daily by syrup-cornflakes and bathtub gin. A really twenty-twenty, all-American product."

"I'm not a drinking man," Larry laughed, "but that bathtub gin is starting to sound good."

And Rick, who normally talked so much, sat quietly, head down, chewing aspirins one after another, washing them down with black coffee.

Outside, a rally was being held by the Corona supporters. They were nervously expectant. Any moment now they thought the verdict for acquittal would be coming in.

The jurors were not at the two tables. Instead, they were here and there, sitting, pacing, not saying much, keeping mostly to themselves. At noon their lunches were brought in and when they sat down to eat Naomi said she could see what they were doing, they were going to give her the cold shoulder until she gave in. She got up and went to the jury room in back. Ernie winked at George and George got up, taking Naomi's tray and his own, and went to the jury room.

Naomi was looking out the window, thinking that maybe she was beginning to understand why Frank, who had been in her car pool with Larry, always looked out windows. It was kind of relaxing not to be talking and just to be looking . . . seeing the sky, the buildings across the street, then the street itself with all the traffic, and here, close, the marchers in front of the courthouse. She sighed and felt very lonely and wondered if Frank was lonely or if he was happy with his wife, and then Naomi remembered having met his wife during voir dire, and she wondered how any woman could possibly be happy with a man who was so miserable he was always looking out windows.

George spoke to her, saying, here, he'd brought their lunches so they could eat together.

Naomi smiled. George was so thoughtful, so nice, so happy, that she just knew that he and his wife were happy, and so she came away from the window and sat down with George but, no matter how she tried, she could not bring herself to eat. Instead she had some coffee, another cigarette, and a few of her pills, and she began to tell George about having lost her last husband and about the neighborhood she lived in, that it was old and run down and yet not far from the old downtown of Vallejo, and that it was mixed with blacks and Mexicans since most of the whites had moved out. Some years back her son had bought her a gun, a Saturday-night special, and her house had been broken into a few months later, and all that had been taken were her incense and her gun. Things like that were always happening to her. All her life. Nothing ever seemed to go right for her like it did for other people. Like that time, just before they retired her, people were stealing a lot of things from her department, and so when she reported the stealing she got fired. Things like that always happened to her. A gun for protection gets stolen. Instead of being given retirement she gets fired for trying to be truthful and honest.

Oh, she was so tired. She began to cry but then she became angry and started talking again.

Here she'd been so happy to get on this Corona case, the biggest mystery of the century, but it had turned out to be a dull, mixed-up mess. With everything pointing to the accused but all the important things, like why these killings were done, and where these killings were done, and what motive was behind all this hacking and stabbing and chopping and shooting and burying . . . now she was told that all these important things were not part of the evidence, were not part of the testimony, and so therefore not to be discussed.

It was crazy.

If Corona did all these things, then why wasn't a plea of insanity put on by the defense?

George listened, not saying much, and she began to tell him how everyone was so afraid—Calvin, Frank—and to look how Jim had changed his mind. Jim, who was so religious and good. Then she looked at George for a long time and asked him how come he had changed his mind? Was he afraid too?

George assured Naomi he was not afraid, but said he couldn't really tell her in words why he had changed his mind. It was a feeling, like Hawk had said. He'd said that beyond reasonable doubt and to a moral certainty was more, had to be more, than a home run, that it had to be like the ball knocked right out of the ball park. That's what the prosecution had to do in order to win their case. And even though the prosecution had made many mistakes, George said, he still had to admit . . . they sure piled up the evidence. It was undeniable.

"But," said Naomi, "that baseball example wasn't Hawk's definition. He said that other attorneys had used that definition, that he personally thought reasonable doubt was like love . . . either you got it or you don't . . . and George, I have the feeling that maybe, just maybe, Corona didn't do it."

"Okay, I get that feeling too but, Naomi, I only get that feeling when I think about the things we *don't* know. Do you see what I mean? When I think about motive, and why didn't Hawk put on a case, and how could Corona be living with his wife and children and yet be crazy enough to be committing all these terrible crimes—it's then, but only then, that I get this feeling. But if I think about the things I *do* know, about the things that were submitted to us as evidence and as testimony, well, then I don't have this feeling."

"You don't?"

"No, I don't. And I can then see why the Judge's instructions are like they are. You know, they make common sense, Naomi, and I can see how everything we know, the facts, all lead right to Corona. Man, the blood alone on those two knives and running down his van is almost conclusive if you just close your eyes and think of the rest of the evidence and see it as one big picture. They got him cold. But you know, I guess that's the way it should be . . . I mean, this is a guy who went around doing his thing, as my kids say, never expecting to get caught, and so when they did catch him they were bound to find all this evidence like they did. Especially that twenty-fifth grave, which was found after he was arrested."

"You really think so?"

"Sure."

"Oh, George, I don't know what to do. Should I tell them I'll vote their way and do it just to get it over with?"

"No," said George, "you can't do that. You got to vote the way you think."

"But you're all against me."

"Naomi, look at me." She looked, and George said, "I'm not against you."

"But George, I heard you talking about your wife. You want me to change my vote so you can go home to your wife."

"Look, Naomi, sure I want to go home but . . . I'll stay with you a week, a month, whatever you want. Hell, with steak and lobster every night, who can complain?" And he laughed and Naomi laughed, and he finished his lunch but Naomi never touched hers. When Ed Hehr came in to get their lunch trays he asked Naomi if she'd like a different lunch, if there was anything he could do, but she only shook her head and said no thank you. As Hehr went out he told Ernie there was nothing he could do. It was like the Judge had said—it was up to the jury, and all anyone outside could do was to suggest that they take it easy, that they try to keep going. After all, it had been a long trial.

After lunch the jurors did not deliberate. They just walked about, keeping to themselves, and now and then made small talk.

Then around three o'clock a few of the jurors began looking at the evidence: the knives, the charts that showed the wounds, the ledger, the photos of the van and the Impala car.

Then one of the men picked up the 9-mm. automatic, another picked up the plaster cast of the tire tracks, and they began discussing the case.

The two meat receipts, one made out to Juan, the other signed by Juan.

The bank-deposit slips.

The small white sock.

The blood on the two knives. And then, as they talked, not really deliberating but just casually going over things, more and more of the jurors came up to the two tables and then Naomi was with them, and she too was talking and things were going smoothly.

Matt smiled and winked at Ernie.

Ernie gave Matt a look to keep it down.

Matt nodded and sauntered over to Naomi. He was going to stay near her and knock down anyone who bothered her.

The talk continued, and the atmosphere was light and very unofficial. Then Ernie said that today no votes would be taken, that everyone should just mingle around and talk among themselves. He suggested that Rick make some more of his great coffee.

Rick looked at Ernie.

Ernie winked at Rick and motioned his head toward the jury room.

Rick finally understood that Ernie wanted him out of the room, so he said, "Sure, coffee coming up," and went out.

Then, as everyone was talking happily, Ernie approached Rogers and said, "Rogers, your cigar is bothering me . . . so could you please go and enjoy your cigar in the back room?"

"Why has it only started bothering you now?" asked Rogers.

Ernie smiled. "Because I'm the foreman and foremen do things like this." And Ernie smiled again.

Rogers gave Ernie a long look, not knowing what to think, but finally realized that Ernie wanted him out of the room so others could talk with Naomi, and he said, "Oh, okay, I get it," and left.

Ernie left the courtroom too. He figured he'd stay with Rick and Rogers for a while and let Matt and Faye sort of keep things going easy-like with Naomi and the other jurors.

At three thirty Ernie told Rick he wanted him to tell Naomi that he had thought things over and was sorry for having yelled at her.

"What?" said Rick.

Ernie repeated himself, and then added that Rick should also tell Naomi that he would never yell at her again because every juror had a right to his or her opinion.

"I can't do that," said Rick, "without sounding like a hypocrite and a liar."

"Believe me," said Ernie, "you can do it and you will do it and you will sound most genuine and sincere because you're not stupid and you know that we got nothing, buddy, if we aren't civilized enough to be respectful of the jury system. You've been to war, you've seen combat, you know that's not justice or truth or morally right or any other kind of . . . shit, man! We each got a responsibility here and that's that!"

Reluctantly, Rick finally agreed.

* * *

When Rick approached Naomi she jumped, she was that afraid of him. When he began to speak she told him to leave her alone.

"I'm sorry," he said.

"What?" she yelled.

He repeated himself and told her he'd truly needed this day of rest, that looking back he could see he'd been getting edgy and he had yelled at her unfairly, and he now hoped she would please accept his most sincere apologies.

Naomi looked at him for a long time and then thanked him and said she too had been edgy, that this day of rest had helped her too, and she appreciated him saying what he'd said and she hoped they could now be friends.

Rick said, of course, why not? After all, they were here doing their duty as citizens. They were not here as advocates, like the lawyers. They were here as persons, as people simply doing a job, and he stretched out his hand.

Naomi saw his extended hand, hesitated, and then smiled and shook hands with him.

Faye was next to apologize. She said she'd meant no offense if she'd ever offended Naomi, that she'd truly enjoyed getting to know her all these months, and she hoped they were friends.

Next Ernie spoke to Naomi, and after Ernie came Matt and George, Jim and Calvin, and then Rogers and everyone else, and soon the atmosphere was warm and friendly. When they started discussing the evidence again Naomi was at ease.

It was almost four thirty, and they decided they would continue just talking and not take another vote until tomorrow.

* * *

Outside the courtroom the bailiffs could hear that the jurors were no longer arguing loudly, and they speculated that the holdout juror had given in. Quickly the rumor spread that the jurors had reached an agreement and soon they'd take another vote and that would be that . . . a conviction.

But the defense, the prosecution, and the Corona family and supporters didn't know about the rumor and so, not knowing, they were sure an acquittal would be coming at any moment.

Especially Hawk. He was ecstatic. Today at noon an elderly woman, a total stranger, had come up to him in the parking lot to shake his hand. She had begun to cry, and had said that what Hawk was doing for Juan Corona, he was doing for all underprivileged people in all the world. And then she'd apologized for taking up so much of his valuable time and had hurried away.

The bus was ready and the jurors were getting their coats when Naomi came over to Faye and Jim and said, "Jim, my vote is the one that's going to count, isn't it?"

"Well," said Jim, putting on his raincoat, "I guess it is, Naomi."

Her eyes became large, "Oh, I hope I'm right."

"Naomi," said Faye, firmly but quietly, "I hope you're right too . . . because if you let this man go, and then a few months from now we read in the papers that he did something to those beautiful children of his . . ." Jim was helping her put on her coat. ". . . God help you."

Naomi looked at Faye, large-eyed, for a long, long

moment. Faye returned her gaze, and then it was time to go. The jurors filed out of the room, going down the hallway to the elevators.

As the jurors came out of the courthouse and boarded their bus the Corona family and supporters, and everyone else, could see they were a very different group from yesterday. They seemed unhurried, less tired, and something else was different—many jurors were openly looking at *them*, rather than straight ahead. Everyone took this to signify that tomorrow the jurors would announce a verdict of acquittal and Juan Vallejo Corona would be freed.

The Corona family raised their voices.

The Corona supporters yelled, "Justice for Juan Corona!"

As the bus was leaving the parking lot Ernie looked out at all the happy faces and felt very heavy inside his soul. Could these people actually be thinking the jury was going for an acquittal? How was that possible? And once again he wondered if they knew something the jury didn't know, and could Corona truly be innocent, and if so . . . maybe tomorrow *he'd* vote for innocent and be the holdout.

He glanced at Naomi and decided that maybe she was the best thing that could have happened to a jury. After all, she was making them talk and explain themselves beyond all reason.

That evening in the dining room Faye did not sit with Matt and George, but in the middle of the table with Jim and Rick. Naomi again sat with George and, surprisingly, she was in a good mood, telling the people around her that tomorrow they could all go home to their wives because she was changing her vote. After she had repeated this several times a couple of the jurors told her she should not be talking about the case here in public, but Naomi could not help herself. Like Jim and Calvin, now that she had finally made her decision she felt so relieved that she couldn't help but feel happy. But unlike Jim and Cal, who regularly spoke to God, she had to speak to people.

As the jurors were going back to their rooms Naomi asked Georgia Wallis if she could make a phone call home, and Faye said she'd like to make one too. Mrs. Wallis said they could not make calls, but if they came to her room she could make the calls for them.

Faye, seeing how anxious Naomi was, suggested that Naomi go first, and went into her room, leaving her door ajar so she could see when Naomi left. Faye waited and waited, and then finally went to the door of Mrs. Wallis' room. When she heard the two women still talking, Faye returned to her room.

Naomi asked Mrs. Wallis to call her sister and tell her she would be home tomorrow.

Mrs. Wallis said she couldn't do that.

Naomi said her sister was leaving tonight or tomorrow, and she wanted her to know she'd be home tomorrow so she would wait for her, and feed the cats.

Mrs. Wallis repeated that what Naomi wanted could not be done.

Naomi asked, "Why not?"

A jury's deliberations were supposed to be private and information pertaining to deliberations could not be given out, Mrs. Wallis replied. "What I can do," she added, "is ask your sister to please continue taking care of your cats."

"But," said Naomi, "my sister will leave if I don't tell her I'm coming home tomorrow. Look, I'm the holdout juror and I've changed my mind and tomorrow I'm going to give them my vote and it will then be a unanimous verdict, and so you can tell my sister I'm coming home."

"Look," said Mrs. Wallis, who was beginning to lose her patience, "I don't want you telling me any more about your jury deliberations."

"I'm only trying to get my cats fed," said Naomi.

"Okay," said Mrs. Wallis, and she called Naomi's sister and said that Naomi wanted her to continue caring for the cats.

Naomi's sister said she was leaving tomorrow.

"I'll be home tomorrow!" yelled Naomi toward the phone.

Mrs. Wallis covered the receiver, glaring angrily at Naomi, and said a few more words to Naomi's sister, and quickly hung up.

Both women were very upset; Naomi was talking and Georgia Wallis was yelling.

Then Naomi said, "Look, what I can't understand is how can a man with such a nice family have done all those awful things with dirty old men?"

Mrs. Wallis, still angry, still upset, said, "Lots of nice people commit awful crimes!"

"But what happened to all his bloody clothes?" asked Naomi.

"Look," said the matron, "I'm not supposed to be talking to you! I don't know! Maybe his wife took them home and washed them."

"Oh, my God . . . then she knew about it all along?"

"Naomi," said Mrs. Wallis, "after this trial is over I can tell you things about criminals that will ease your mind!" She was screaming. "But I'm not going to talk about this case now!" She was so upset she was still shouting. "I wasn't in the courtroom every day but you were, and so if you don't know by now, you'll never know!"

"Know what?" asked Naomi. "Do you have information we don't have?"

"Oh, God!" said Mrs. Wallis, rushing to the bathroom and closing the door.

Naomi asked what was the matter.

Georgia Wallis screamed that she wasn't supposed to be talking to her and she wasn't going to talk to her anymore.

Naomi was large-eyed with disbelief and said she was sorry if she had offended her but . . . she'd only wanted to have a little talk, woman to woman.

Mrs. Wallis was so upset that she locked the bathroom door.

Naomi shook her head, not believing what had just happened, and left the room.

Faye saw Naomi leave, waited a moment, and then went to have Mrs. Wallis call her husband for her. The matron was trembling, but she tried to smile and be cheerful, and Faye asked her if she was all right.

"Faye, talking to Naomi for five minutes is knowing her, and knowing her is . . . oh, God." And Mrs. Wallis shook her head, again and again.

Faye's husband was not at home, so Faye talked with Mrs. Wallis for a while, trying to calm her. But after hearing what Georgia Wallis had to say, she wondered again if Naomi was changing her vote just because she was worried about her cats or . . . if she truly thought Corona was guilty.

Before going to sleep Faye decided that tomorrow she would confront Naomi with this question, and if Naomi was changing her vote because of her cats then Faye would not accept her vote, and that was that.

Eighth Day—
Thursday, January 18, 1973

On Thursday morning the jury decided to vote before discussing the case at all. They voted as usual on torn pieces of paper, and the result was unanimous: twelve votes for guilty.

Faye was the first to speak.

"Ernie," she said, "before you sign these twenty-five cards I would like Naomi to tell us how she feels. Did she change her vote out of some sort of convenience or does she now believe Corona is really guilty?"

"Yes," said Jim, "this is important. Because I personally won't accept someone changing their vote just out of exhaustion or convenience."

"Well," said Naomi, "I think I've changed my mind. Yesterday you gave me a day's rest and I relaxed and I saw things differently. Like when George spoke to me and, basically, I now think you people are right and I do think Corona is guilty."

"But you used the word 'think,' " said Rick

Matt kicked Rick under the table.

Ernie stood up. "What's wrong with the word 'think'? Only God *knows*. All we mortals 'think.' And we all agreed to follow the law and think, use common sense, and arrive at a verdict beyond reasonable doubt . . . I believe Naomi is a most humane and just individual and her usage of the English word 'think' is most appropriate.

"Okay. Now, before I sign these individual counts of murder, do we also all agree that these were first-degree murders?" Everyone agreed. "All right, now, before I sign each of these I want us all to say verbally that we do in fact, at this point in time, agree on the verdict of guilty."

And so the foreman polled the jury before signing each paper, and all the jurors said yes, guilty, for each of the separate twenty-five counts of first-degree murder.

Then they were done, and so Ernie called Officer Ed Hehr and told him that the jury wished to summon the court. They were ready.

The court was summoned, and everyone was rushing to the courtroom. Deputies and policemen tried to control the waves of onrushing people. Everyone was sure that a verdict of acquittal was coming in, and that Juan Vallejo Corona would be free within the hour.

By a few minutes after noon on January 18, 1973, the courtroom was filled to capacity and was exceptionally noisy with jokes, cheerful conversation, and greetings between members of the press, the Corona family and supporters, and the general public.

Hawk, nervous but poker-faced, patted Juan Corona on the shoulder. "We're doing fine, amigo, we're okay.

We got it in the bag. Hell, even if we lose we'll get an automatic appeal. You saw how I tore them apart."

Juan Corona looked at his attorney, not saying one word, and Hawk saw Corona's eyes and he grew so uneasy that he stopped patting Juan Corona on the back and stepped away.

The Corona supporters were jubilant, calling across the room to Juan Corona.

The prosecution team just stood there, very quiet, looking at no one.

At nine minutes after twelve Judge Patton said, "The defendant and all counsel are present." The courtroom did not quiet down, so the Judge raised his voice. "I would remind those in the audience that the court expects that order be maintained during these proceedings, and the courtroom doors are closed, and no one will be leaving the courtroom until the doors are opened by order of the court. The defendant and counsel being present, will you bring in the jury, please, Mr. Bailiff, and also the alternate jurors."

One juror, Larry Gallipeo, came in and sat down, swiveling in his juror's chair, before he realized the other jurors had not followed. He stopped swiveling. Everyone was staring at him. He lowered his head and the courtroom vibrated with quiet whispering; everyone thought he had come in alone because he'd been the holdout for guilty.

The Corona supporters began making ugly noises at him.

Then the other jurors entered and the room became silent. The jurors were stone-faced, not smiling, looking straight ahead.

A sudden coldness began to fill the courtroom.

It took three long minutes to bring in the entire jury.

The Judge then spoke. "May it be stipulated, gentlemen, that the regular jurors together with the alternate jurors are each present?"

"So stipulated," said Bart Williams. Dave Teja and Ron Fahey were staring into space.

"Yes, Your Honor," said Richard Hawk.

"And, Mr. Phillips," continued the Judge, "does the jury have a communication for the court, sir?"

"We have, sir," said Ernie, standing up.

"I see papers in your hand. May I inquire: Has the jury reached a verdict in this matter?"

"We have, sir," said Ernie, and he almost turned to see if maybe Naomi was shaking her head. But he didn't turn. He held . . . stone-faced, and very nervous.

"Will you hand the verdicts to the bailiff, please, who will present them to the bench." Ernie handed over the cards, and then the Judge said, "You may be seated, sir."

Ernie sat down, glancing at the spectators—they all seemed so happy . . . he couldn't believe it. He turned to Corona and Juan Corona was staring at him and they held, eye to eye.

The Judge was speaking. "There has been presented to the bench twenty-five forms of verdict in this proceeding. The court will proceed to read the first verdict offered." Judge Patton glanced at the first card, saw the verdict of guilty, and coughed, trying to proceed calmly. He decided that he would not ask Juan Corona to stand for the reading. That would be unjustly cruel.

He began to read: "Superior Court of California, County of Solano. The People of the State of California, Plaintiff, versus Juan Vallejo Corona, Defendant, No. 8251. Verdict, first count: As to Count one of the indictment herein, which said count accuses the defendant, Juan Vallejo Corona, of the murder of Kenneth Whitacre, an alleged violation of Section 187 of the Penal Code of the State of California, we, the jury, find as follows: Guilty of murder in the first degree. January 18, 1973. Ernest Phillips, foreman."

The courtroom was frozen in disbelief.

"And I'm going to ask you, ladies and gentlemen," continued Judge Patton, turning to the jury and smiling, "if the verdict as just read by the court pertaining to the first count is the verdict of this jury. If this be your verdict as to the first count, you will please respond by answering yes. I will ask you: Is this your verdict as to the first count?"

Rick was looking at Naomi, who had her head down, looking at the floor. The jurors all answered together, "Yes."

"Is there any member of the jury," continued Judge Patton, "who did not vote for the verdict as to the first count as just read by the court?"

Rick stared at Naomi and held his breath. But no one said anything.

The Judge turned to the attorneys. "Does either counsel desire to have the jury polled?"

"Yes, Your Honor," said Hawk, finally realizing that the one holdout had been for innocent and maybe this person would still speak out.

"Very well," said the Judge. "Ladies and gentlemen of the jury, as to the verdict just read by the court, your name will be individually called, and as your name is called, if you voted for the verdict as read by the court as to the first count finding the defendant guilty of murder of the first degree, you will please respond yes."

Rick's feet were dancing under his chair. George, who

was sitting next to him, put his hand on Rick's knee, and Rick strained to keep calm. He just knew that Naomi was going to blow it.

"If you did not vote for the verdict as read, you will respond no. The clerk will call your individual names."

And as the clerk began, the Corona family now understood. At first because of language problems, then because of hope, because of so many months of saying that Juan was innocent and having gotten so many people to believe in it also, they had not been able to understand, but now they did and Gloria's eyes were huge. Martha, her oldest daughter, who spoke English, was crying, and then Gloria was crying too, and Doña Candida Corona was gasping, choking, as the clerk read on and the jurors could hear the Corona family and yet they stood up, one at a time, and answered the clerk.

"Mr. Calvin Williams?" said the clerk.

Cal stood up. "Yes."

"James R. Owen?" said the clerk.

Jim stood up. "Yes."

"Victor Lorenzo?" said the clerk.

"Yes," said Victor, standing up.

"Matthew G. Johnson?" said the clerk.

"Yes," said Matt, standing up.

"George W. Muller?" said the clerk.

Quickly George stood up and said, "Yes."

"Richard Bremen?"

"Yes," said Rick.

"Ernest Phillips?"

"Yes," said Ernie.

"Faye M. Blazek?"

"Yes," said Faye.

"Donald Rogers?"

"Yes," said Rogers.

"Frank J. Broksell?"

"Yes," said Frank.

"Naomi Underwood?" said the clerk.

Naomi stood up and said, "Yes," and no one would have thought she had been the holdout.

"Laurent Gallipeo?" said the clerk.

Larry stood up and said, "Yes."

"Very well," said Judge Patton, "all twelve have responded in the affirmative; is that correct, Mrs. Clerk?"

The clerk said, "Yes, Your Honor."

The Judge continued, "The court therefore finds that the verdict as to the first count as read by the court is the verdict of this jury and orders the clerk to record the verdict." Judge Patton cleared his throat and read the second count.

". . . As to Count Two of the indictment herein, which said count accuses the defendant, Juan Vallejo Corona, of the murder of Charles Fleming . . . we, the jury, find as follows: Guilty of murder in the first degree. January 18, 1973. Ernest Phillips, foreman.

"And I ask you, ladies and gentlemen, is the verdict as to the second count as read by the court the verdict of this jury and, if so, and you voted for it, respond yes.

"Is this your verdict?"

The jurors all answered, "Yes."

The Judge continued, "If any member of the jury did not vote for the verdict as to the second count as just read by the court, you will respond by saying no."

There was no response and Rick began to cough.

"Hearing no response," continued Judge Patton, "is there any request to poll the jury as to the second count, gentlemen?"

Hawk hesitated and then said, "Yes, Your Honor."

"Very well . . . Ladies and gentlemen, the clerk will again call your names as was done after the first count and you will respond yes if you voted for the verdict as read; you will respond no if you did not. It will not be necessary for you to arise when announcing your vote."

"Calvin Williams?"

"Yes."

"James R. Owen?"

"Yes."

"Victor Lorenzo?"

"Yes."

"Matthew G. Johnson?"

"Yes."

"George W. Muller?"

"Yes."

"Richard Bremen?"

"Yes."

"Ernest Phillips?"

"Yes."

"Faye M. Blazek?"

"Yes."

"Donald Rogers?"

"Yes."

"Frank J. Broksell?"

"Yes."

"Naomi Underwood?"

"Yes."

"Laurent A. Gallipeo?"

"Yes."

The Judge said, "All responded in the affirmative, did they not, Mrs. Clerk?"

"Yes, Your Honor."

"Very well . . . the Court finds the verdict as to the second count as read by the court to be the verdict of this jury and orders the clerk to record it."

Gloria was hugging her daughters. Many of the Corona supporters were also crying. Pedro Corona was on the edge of his seat, ready to leap. Uniformed deputies were everywhere. Plainclothes deputies were also sitting watchfully among the audience. Everyone was on edge. Or, as Ernie would say later that day at his home, the only one who didn't seem at all on edge or surprised was Juan Corona himself.

The Judge was continuing: ". . . As to Count Three of the indictment herein, which said count accuses the defendant, Juan Vallejo Corona, of the murder of Melford Sample . . . we, the jury, find as follows: Guilty of murder in the first degree. January 18, 1973. Ernest Phillips, foreman.

"Now, ladies and gentlemen, if the verdict as to the third count as read by the court is the verdict of this jury, please answer yes. Is this your verdict?"

The jurors all answered, "Yes."

"If any member of the jury did not vote for the verdict as read by the court will you respond no?" said the Judge.

There was no response.

"I want them polled!" snapped Hawk.

"Very well," said the Judge.

And once more the jurors were polled, and once more each of them answered yes.

Then the Judge continued, reading the fourth count: ". . . which accuses the defendant . . . of the murder of an unidentified male adult. . . . We, the jury, find as follows: Guilty of murder in the first degree.

"I ask you, ladies and gentlemen," said Judge Patton, "is

this your verdict as to the fourth count as read by the court? If so, answer yes.

"Yes."

"Any member of the jury who did not vote for the verdict as read, please respond by saying no."

No one responded and so Hawk threw up his hands and said, "I waive, Your Honor."

"Very well . . . the jury having responded unanimously that the verdict as to the fourth count was their verdict, and there being no request to poll the jury—"

"That is correct," said Hawk, looking disgusted and angry.

"—the court finds the verdict as to the fourth count as read by the court to be the verdict of this jury as to the fourth count and orders the clerk to record it."

And the Judge continued through the rest of the twenty-five victims:

Fifth count:	Donald Smith
Sixth count:	John J. Haluka
Seventh count:	John Doe
Eighth count:	Warren Jerome Kelley
Ninth count:	Sigurd Emil Beierman
Tenth count:	John Doe
Eleventh count:	William Emery Kamp
Twelfth count:	John Doe
Thirteenth count:	Clarence Hocking
Fourteenth count:	James Wylie Howard
Fifteenth count:	Jonah Raggio Smallwood
Sixteenth count:	Elbert T. Riley
Seventeenth count:	Paul B. Allen
Eighteenth count:	Edward Martin Cupp
Nineteenth count:	Albert Hayes

Twentieth count:	Raymond Muchache
Twenty-first count:	John H. Jackson
Twenty-second count:	Lloyd Wallace Wenzel
Twenty-third count:	Mark Beverly Shields
Twenty-fourth count:	Sam Bonafide, aka Joe Carriveau
Twenty-fifth count:	Joseph Maczak

"Now, ladies and gentlemen of the jury, is the verdict as to the twenty-fifth count as just read by the court the verdict of this jury?"

The jurors answered, "Yes."

"Did any juror not vote for the verdict as read?"

No one answered.

"The court finds that the verdict as to the twenty-fifth count is the unanimous verdict of the jury as to the twenty-fifth count. The court so declares it and orders the clerk to record the verdict as to the twenty-fifth count.

"May it be stipulated, gentlemen, that each of the verdicts as recorded not be read to the jury and that the jury may be now discharged prior to the recordation of each of the verdicts in this matter?"

"Yes, Your Honor," said Hawk.

"Yes, Your Honor," said Williams.

"Very well . . . ladies and gentlemen, that completes your services in this matter. Certainly you are aware of the sacrifice that you were each called upon to sit as jurors through the many hours and many days and weeks and the months that have been involved in the trial of this case, and on behalf of the State of California and of the County of Solano, I thank you for your conscientious services and you each leave this courtroom with the satisfaction of knowing that you have made a substantial contribution to the administration of justice in the State of California. And I thank each and every one of you for your diligent and conscientious attention in the performance of your duties in this matter.

"The jury and the alternate jurors are discharged and will be taken out from the courtroom."

The Judge was keeping everyone in the courtroom so the jury could get on the bus and be well on their way. As the jurors were getting their things and putting on their coats, Naomi said, "Oh, Ernie, please don't tell the press that I was a holdout. I'm so tired, I just couldn't stand it if they came asking me questions."

Ernie nodded, and Matt said, "Listen, I don't know about anyone else, but I'm sick and tired of this case. I don't want any newsmen bugging me. I want to go home, get drunk, and not say a word to anyone for a week. And Ernie, being the foreman and liking to talk"—Matt was smiling—"I think he should meet with the press and answer all their questions for all of us."

"Right," said Rogers, "Ernie's got a good memory, he could tell them everything. By the way, Ernie, I want to shake your hand and say you did a fine job."

"Ernie," said Larry, "I'd like to sincerely say the same thing. If we'd searched all over this country, I don't think we'd ever have found a better man than you. You did a great job."

"Ernie," said Frank, "I've always had trouble expressing myself . . . I'll write you a note."

"Wow," said Ernie, looking at them all, "you all didn't have to bribe me, I'd already made up my mind to meet the press and answer their questions.

"But, coming back to what Naomi asked, I'd like to say

that I do believe it's best for us to never say who was the holdout. Once these reporters get a story going, they want another and another, and we'd be hounded for days, and we'd have to go all over this case in its entirety.

"Believe me, if you all want to rest, we best keep our mouths closed."

"Yes," said Naomi, almost in tears. "Please, do that. I'm so . . . so tired and scared, I guess. In my neighborhood, the people are . . . well, right next door in this old beautiful two-story home—but it's all run down now—is a house of ill repute."

A couple of jurors laughed. Naomi looked from one to the other and then laughed too.

"Okay, then," said Ernie, "no one talks. It's our secret."

And so they left the room, going down the hallway to the elevators. There were Corona supporters everywhere, but they did not yet know the verdict.

George saw a group of large, dark men with beards and hip clothes by the stairs. "Who are all those big weird guys?" he asked Ed Hehr.

"Don't worry," said Hehr, "those are cops."

"I'll be damned," said George.

As the jurors got into the two elevators, uniformed deputies got in and rode down with them and ushered them quickly to their bus. By now the Corona supporters were beginning to sense the situation, but the jurors were already on the bus. Then another bus pulled up in front of them, causing a minor traffic jam, and it was a long two- or three-minute wait, with Corona supporters all around them, before the jury's bus could continue.

In the courtroom, Gloria was weeping, and Martha was weeping.

The Judge left the bench and instructed the bailiffs to keep the doors closed for five more minutes.

Suddenly Martha went into a convulsion. Deputies tried to help her but Pedro Corona told them to keep their filthy hands off his family. An ambulance was called and later it was disclosed that Juan Corona's eleven-year-old daughter had an ulcer and had gone into a state of shock.

With one police car ahead of them and another behind, the jurors' bus drove to the fenced-in lot where their vehicles were parked. The jurors immediately got out of the bus and into their cars to leave. Newsmen tried to stop them as they came out of the gate. Matt, driving a camper pickup, said to George, who was with him, "You want to knock off a newsman?" And he drove right through them. The reporters and photographers scattered. Matt laughed. "Let's go to your place, George, and lift a few."

George wasn't talking. He felt sick. He thought he would vomit. For some reason, the whole thing now seemed more real. Inside the courtroom everything had been so clean, so air-conditioned, so removed from reality, that these crimes had been no more than something one read about in the papers, but now George could feel in his gut that these murders had really happened and they, the jury, had really convicted Juan Corona of twenty-five brutal murders.

Ernie was the third juror to leave the fenced area. He stopped and told the newsmen, "I'll park down the street over there."

A uniformed deputy came rushing up, telling them to leave the juror alone.

Ernie turned to the deputy. "Boy, I stopped my car. I can take care of myself. Don't be so overzealous in performing your duty!"

"I was only trying to help."

"Fine. Just fine. Any good intentions have paved the road to hell a thousand times."

Ernie drove up the street and parked. Some of the reporters sprinted up the street. Others drove. The foreman got out and began answering questions. What had been the most incriminating piece of evidence? What this, what that? What this, why that? And Ernie, speaking softly, politely, answered all their questions except when they asked who had been the holdout. To this question he replied:

"This was a long and complex case, our deliberations were long and arduous and a certain person among us jurors became so mentally exhausted that any more pressure could cause this certain person to have a nervous breakdown. No, I will not tell you who the holdout was. That would be inconsiderate of me. Now ask me your other questions."

Across the way Rogers said to Calvin, "Cal, I'd like you to know that I'm glad how things turned out. I'm talking about us being roommates. I learned a lot and I like you . . . I want to shake hands with you."

Slowly, Cal took Rogers' hand and said, "Thank you."

"Thank *you*," said Rogers, then, taking his hand back, "Oh, well, I guess I better be going."

"Yeah, I guess so," said Calvin, and he watched Rogers walk away and he shook his head, shrugged, and got into his car.

* * *

Naomi, Frank, and Larry were driving to Vallejo in Larry's old pickup truck. Naomi was sitting in the middle, talking nervously. Frank wished she'd stop. So did Larry.

Larry went to Frank's house first. There were many things Frank wanted to tell Larry but he couldn't with Naomi present. When he got out, Frank said two or three words, felt confused, upset, and angry at himself and Naomi, so he slammed the door of the pickup and went up the driveway. His wife opened the door for him and he walked in and stared at her, not knowing what to do, so finally turned, locked the door, and then stood there looking at the locked door.

He stood there two full minutes before his body began to tremble, then a cold, terrible feeling began making him feel sick. His wife asked him if he was okay. Softly he said that he'd be all right, he just needed time to unwind. His wife understood and left him alone, never even asking what the verdict had been.

Frank remained there, just staring and shaking, for twenty full minutes, then he rushed to the toilet.

At her home, Naomi asked Larry please not to leave until she was safely inside, and Larry said he'd go to the door with her. Naomi's sister wasn't home and Naomi didn't have her key. Finally, after much confusion, Larry tried the door and found it open, to Naomi's relief. She went inside. It was an old house and it was small and poor and very much in need of paint. Naomi was talking to Larry quickly and looking for her cats, then looking for her gun. No, not her Saturday-night special, no, that one had been stolen, yes, this was another gun her son had bought her. She asked Larry not to leave until she'd found her gun or until her sister came back.

Every reporter in the courthouse was on the telephone, most of them calling various jurors. One called Naomi, because somehow he felt she had been the holdout. When she answered, he immediately said he knew she was the holdout juror.

"Who told you?" demanded Naomi. "They promised not to tell."

The reporter gave the phone to his partner, saying, "Keep her talking, I'm driving!" And he took off, laughing with the thrill of having bumped into a good lead.

A few other newsmen followed, and soon the entire block in front of Naomi's house was filled with television mobile units and press cars.

There were forty-some newsmen in Naomi's living room asking her questions and taking her picture. She tried to answer as well and as truthfully as she could but there were too many questions coming at her at once.

Later she said, "I swear, there were reporters in my house from everywhere. From San Francisco, New York, London, and all places in between. And they'd ask me questions, take notes, and leave before I'd said enough for the answers to have any meaning."

Naomi said this later, but at the time she was so exhausted and yet so high on nervous tension that she could not keep from talking.

She told the reporters that she still had doubts, that she had a list of them. Four more than Rick's list for conviction.

They asked her who'd run the jury, was it this Rick?

She said he was so loud, always screaming.

They asked her if he was the leader.

She said yes, he'd ramrodded the jury's verdict.

They asked if she'd been pressured.

She said, oh, there was pressure, all right. Every day, every hour, more than anyone could ever imagine.

They asked what were her doubts.

She said that her list of doubts was right here.

Reporters asked if they could use her phone, and she said yes. Television men asked if they could bring their camera crews inside, and she said yes. And that night the other jurors watched as Naomi became the star of the television news across the nation, and they were amazed. There she was, just like she had been in the jury room, except now she sounded very convincing as the people interviewing her asked her the right questions.

Rick was sick. His friends were asking him how he could have convicted an innocent man.

Faye's husband told her that she had truly surprised him. He'd thought Corona was innocent.

Victor's wife said that what Naomi was doing was an outrage, and she was going to write a letter of protest to the Judge.

Ernie had his hands full. Newsmen were calling him every minute, asking him if it was true that he had not been able to handle the jurors and that several of them had pressured Naomi into her vote for conviction.

Matt laughed and said he'd expected as much, turned off the TV, went to a friend's house to get away from the ringing phone, and got very drunk.

Later most of the other jurors called Ernie to ask what they should so. Calmly, he told them to do absolutely nothing, for they did not have to explain themselves to anyone. Two jurors were especially worried about what people would think of them, because Naomi was making them look like fools. Ernie told them that they had not been fools; they had been conscientious and forthright, and they should just hold tight and say nothing.

The next day the headlines read, "Holdout Juror Still Had Doubts," "Holdout Juror Was Pressured," "Confusion Follows Corona's Conviction," "Juror Now Says Corona Is Not Guilty," and that night Naomi Underwood was once again a TV star, and among the things she happened to mention was that the matron, Georgia Wallis, had talked to her during the jury's deliberations. Mrs. Wallis had told Naomi not to worry about changing her vote because after the trial she, Mrs. Wallis, could tell Naomi things about Juan Corona that would ease Naomi's conscience—that, for instance, Juan's wife had washed out all his bloody clothes after each and every murder.

That night watching herself on television Naomi became scared. As she said later, "Yes, I said those things to the newsmen but I didn't say them like they came out on TV."

Then a woman stopped by to see her, saying that Richard Hawk would like to talk to her at his home. Naomi agreed, and went with the woman to see Hawk. He spent two hours transcribing Naomi's account of her conversation with Mrs. Wallis.

The next morning Hawk held a news conference, and the resulting headlines screamed about jury tampering in the Corona case. Now Hawk was not only a hero, he was a man fighting single-handedly for justice against a corrupt Sheriff's Department and the whole judicial system. The Corona case had gone beyond being a murder trial, even a mass-murder trial—it had become a cause of justice and liberty for all Chicanos and other minority groups. The prosecutors, on the other hand, began to look very bad, if not downright unethical.

For the next three days Naomi had to take her phone off the hook so she could sleep. It was difficult to get a night's rest, with newsmen calling her night and day, and she had to take even more of her nerve pills. Her sister, however, thought the whole thing was fun, and answered all the phone calls, saying she was Naomi and telling the callers great stories.

Judge Patton held hearings to decide the matter of the alleged jury tampering, and finally ruled that there were no grounds for declaring a mistrial. Because of the confused nature of Mrs. Wallis' testimony and because the Judge was convinced, in any case, that Naomi had decided to vote for conviction before her conversation with the matron, he ruled that she had done so freely, of her own volition.

This decision enraged the defense attorney and the supporters of Juan Corona's cause. They were now absolutely sure that the trial of Juan Vallejo Corona was a mockery, a travesty of American justice, and had set back the struggle for equal rights for the poor and minorities by at least fifty years.

Several weeks after the court hearings, when the public once again began to lose interest in the case, Ernie Phillips received a letter from Frank Broksell which said: "In all my life I've met a few people who are my superior in some ways but I've never met a man who was my superior in all ways. Believe me, you did a fine job as foreman and it was a pleasure and honor to meet you."

Larry Gallipeo later said: "Being a juror was a terrible thing. I'm not smart and I'm not educated, and I don't know if it's right to put a person like me in that position of being the judge.

"It was awful. I had to think like I've never thought before. I had to try and understand words like justice and truth and . . . if it hadn't been for Ernie I don't know what we would have done. He didn't finish high school, you know, but . . . if we'd looked the streets all over town I don't think we'd ever find a better man. He kept us all together and let us all do our own thinking and talking. Especially Naomi, he helped her—he helped all of us, but . . . still, why do they make people like us the judges? It was terrible!"

"Ernie," said Matt Johnson later, "he's a good man. Too bad we don't have more good, honest, average people running the country."

"He talked too much," said Faye Blazek, "but, looking back, I don't know if anyone but Ernie could have kept us together—we were so far apart. But maybe that's why we have the jury system."

Afterword

On Saturday morning, February 1, 1975, I received a telegram. It read, "ERNEST PASSED AWAY 1-31-75 AT 5:20 A.M. WOULD LIKE YOUR ATTENDANCE AT THE FUNERAL. PLEASE CALL. MRS. PHILLIPS." For months I'd known that the foreman was in the hospital in critical condition but still . . . I had to re-read the telegram several times before I believed it. I called, spoke to Ada, Ernie's wife, and then wrote a long letter to his four children. I wasn't able to attend the funeral, but I did drive up the following month to visit Ernie's family. They all seemed okay. They said that Ernie had often spoken of me and that book I always kept rewriting. I laughed and told them the book was finally done and that *we* just needed to get it published. That made them happy. I asked if any of the jurors had attended the funeral. They said no . . . but then quickly added that Ernie's death had come out in the paper just before the funeral, so, most probably, none of them had known about it in time.

Leaving the Phillips home I drove over to Matt's house—twenty-six miles away—and when I told him about Ernie's death he shook his head, got up, fixed us each a drink, and then said, "Ernie told me about his cancer before deliberations. He told me he'd known for over a year that he was terminal. He asked me to be ready to help him out if he was made foreman." Matt drank his drink. I nodded and then drank mine.

A lot had happened since the trial ended. Defense attorney Richard Hawk was arrested for an old traffic violation immediately after the trial was over, then a year later he was charged and found guilty of federal income tax evasion. He spent five months in prison at Lompoc, California, and then was placed on two years' probation.

Dave Teja took a long vacation, then, instead of running for re-election when his term as D.A. expired, he joined the Criminal Justice Department at California State University in Sacramento as an associate professor. Since then he has been appointed Judge of the Municipal Court in Yuba City by Governor Brown. Prosecution attorney Bart Williams was elected District Attorney of Marysville, in Yuba County. Ron Fahey quit the D.A.'s office and took a free-lance contract—an unusual arrangement—with the Public Defender's Office of Sonoma County.

Juan Corona was kept at Vacaville for observation for a time. While he was there, he was brutally attacked by four inmates as he was writing a letter to one of the supporters who still believed in his innocence. He suffered over thirty wounds to the face alone. But none were very deep. It seemed as if his attackers had not wished to kill him, but to disfigure him. Corona was moved to Soledad prison, south of Salinas, California. He still hopes for a retrial, but he doesn't write many letters to his supporters anymore. His wife has divorced him, changed her name, and moved away.

For the surviving jurors, the trial of Juan Corona has become part of their past and they have returned to their normal lives, swept up in the problems of the present. Only Naomi still concerns herself with the case and writes to me often. She wrote me that last Christmas, 1975, she received a card from Corona. On it was a picture of the Christ child. A week later she received a letter from Corona, asking her to write to Judge Patton on behalf of a retrial. Naomi did write the Judge, and then she wrote back to Corona. But she hasn't heard from him again.

V. V.

May, 1976